FATE OF DEVOTION

ALSO BY K.F. BREENE

Finding Paradise Series

Fate of Perfection

The Warrior Chronicles Series

Chosen

Hunted

Shadow Lands

Invasion

Siege

Freedom (coming soon)

Darkness Series

Into the Darkness

Braving the Elements

On a Razor's Edge

Demons

The Council

Shadow Watcher

Jonas

Charles

FATE OF DEVOTION

K.F. BREENE

Text copyright © 2017 by Hazy Dawn Press, Inc.
All rights reserved.

No part of this book may be reproduced, or stored in a retrieval system, or transmitted in any form or by any means, electronic, mechanical, photocopying, recording, or otherwise, without express written permission of the publisher.

Published by 47North, Seattle

www.apub.com

Amazon, the Amazon logo, and 47North are trademarks of Amazon.com, Inc., or its affiliates.

ISBN-13 9781503943636
ISBN-10: 1503943631

Cover design by M. S. Corley

Printed in the United States of America

FATE OF DEVOTION

Chapter 1

The small orb opened with a gush. Millicent leaned forward, surveying the interior for what seemed like the millionth time. The object was from Toton, one of the three conglomerates in control of Earth, and she'd been analyzing it off and on since she'd settled on Paradise. Until recently, she hadn't taken as much time as she'd wanted to really dig into it. She had many demands on the new planet, but Toton was waging a destructive, high-casualty war on the other two conglomerates, and Millicent's gut told her the orb was important.

It was one of three items she had stolen from a warehouse when she, Ryker, and their little girl, Marie, were escaping Moxidone, the conglomerate they used to work for. While she could get data on some of its elements, the larger picture of the device eluded her.

The inside of the metal casing wasn't a perfect circle, unlike the outside. It was more oblong, with a little groove at the bottom for Holy knew what. The receptors jutted into open space like needles.

She checked her computer screen, going over the readings yet again. There was a solution within this puzzle, she could *feel* it.

"Hey, Millicent?" Trent wandered in, his unruly hair curling around his ears and his clothes baggy on his thin frame. He ignored the organized room full of tech pieces, screens, and nearly completed weapons. Unlike the other people on Paradise, he had no interest in Millicent's tinkering. It was refreshing to her, and one of the reasons he was allowed to enter her work space. "I'm headed to the park with a few of the resident kids. I was going to take Marie with me to help corral the younger ones."

"Sure, sure." Millicent waved him away distractedly.

"Working on that Toton thing, huh?" He bent toward it, squinting his brown eyes. "I haven't seen it opened before. Does this mean you've figured out what it's for?"

"I still don't know. From what I've found, it almost seems like a motherboard. Considering the size, it would have to be for a supercomputer. One that might take up half a room. But . . ." She stared at the opening of the sphere. "No way this interior could be for the central processing unit. It's way too big in comparison to the motherboard. But if it's not a motherboard, what could it be?"

"I don't know what any of that means, except that something is amiss."

Millicent ignored him, now hashing out the problem verbally. "It has the receptors I might expect from a motherboard, but then it has these strange prongs, almost like they would connect to a port. I just can't . . ." She tapped her chin in frustration. It didn't make sense. This sort of system was unlike anything she'd seen before.

Trent's brow scrunched as he looked at the inside of the casing. He put out his hands in a measuring kind of way. "I'm sure this has already occurred to you, but we used those types of prongs in the research lab back in Moxidone. Not that I did the actual research, you know, but I did see some of the machines they used—"

"What's your point?"

"Oh right. Just that those types of prongs are good for reaching different areas of the brain. And the size is about right. So . . ."

"Wait." Millicent held up her hand and stepped back, taking in the whole situation. "Different parts of the brain . . ."

"Yeah." Trent crossed his arms over his chest. "It's the right size for a brain, too. But Moxidone's equipment was larger. There were computers, and screens, and—"

"*Shhh.*" Millicent rubbed her temples as a sickening realization overtook her. The final piece clicked into the overall puzzle. She had no idea how she hadn't seen it sooner.

She took another step back.

"They use brain power for their central processing unit," she said in a hush. "Human brain power."

"What do you mean?" Trent turned toward her in confusion.

"This is a motherboard, as I'd thought, encasing a CPU. A CPU that no computer could duplicate. Computers have limits. They are only as smart as their programming. Even artificial intelligence—even the learning computers—hits a wall at some point. But this . . ." Millicent started to pace. "In comparison to a computer, a human brain has no limits. And now it has a means to reach its full potential."

"I don't know about that," Trent said with a snort. "Even with Marie's advancements, evolution is still inching forward a tiny bit at a time. It'll be a long time before the human brain reaches its full potential."

Millicent shook her head and bent over the sphere again. "You don't understand, Trent. They're not trying to further evolution with the help of machines; they're trying to further machines with the help of biology. They are using a human brain to help computers think. This is—" Millicent braced her hands to her hips. "My first impulse is to try it out. To test this. But how could I? How could *they*?"

"They're taking the brains—the consciousness—from clones?" Trent breathed, a look of horror crossing his face.

"No—" Beeping caught Millicent's attention. Something was entering their upper atmosphere. She watched the monitor for a moment. The rocket they were expecting was on schedule.

She shifted her attention back to the matter at hand. "Not clones, unless the clones were educated for the purpose. The designer of this computer would probably look for a certain type of mind. Like you did for Marie's experiment. Someone smart, educated, good with systems—"

"Someone like you."

"Someone like me, yes."

A pregnant pause stole over their conversation. Millicent didn't want to voice her next thought. Based on Trent's silence, he'd shared her apprehension—and uncharacteristically swallowed his words.

Someone like her . . . and someone *exactly* like Marie. Not just Marie, either. In the five years Millicent and her partner, Ryker, had been on Paradise, they'd had two more children. Mason had recently turned four and little Jessa was two and a half. Like their elder sister, both children had benefited from Trent's prenatal concoction that enhanced certain areas of the brain. Trent had devised the formula on Earth, but he'd duplicated it with resources found on their new planet. For Jessa, he had even accentuated the effect.

Any of Millicent's children would be supercomputers all on their own. Intelligence without limits.

A shiver ran through her body.

"No," Trent said, the boldness in his voice shocking in the silent room. He shook his head before heading for the door. "I think you're wrong. There is no way Toton could get away with using humans as components in their machines. They'd have to have live volunteers. Why would anyone volunteer to come to consciousness in a machine?"

"Do you honestly think they'd ask for volunteers? Does Moxidone ask clones for their organs? No. If a heart is needed for an upper-level staffer, the clone is called, and they die for someone else to live. Toton didn't ask, they took. I guarantee it. But how did they keep it quiet?"

"But the clones were—"

Millicent shut out Trent's argument as a new idea struck her.

She turned toward the door, letting the thoughts and various memories slide through her mind, fitting together to create something new. Her feet crunched onto gravel after she let herself out of the house. The code she'd copied from Toton's vessel all those years ago was more advanced than anything she'd ever seen—and she had been Moxidone's preeminent coder. Then there was the metal of the sphere, a type of material not found on Earth.

It had been found on Paradise, however, which was an alien planet.

The breath rushed out of her lungs as she came out of her fog, realizing she was all alone in a beautiful green field. Trent hadn't followed her.

That metal wasn't from a land inhabited by humans. That code had come from a more advanced being. A being that didn't care about harvesting human brains for its machines, just as humans didn't care about harvesting clones—organisms deemed *lesser*.

"Couldn't be," Millicent said, looking around the world on which she stood. A world that supported life, just like Earth.

A world humans had the tech to travel to.

A more advanced being would be able to go much farther. Already, Roe's people had improved the travel time between Earth and Paradise from two years to eighteen months. The new rocket Moxidone had built could span the distance in a year. It was only a matter of time before humans expanded outward to the next habitable planet.

"Couldn't be," she said again, remembering those smart doors they'd seen at Toton. Remembering the black craft moving through the travel way like a shark.

Toton's economic position had been failing before Millicent left Earth, which was laughable given the advanced coding and tech she'd seen at their building in Los Angeles. From what she'd learned through analysis, they'd developed some truly groundbreaking weaponry and machines. It was like they were working with stronger building blocks.

She turned toward the rocket site, way in the distance. Without consciously thinking about it, she started walking toward her transportation.

Millicent jumped out of the ground vehicle. Smoke billowed from the newly landed rocket two miles in the distance, a bit off target from the preferred landing site, but good enough. She imagined the landing crews were still waking the passengers.

The small landing office was nothing more than four walls and twice as many windows. The two ground vehicles outside belonged to the men she was looking for. The larger transportation vehicle that was normally parked out front must've already been dispatched to pick up the newly landed passengers.

Not bothering to knock, she pushed into the building. Sunlight streamed in through the windows and splashed across two desks nestled close to the wall. Ryker glanced up, and a flash of joy raced across his face before his expression returned to a stoic sort of intensity. His black hair was piled on the top of his head in a messy bun, and lines of fatigue showed around his electric-blue eyes. Roe, the man who'd created the Rebel Nation, a group dedicated to fighting the various conglomerate powers on Earth, and who had helped Millicent and Ryker get off-planet, wore his customary expression of impatience.

"Any news?" Millicent asked, walking straight to the communication device to answer her own question. She'd been right. The passengers were being helped out of the pods that had kept them asleep and saved them from aging on the eighteen-month journey. "How'd the flight go?"

"We lost one," Roe said as he stared out the window. "She was on the older side."

Millicent pulled up the name, immediately recognizing it. "Shame. She was a ruthless pirate. I would've liked to speak to her about the new intranet I designed."

"Her lover made it. You'll still get that knowledge." Roe clasped his arms behind his back. He hated losing anyone, Millicent knew, but did an excellent job of not showing it. He'd always put up a hard front. It inspired confidence in his leadership, he always said. It sounded like a personal hang-up to her.

She checked everyone's vitals. "The children seem good. Energetic."

"We received a report earlier." Ryker moved closer to her. He flicked her loose, wavy blonde hair over her shoulder. "We captured another group of children recently. They weren't guarded as well as we'd expected. It made our job easier. The reports say they are extremely intelligent, all of them."

Millicent's hand stilled on the console. "Where did you file the reports? I didn't get a notice of new information . . ."

One of his hands slid down her back as he leaned over her to work the console. His warm breath fell across her neck, giving her shivers. "I didn't get around to filing it yet, princess." His firm touch moved over the small of her back and kept going until it came to rest on her butt. He squeezed.

"Would you"—she wiggled to dislodge his hand—"stop? I'm working."

Roe sniffed. "How could you be working? I don't see a dead plant in your hand."

Ryker laughed. It was no secret she wasn't great at growing things, but since she'd have to be elected to head up the weaponry department on Paradise, and even then, the community would get to choose what she worked on, Millicent had decided she would do something else and treat her tech and code work as a pastime. Her "hobby" was outside the jurisdiction of the people, who had no idea what she was making, let alone why it was so important. Botany was the only profession she could simply walk into without getting bossed around the entire time. She wasn't great at it.

Ryker thought the whole thing was hilarious, and continued to call her princess because of it. Absurd really.

Lips pressed together, Millicent slapped his hand away as the report came up. "The conglomerates are basically breeding their arsenal now. Why weren't they more heavily guarded?"

Ryker leaned a muscled shoulder against the wall, watching her. The sparkle in his eyes dulled. "Mostly, I think, because Earth is a mess of violence. Since Toton's first attack was timed to hit during the economic summit in Los Angeles, where a great many of the conglomerates' leaders had gathered, they successfully crippled the chain of command. The upper-level staffers who escaped are trying to hide to save themselves, so they're not leading as they should be. Add to that the fact that people continue to disappear across the world, and there's widespread panic and hysteria. It doesn't take much for the downtrodden—the lower-level staffers—to riot, and mass fear has created end-of-the-world type behavior. Our people are staying calm, in their ranks. They went in with level heads and came back out, no problems they couldn't easily deal with."

"Do we have any new reports from Earth-side?" She flicked through the rest of the information. "Anything regarding Toton's movements? Their intentions?"

"Nothing new. They continue to have a presence across the world, but their major activity seems to be in LA. We're still guessing this has to do with all the high-level staffers hiding there. Another possibility is that their headquarters are stationed in that city, which makes sense since they launched their first large-scale attack from there, and they have yet to fully branch out. Ultimately, however, we're still not sure. With major info drops coming in only occasionally with the rockets, and your light-speed communication device regularly malfunctioning after your network updates, we have a lot of guesswork."

Millicent knew all of that, of course, but it was good to hear it spoken aloud from time to time. Blowing out an annoyed breath, she glanced around the hovel that was the check-in point for the landing crew and passengers, then crossed to the portable screen and accessed the catalog of communications reports. Like Ryker had said, they hadn't received a real update in months through her shaky dish- and satellite-driven communication device, but when the news came, it was all the same—heavy artillery, massive death tolls, and desecrated sections of cities. Enormous buildings had crumpled, taking out huge sections of Los Angeles's skyline. Moxidone had employed the most vicious weapons Millicent had created for them, and Toton's return fire had wiped out half of the conglomerate presence in that city.

As far as anyone knew, Toton had never acknowledged the other conglomerates' pleas to work out an economic and land-sharing compromise. Worse, no one really knew what Toton wanted. The other conglomerates didn't know how to end the tyranny. What to offer up.

"Have any of the higher-level staffers gone missing?" Millicent asked.

Ryker was still staring at her. Reading her.

"Just come out with it," Roe growled. "Clearly something is bothering you, so out with it. I don't have the patience to play the question-and-answer game with you."

"Many staffers have gone missing. All presumed dead," Ryker answered calmly, ignoring Roe.

She chewed her lip. Was her theory mad? Possibly. It certainly sounded insane.

"What's the situation with Moxidone's rocket?" She stalled, pulling up more reports that she knew wouldn't help her. After all, if there had been more clues, she would've figured out the riddle long ago.

"Same as before. Grounded and defended by Toton," Ryker said.

"Toton has a rocket at their disposal. They have the opportunity to get off that war-riddled planet, yet no one is taking it." Millicent looked at Ryker. "Doesn't that seem odd?"

"Toton is the one riddling the planet with war," Roe said. "They don't want anyone to escape. As the aggressors, that seems normal to me. Whatever they want is on that rock. And it seems they want to keep it on that rock."

"Have we scanned the planet for any other rockets or flying devices?" she asked, leading them toward her line of thought.

Roe's brow furrowed. "Gregon Corp. didn't have a chance to get their rocket under way. They're ground bound."

"Toton stopped Moxidone from leaving, but we can come and go as we please," she said softly. "Why has this never seemed odd before now?"

"It has." Ryker shifted. A glimmer of malice sparked in his eyes. "I've set defensive measures to keep outsiders from commandeering our rocket. The fact that I haven't had to use those measures has constantly poked at me."

She should've known Ryker would fill in any holes she'd missed.

"Look, woman. What are you getting at?" Roe demanded.

"You remember when I told you that the long metal piece we took from Toton's warehouse is a mental warfare weapon, correct?"

"Mostly causes pain or blacking out, right?" Ryker asked.

"Correct. It emits a sort of signal directed at human brains. We never went that route at Moxidone, not with any of the weaponry I developed, or anything that came before me."

"So?" Roe asked, shifting.

"That sphere we took out of Toton's warehouse . . . ," Millicent went on, feeling the shiver down her back. "I couldn't shake the theory that it was a motherboard. A motherboard that size would have to be for a giant computer, so that discounted my theory, in addition to the strange size ratio of the CPU in comparison to the motherboard. But . . . I'm thinking that a motherboard is exactly what it is."

"Did you figure out a way to test it?" Roe asked before leaning toward the communication device. The first of the new residents were being helped out of the rocket.

"I did figure out a way, yes," Millicent said slowly. "But I don't know how I could follow through without a human brain."

Roe's head snapped around. Ryker continued to stare, showing absolutely no emotion. It meant he was processing. He'd probably been waiting for a reveal of this magnitude—it was the only time she drew out her explanations.

"A human brain?" Roe asked.

"I didn't realize it until today, but Trent poked his nose in and identified some of the prongs in the sphere as the same ones Moxidone's lab used for brain research. The size is about right. The idea is . . . about right."

"About right for what?" Roe's tone turned aggressive. Disgust lined his face.

"The smart doors," Ryker said evenly. "When they took that girl, she disappeared. There was no blood left behind. It would've been easy to deliver a dose of poison, rendering her unconscious, before lifting her body away."

"Not a dose of poison . . ." Roe turned to face Millicent. "The tech you were trying out. The poor bloke who wandered into one of your makeshift experimental sessions screamed bloody murder."

"Yes, that's right." Millicent closed down the reports. "The default frequency first causes a flash of pain before changing to render the victim unconscious. I'm not sure why that is. It seems unnecessary to me. I was playing with the setting when he walked in, and at the time, it was solely set to cause pain. Maybe they've since changed their schematics."

"Only if they're concerned about stealth, and from what I've heard so far, I don't think they need it." A sparkle of violence lit Ryker's eyes. "The only way to test this sphere is with a live human brain?"

Millicent glanced at Roe. "I image we'd get some sort of signal with any organic brainlike material. The computer might not be able to read it, but it should still try . . ."

Roe shook his head. "You can't chop up that woman that didn't make it." He glanced at the screen—at the people being loaded into the ground transportation. "She had a loved one. We can't welcome her to Paradise and then tell her that we need her lover's brain for an experiment."

"What if we ask nicely?" Ryker asked.

Roe ignored him.

"That isn't the end of my theory, it's just the most believable part." Millicent ran her thumb along the table, stalling. Then she told them about her other thoughts, and what the visitors might be doing on Earth.

"If this is true," Ryker said, his expression blessedly closed down, "how would our situation change?"

Millicent shared her thoughts on which kinds of minds would work best for those machines. "My kind of mind, Ryker. Yours." Again, she paused. She couldn't bring herself to name their children.

A killing edge flashed in Ryker's eyes. It was hard not to make the connection.

Roe bowed his head. "Danissa's, as well. And about a dozen others I can think of off the top of my head. All of whom were probably in LA for that summit. The conglomerates always liked to flash their best and brightest at the others as an attempt at intimidation. Toton knew what they were doing with their timing."

Millicent felt a twinge of discomfort at hearing her sister's name spoken. Because Roe was right—if Millicent's brain would work perfectly, so would her sister's. As of yet, Toton hadn't captured her. *Yet* being the operative word.

"But they aren't trying to use the rocket to come get us," Ryker said fiercely. "They are allowing us free rein of space travel."

"Why is that, do you think?" Millicent asked. "It doesn't make sense."

"If any of this is correct"—Roe scratched his chin in thought, a sound like rubbing sandpaper—"then we're just helping them out. We're sneaking on to Earth and stealing the best and brightest children, not to mention the hardy, smart people who've evaded Toton. Who's to stop Toton from shutting down our operation and coming to collect?" He paused with a grim face. "Or maybe we have this all wrong."

"Hopefully we have this all wrong," Millicent said softly.

"Wrong or right, it's a risk. One we need to combat." Ryker pushed away from the wall, standing tall and firm in the center of the room. "If not Toton, then someone will eventually come for us. Moxidone was in the process before Toton started their campaign. We created that need when we took the three most sought-after minds from them. So we can either wait for one of them to come for us, or we can destroy them on their home turf."

"The conglomerates are already in pieces," Roe said, his expression grim. "They're vulnerable. We'd really only need to focus on tearing down Toton. Once that's accomplished, *if* we can accomplish it, ripping out the rest of the conglomerate hierarchy would be a breeze. We can keep peace until the government rebuilds and steps in."

"Do you hear what you're saying?" Millicent stared at them incredulously. "This is a huge undertaking you're talking about, and it would mean leaving our home and children to wage war on another planet. One we left for a reason. Think this through."

"In what world would I let someone threaten our children without trying to stop them?" Ryker asked savagely. "You're never wrong when you finally lock on to an answer for a riddle. In all the time you've been searching, however sporadically, this is the only conclusion that has made sense. And it does make sense. Perfect sense, with all we've learned since Toton has emerged from hiding. We can't know for sure if you're correct, but there is a risk. A large one. So the next step is combating that risk. I know we can take Toton down."

Millicent wiped the comment away. "Of course we can—we're both highly skilled in systems, warfare, and combat. Toton won't know what hit them—"

"There's that royal confidence you accuse her of," Roe said with a snort. "Too bad it's made up of dreams and unicorn farts."

"—but a great many things could go wrong. We'd miss years of our children's lives for a what-if?"

"Like I said, Millie." Ryker stared at her gravely. "Someone will come eventually. This is a beautiful planet with bountiful resources—intelligence and nature both. If not Toton, someone else. That is a certainty. Only Toton is a what-if, and a big one at that. Right now, the world is in upheaval. They're vulnerable, as Roe said, so this is the best time to make a move."

Millicent cocked a hip, not wanting this to be the solution, but already knowing Ryker was right. "What about establishing a government? That is not something either of us has had training for. We can't possibly hope to make a positive difference."

"We're going to clear the way for democracy," Ryker said, moving toward the console. "The Rebel Nation can oversee the formation of that democracy so we don't have a repeated threat down the line. From there, we can keep watch. Snip any uprising threat before it becomes troublesome. No big deal, princess."

Millicent rolled her eyes. "*I'm* the one with royal confidence?"

"Roe," Ryker said, his hands flying over the console. "I temporarily accept your offer of employment to lead the rebels and the pirates on

Earth. I'm going to take those conglomerates down, and, cupcake, I want you to join in the fight."

"Obviously I have to join in the fight or you won't know where to point your gun," she said.

"About damn time," Roe growled. "I was getting tired of asking. Though how you plan to take down Toton, I have no idea. They rule the roost . . ."

"I always know where to point my gun, sweetheart," Ryker said with an extremely suggestive tone, ignoring Roe. "And where to fire it. My ammo has proved extremely effective."

Millicent shook her head as a thrill accosted her, both from his tone, which still affected her after all this time, and from the enormity of the undertaking they were planning. She did believe in their abilities, and a large network of people around the world had joined the rebel ranks—some of the very best—but Toton was a foreign entity with a lot of devastating tech. Tech that could possibly think like a human.

She stared out the window and into the bright sunshine, soaking in the beauty of her home. Only a fool would think it was a safe haven.

A pang pierced her heart at the thought of anything happening to her children. She'd left Earth to save one. Now she had three, and they were no closer to being safe. Their family wasn't in immediate danger, no, but Ryker was right. They'd always known someone would come calling. No conglomerate would lose three expensive staffers and just let it go. If Toton hadn't started this war, Moxidone staffers would've already been on Paradise.

She took a deep breath. "We do this once and for all." She looked Ryker square in the face. "We take them all out. We'll cripple the conglomerates, like you said. Roe's people can help set up this democracy and start fresh, I don't care. But regardless, we do that, we get out, and we stay out. When we get back here, I will get free rein to create a planetwide defense system, complete with heinous weapons that no one will want to approve until it's too late. I want my peaceful life, with you and my children. I want this threat to finally end."

"I've been planning for this since we got here, cupcake. Trust me. We got this."

She huffed and turned toward the door. "Yeah, right. You probably plan to just show up and figure it out from there."

"She knows me so well."

"Wait, where are you going?" Roe called. He filled the doorway after she walked through. "Don't you want to debrief the rocket passengers?"

"I'll get to it later. I bet a pig brain might fit into that sphere, and one of the animals is ready for slaughter. Two birds with one bullet, as the old saying goes. Then I have to get creative with our arsenal. I have a superpower to bring down—I want the best game in town."

Chapter 2

The floor groaned in the wake of the blast. Smoke swirled through the door.

Danissa's breath was loud in the quiet that followed. Dust floated down from the ceiling and sprinkled her stained suit. She touched her head and winced. Red coated her fingers.

"Are you okay?" Puda whispered in a thick voice from the other side of the room. A pile of rubble lay beside him.

"Yes." She glanced up at the cracks sprawling above them. "That was close."

"What set off the bomb?"

Danissa guessed it had been the last of her security. Even if they hadn't accidentally set off one of the hidden bombs, the silence outside the door was a pretty telling indicator that they hadn't survived the blast. Meaning Danissa and Puda were now on their own.

She looked at her wrist, then swore. Black-and-white static filtered across her skin. "My implant should be able to activate this hard port at close range . . . Why isn't it working?"

"Hard port? That's the thing you call the protected part of the intranet, right?"

Danissa schooled her patience as they crouched on a middle-level floor of a Gregon Corp. building, in the heart of the Los Angeles battle zone between Toton and the other conglomerates. She'd explained it a few times already, but Puda wasn't on her level of systems knowledge. Hell, no one was on her level anymore. Except for Toton. And they were systematically taking down all the coding spiderwebs and traps she'd set up. She was a match for their best if she had time and focus, but now, always on the run with strange thinking machines chasing her, she was out of her league.

Not for the first time, it made her appreciate just what Millicent Foster had done when she'd made her escape.

"Yes," she said, picking through various cables before finding one that might work. She plugged one side into a beat-up hologram machine and the other into a console outlet. "It's the secure line I set up before we had to evacuate our—my—level. I had my team root the line to various landline ports around the city. Toton's scramblers won't work on them, and I beefed up the firewall to the point that no one is getting through anytime soon. I want to create a network out of these roots, like Ms. Foster did with that pirate network, but it's not working with my implant for some reason . . ."

"I don't . . . understand any of that. You're so smart, baby. But I thought they took over everyone's implants." Puda coughed. "Man, I don't feel great."

"They took over a great many, yes. Mine was not one of them, remember? I blocked them out."

"Of mine, too?"

Danissa turned back in confusion, and then started. Puda's hand covered his head, and his back was bent forward. A thick line of red dribbled down the side of his face. Her stomach pinched in terror. "Oh Divine, are you okay?"

She rushed to his side before pulling him farther into the flickering light. A huge gash had opened up at the top of his skull. Her stomach squirmed at the gruesomeness of it. "Oh no. We need to put something on that."

"Huh?" He shook his head before leaning forward and retching.

"A concussion. I bet you have a concussion. Shit. Ummm . . ." Stealing a glance at the ceiling—the cracks weren't spreading yet—she dashed to the door. A severed leg was five feet from the body from which it had originated. That guard was clearly the one who'd set off the hidden explosive. Another crumpled heap lay off to the right, dead, but not in pieces.

"The security is down," she said, swallowing back bile. She wiped her hand across her face, clearing away the moisture. "Okay. That's okay. We're still alive. We need to apply pressure to your wound, Puda."

A thud caused her to turn back. Puda lay sprawled across the ground.

"No! Oh no. Please," she begged, a thick weight lodging in her chest. Without thinking, she ran to the more intact guard, pulled his knife out of his belt, and then cut off a part of his suit that didn't have blood. There wasn't much to choose from. She returned to the small office, pressed the fabric to Puda's head, and racked her brain for where they might find a Medi-Kit on this floor.

"It probably has the same layout as a floor ten stories up, right?" she asked the silent room. "Ten floors isn't enough to skimp on medical supplies, is it?"

Granted, while her department had been housed ten floors higher, it had also been in a different building on the other side of town. The layout seemed vaguely similar, but not the same.

"You have to hold this, Puda, okay? Can you hear me?" He didn't move or make any sound. She felt his pulse and, to reassure herself, the rise and fall of his chest. He was still alive, but if she didn't get something to help, he wouldn't stay that way.

"I'm going to go for supplies, okay? Just hang tight." Out of blind hope, she waited for a response she knew wouldn't come. Struggling for breath against her panic, she pushed up from her knees and jogged out of the office and around the corner, trying to avoid stepping on any piles of debris. There was no telling where explosives were hidden. Or discarded. There was also no telling why, since Moxidone never seemed to have a clear strategy when employing their various weaponry.

Wires and ceiling tiles hung down, looking like the root system of a giant plant. Piles that had once been work pods littered the floor with an occasional cracked screen standing erect in a sea of desecration. Green light flickered from an exit sign across the large space.

She stopped next to an alcove and stared at the heap of stuff blocking her way. A black hole where the ceiling had caved in loomed above a counter. Beams cut through the darkness.

After a deep breath, then two, she glanced back in the general direction of Puda. He needed help. She had to do this.

Gathering her courage, Danissa stepped onto the mound. Not stopping, she took another step, and then another, her heart clattering in her chest. Something clicked. She tried to get footing to jump, but a piece of rubble fell away, making her struggle for balance. She squeezed her eyes shut, knowing this was her only chance to get clear.

No explosion.

"Oh thank the Holy Divine," she breathed.

C'mon, Danissa. Almost there. You can do it.

She half slid down the other side of the pile and crashed into cabinets. Frantically, she pulled on the plastic handles one by one, only able to open each cabinet a fraction. Computer parts and hardware sat in neat piles, not affected by the blast. Moving on, she ripped open higher drawers. No medical supplies.

After continuing to all the other cabinets and drawers, she eyed the last, a cabinet door that was mostly blocked by the fallen ceiling. Exhaling loudly, she thought of where else medical supplies could be.

Then shook her head. On her floor, they had been with all this stuff. All supplies, no matter what kind, were kept in the same places on each floor for efficiency so employees only needed to make one stop to stock up.

Maybe they've all been used . . .

"No, they're here," she answered her wandering thought aloud. They had to be, or else Puda was in real trouble.

Swallowing back a frantic sob, she kicked at the rubble, trying to clear a space in front of the remaining cabinet. She took to it with her hands, clawing and yanking, using all her strength. Finally able to pull the door open a fraction, she peered into the dark space.

Gritting her teeth, she reached in and pulled everything out so she could see what she was working with. Panting, she poked through her spoils and then cried in frustration.

Nothing.

Standing in desperation, she looked up with the intent to pray out loud. There, on the top of the cabinets, was a dented metal box emblazoned with a large red cross.

How stupid of her not to look up.

Struggling, she managed to get it down, knocking something else off the shelf with it. A round metal disc bounced off the counter and then lodged at the base of the debris.

It made a sound like a snap.

Her breath caught. *A bomb!*

"Shit!" She threw the Medi-Kit over the rubble and scrambled after it, a countdown ticking away in her mind. Panic flaring, she hit the ground and rolled to the side just in time.

The world lit up in sound and light. Heat trundled by, searing her, as flames coughed upward, shooting out of the small alcove. A piece of ceiling crashed down next to her head. The wall groaned.

Struggling up, now with a searing pain in her right thigh, she snatched the metal box and hobbled back the way she'd come. Another long-suffering groan from the building had her pushing harder. Since Moxidone was the world leader in large-scale weapons, leaving the market share of personal weapons to Gregon's manufacturers, they had headed up the majority of the conglomerates' combined retaliation. They'd struck this building and many others with a frantic bombard-ment, trying to eradicate Toton's invading robots. After the fighting died down in each location, Moxidone had then gone through and seeded the evacuated and damaged buildings with delayed-trigger bombs. The idea was that any humans who happened through could get to safety, knowing what the click preceding an explosion meant. The robots would not "learn," and hence would continue to trigger—and be blown up by—the hidden weapons. Fear had made the decision a no-brainer, but now, in the aftermath, the bombs were more detrimental than helpful.

Back at the office, she half kneeled and half fell to Puda's side. "We're going to get you fixed up in no time," she said, opening the box. And sighing in relief. It was fully stocked. "Just hang on."

Having no idea if Medi-Seal was okay for head injuries, she tried that first. It started to stitch his gash nearly immediately. So far, so good.

That done, she injected him with Cure-all, terrified it wouldn't work. Stricken with fear that he would leave her.

With frantic breath, she waited. And waited.

The other countdown was running in her mind. The one that always seemed to start when she landed in a new location—and end when Toton's robots showed up. The countdown shortened with every new venture. Toton always seemed to know where she was, and lately, each escape was a close call. Now, with no security, they were completely vulnerable.

Taking calming breaths to still her tremors, Danissa shot herself with some Cure-all. Wanting to make the best use of her time while Puda healed, she limped to the hologram machine. There she powered everything up and attempted to get some sort of image besides the accursed black-and-white static.

She bit her lip in concentration. There was obviously power, just no connection.

Another ten minutes went by as she checked the cables and stared at the wall, having no idea how to fix the hardware. One explosion or another must've taken out the rooted hard port.

Danissa started laughing as tears of defeat ran down her face. "Damn it. I'm so stupid."

"Danissa?" Puda wheezed.

"Oh thank Holy. Thank you, Divine." She rushed to Puda's side. "Are you okay?"

"My head hurts really bad. What happened?"

"You have a head injury. But we have to go."

"You aren't stupid, love. You're the smartest woman in the world."

Danissa laughed, trying to summon determination. "I came here because I didn't think Toton took out the connection. And maybe they haven't, but it's inaccessible."

"Now what? Where do we go? I could use a little sleep."

"No, you can't sleep until you're further healed." She shook her head. "We need to find our—my—superiors. I have no idea what to do next. Where to go. Where I'm needed . . ."

"It's okay. Shh." Puda patted her hand lightly. "This will be fine. Don't worry."

She couldn't help but smile. That's exactly why Puda was mostly responsible for keeping her alive. He believed in her, without question, without reservation. He honestly believed that she could do anything she put her mind to.

So far, with the help of his faith, she had.

When would her luck run out?

"Let's move on. We have to keep moving." She tried to hoist up his dead weight. Her leg screamed in agony.

"Where are we going to go?" He struggled up and then wavered. "They're looking for you. Shouldn't we stay here and hide?"

Danissa held him upright and batted down another surge of hopelessness. Those types of emotions were invasive these days, and they weren't doing any good. "They're looking for all high-level staffers, not me specifically."

Puda tilted his head in that way he did. He knew she was blowing smoke. It certainly did seem like Toton had a price tag on her head. And why wouldn't they? She'd been the sole systems resistance for both Moxidone and Gregon. After learning what she could of Toton's complex codes, she'd tweaked and manipulated them to section off some of the companies' most sensitive information. Strangely, Toton seemed more interested in the conglomerates' files on staffers, as well as information about food-processing plants and supplies, than they did in finances. Which meant the superiors in Gregon and Moxidone weren't sure of Toton's long-term goals.

It was hard to strategize a defense when you didn't know what the offense was ultimately after.

"Okay, let's get to another hard line. Or whatever." Puda stepped forward tentatively. He put his hand to his head. "Is there a pain deadener in that box?"

She was already on it. She shot him with a dose and then dosed herself before packing up the rest. Together they moved through the door.

"Will you grab a couple guns for us?" Puda gestured to the crumpled guards. "We might need them, since . . ."

"Sure." Danissa snatched them up and stuffed them into her utility belt. When they started moving again, he staggered. "Maybe we should stay for a moment. Just until you're a little more solid."

"It's okay. If we can get to the craft, I'll be fine."

They hobbled through the empty space together, sticking to the clear path. A strange, rhythmic thrush sounded in front of them, a ways off to the left. A fizz from a wire in the ceiling made Danissa jump.

"It's okay," Puda said through heavy breathing. "That was nothing."

"You should be in the secured levels. Not in danger because of me. This isn't your job."

"It's not your job, either, baby," he whispered with his eyes closed, his voice pained. "You should be in the secured levels with all your people, fighting this on a console. You aren't security. You weren't trained for this."

"I was in the secured levels, remember?" She stopped him and looked into his dilated eyes. "Do you remember?" She squeezed his upper arms. "Are you with me, Puda? Should we stop?"

"What's that?" He blinked rapidly. "Oh yes, that's right. The secured places. And they cut the intranet again."

She sighed in relief and resumed walking. "Exactly."

Time sped by as they slowly progressed. They'd been in the building for too long. Toton was bound to show up any minute.

She stopped as they neared the stairs. They were safe—they'd walked down these same stairs to get to this floor. But there was no way to get Puda up the steps. He could barely walk in a straight line on flat ground, and he was too heavy to carry.

She ground her teeth as she swiveled toward the elevator. It worked as often as it didn't, and while Moxidone didn't rig anything to blow the breaks, occasionally Toton took control. Sometimes people went into the elevators and never came back out. The doors would open but no one was home.

That was before the heavy artillery started, though. Years ago. And it was in the lower, less defensive levels. They should be fine.

Not like they had a choice.

Taking what must've been her hundredth deep breath, she led Puda to the metal doors and then gingerly pushed the button. The light blinked on. The elevator started to whirl.

"It's running, at any rate," she muttered, eyeing the still-flickering lights behind them.

"Can't we just use the pirate network?" Puda's words were slightly slurred.

"No, I can't get into the pirate network, remember? I haven't had the time to break through the ironclad firewall that Ms. Foster has devised from Holy knows where. I can only do so much."

The doors shuddered open. Danissa pointed the gun, ready to fire. Emptiness greeted them.

"Here we go," she said softly, helping him along.

"My legs feel a bit weak," he said, draping his arms around her neck. "We're almost there, though. I can make it."

The wispiness of his voice made her heart ache in fear. He was barely hanging on. There was no reason he should be so optimistic. In fact, he should be blaming her.

"Here we go," she said again, clicking the button to their floor.

The doors shuddered closed. A soft whine filled the space, competing with Puda's haggard breathing. Ninety-one. The lift jolted as it came to a stop.

Her mental alarm was screeching at her to get moving. To run! It had been way too long.

"Almost there now," she said quietly as she supported most of his weight out of the elevator. "We just need to go as fast as we can, okay?"

They staggered through the empty space of the floor, staying on the cleared path devoid of hidden explosives. The legs of an overturned chair jutted into their walkway.

She hooked her shoulder more firmly in Puda's armpit to better navigate his weight around the obstacle.

"Someone fell over?" he asked lethargically.

"Are you tired?" She squeezed her arms around his waist. "Because you sound tired . . . Or do you need more Cure-all? I think we have more . . ."

Tendrils of fear curled up her spine as time ticked by.

"I hope they didn't bump their head when they fell like I did." Puda coughed. "My toes are numb, love. I don't think that is good."

"It's just blood loss." She hoisted him up a little higher, trying to move as fast as possible. He was staggering freely now, leaning heavily on her. The mental countdown clicked to zero. Her mind silenced. Her heart hammered. "I think there is something to help that . . ." Movement registered out of the corner of her eye. Her mind zipped back to the chair, and then to the memory of what this path had looked like when they'd first come through.

The fallen chair hadn't been there. It was recent. They weren't alone!

"Run!" she screamed, trying to pick up the pace. "Hurry!"

A machine that looked like a spider, half the size of a human, skittered out from the side on ten legs. Three blunt claws at the end of each leg lightly ticked as they hit the hard floor. Its body was metallic and its face looked like a data port. Another crawled out from the other side. Up ahead, something dropped down from the ceiling.

"Oh no," she said as she dragged Puda along. Her implant started to hum. Soon her head would throb. After that, her defenses would surely fail. "C'mon, Puda. Please. We have to hurry."

Each step took too long. His hands, nearly limp, fell away.

"No, Puda. Please, hang on. One sprint and we'll make it."

"No, love," he wheezed. His eyes were hooded. "No we won't. I can hear your resignation."

The elevator dinged behind them. Accompanying the sound of doors opening was the thrushing from before, only louder now.

Heart in her throat, Danissa dragged Puda for all she was worth as the robotic spiders advanced on them. Adrenaline pushing her on, she lugged him along, ready to fight but having no idea how. Not without a console.

Puda stopped trying to run with her.

"No! Are you trying to kill us both?" She heaved, glancing behind them.

Horror punched her.

The newest robotic creature had four sturdy legs and a robust body. Like a barrel-chested human mixed with a cockroach, it crawled along, slower than its spider counterparts. Along its plated back sat three shiny metal spheres.

"What the hell is that thing?" she asked, trying to pull Puda.

"No." Puda fought her.

"What are you doing?"

"Run, baby." Puda ripped away and crumpled to his knees. He weakly snatched a gun from her suit's utility belt. "Run."

The spiders advanced, slowing now. She'd had enough narrow escapes in the past to recognize their strategy. The spiders would try to surround their prey, and then they'd come all at once. Danissa knew where to shoot, though. The vulnerable spot to kick.

She just didn't know if she could hit either place. She had no practical experience—the security staffers had always defended them.

"Run, love." Puda opened fire, his shots going everywhere. One hit the thrushing robot as it walked toward them. The bullet had no impact.

"No!" She snatched at his suit. "Crawl, Puda. Crawl out and I'll cover us."

"I don't have much left, Danissa. I love you. Thank you for forcing them to let me be with you all these years. Now run, please. I can't bear thinking you won't make it." He sagged. His arm wavered. "Hurry. I'm so tired."

Breathing raggedly, panic nearly blinding her, Danissa ran at the closest spider and kicked as hard as she could. Her steel-reinforced boot toe hit the metal undercarriage.

Dunk.

The robot shivered, then staggered like a ten-legged drunk. She kicked again, harder, trying to hit that one vulnerable spot that would make it fold up.

Another spider dashed forward and slashed with one of its legs. A shock of pain announced a tear in her skin. She cried out before grabbing her gun, pointing down at the robot, and squeezing the trigger. A bullet tore through its makeshift face. A tendril of smoke curled up from the hole as the other spider rushed in again.

A hoarse scream made her whirl toward Puda. The third spider slashed at him for what must've been the second time, getting his side. He twisted, giving the spider access to his neck. The spider moved in.

She squeezed the trigger before she'd even known she'd aimed her gun. The bullet hit the spider's body and sent it skittering away. The thrushing robot still advanced slowly, closing the distance.

Danissa spun and kicked in one fluid motion, surprising herself with her ability. Her boot hit the undercarriage of the nearest spider. A buzz announced the puncture, followed by a strange whine, almost like a robotic death scream, as it curled up. Its legs folded and it dropped to the ground like a stone. Two faint green lights on the disgusting makeshift face flickered and went out.

She'd never noticed those lights before.

Another slash had her grunting and stumbling. Puda screamed again. He fell to his side as the spider behind her readied a jab to his ribs.

"No!" She kicked the nearest robot before marching at Puda's assailant like a woman possessed, firing repeatedly. The bullets hit, her aim true, punching holes along the top and side. Tiny sparks lit up and spread out over the bulbous body before it sank to the ground and curled up with a whine.

Not wasting any time, she turned back to the final spider. It stared at her. Watching.

"I'm going to kill you, you piece of shit," she said through clenched teeth as she walked toward it slowly, ready for it to strike.

It waited. Seemingly patient.

Why, she wondered. What was the strategy it had been programmed with?

A glance back, and confusion stole over her again. The thrushing robot had stopped advancing. It was waiting, too.

For what?

A surge of expectation filled her.

Reinforcements. It must be. They had access to their intranet. She didn't. They could call for help. She couldn't. They had all the time in the world.

Or so they thought.

She ran forward, squeezing the trigger repeatedly, pummeling the last spider with three bullets. To her amazement, her aim was true. The robot tried to retreat, but its legs weren't working properly and it veered sideways. She was on it in a flash, beating down on its top with the grip of the gun and then stepping back so she could kick. And kick again. The thing crumpled, not able to get away.

Looking toward Puda, she saw the other machine was backing away.

"No you don't. You're going down, too." Gritting her teeth against the pain in her legs, she chased it. Two gunshot blasts were followed by a click, click, click. No more bullets. "Shit!"

She snatched Puda's gun from his limp hand, trying to ignore the aching fear for him as she turned back to the robot. "C'mere, you little sucker," she said, wild. Her adrenaline was running out, but unexpected rage took its place. *"C'mere!"*

She sighted and fired, missing the first time but getting it the second. And third. She ran at it before having to jump back from a swinging, razor-sharp claw at the end of its blocky, humanlike arm. She kicked its undercarriage, like she'd done with the spiders. Pain vibrated up her leg. The thing didn't seem to notice.

She aimed at its flat face and shot. The lighter metal spheres were next. The robot didn't react.

"How do I kill you?"

A thrum of a large carrier craft vibrated through the building. She'd heard that sound before, right before robots attacked, and she and the higher-level staffers had to be moved.

These robots *had* sent for reinforcements.

She shot at the humanoid cockroach again, dodged its swinging arm, and stepped in to kick. No matter where her bullets punctured, or her kicks landed, the robot didn't seem affected. It was slow, too. Clumsy.

Click.

She looked at the gun. "No," she whispered. Out of bullets. *Now what?*

In a last effort, she dodged an arm, reached over, and ripped at the metal spheres on the thing's back. One popped off. She dropped it, letting it roll away. Under it was a sort of crater, as though this cockroach creature had only been designed to transport the spheres.

She danced around the turning body, then slammed her heel into the crater. The whole butt end of the thing banged against the ground. One of its legs cracked.

It hobbled—if a robot could hobble—still trying to turn and face her. Its humanlike arms swung, but couldn't reach.

She slammed her heel into it again. And again. A fissure point opened up along its side.

Angry tears dripping down her face, she kicked at that tiny vulnerability with all her might. A spark spit out of the body before smoke curled up. Crackles and a shimmer ran through the robot.

It had to be enough. She didn't have any more time.

She jammed the empty gun into her suit's utility belt and ran to Puda.

"Sweetie, are you okay?" she asked as she applied two fingers to his neck. A weak pulse pushed against her touch. "I'm going to get you out of here."

The thrum lingered, the carrier probably stationed right next to the security hovercraft. She'd never get out that way.

After threading her arms under his, she started to drag Puda across the floor. They made a wide sweep around the shaking robot, tried not to hit any rubble, and made it back to the elevator. Her only option was to hide and try to break into any intranet she could in order to call for help. It was a futile effort, but it was all she could do.

Chapter 3

"What has happened to this world?" Millicent asked as she stared at the gray destruction spanning out in front of them. Where once Los Angeles had been a collection of jagged building peaks rising above the constantly hovering cloud of pollution, now only half of the spires still stood. As though a huge animal had flown through and randomly bit off chunks, ragged holes had cut out sections of skyline. The light that had once glimmered off windows was now fractured, since many of those surfaces had apparently been blown out or broken.

"It looks like they just unleashed the weapons without thought or regard for human life." Millicent shook her head in sickened awe.

"This screams of desperation," Ryker said, staring through the window. "A desperate people are a dangerous people."

They rode in a large craft filled with the small group of fellow passengers from the rocket, and a much larger group of rebel troopers who were transporting them to the headquarters. The wall surrounding LA, acting as a barrier between the city and what lay beyond, loomed large behind them, nearly deserted of crafts entering the partially desecrated city in front of them.

"No more dangerous than what we're facing, right?" Trent asked. He clutched Marie tightly to him, resuming his duties as caretaker for the time being. Soon, however, he'd be in charge of tracking down the enhanced children the conglomerates had hidden from Toton, as well as acquiring any information or equipment he could gather regarding the progression of the breeding projects since they'd left.

Millicent glanced at her little girl and then away, her anxiety over bringing her child into this dangerous city threatening to derail her focus. At nearly seven, not including the three plus years of cyber slumber she'd spent on rocket trips, Marie had the intelligence and intellect of someone twice her age. But she was still a child. She'd begged and pleaded to be brought along on the mission, citing the many reasons she'd be useful. While her arguments were all justified, since she *was* the only one as good as Millicent, or better, at manipulating systems, and she could do it from a distance, she was continually met with a hard no. Appealing to her daddy hadn't helped in this case. Millicent and Ryker had forbidden Marie to come along.

Before leaving, they'd discovered one of the rocket pods had been locked with Marie's special abilities. It didn't take a genius to realize Marie had taken matters into her own hands, but Millicent hadn't been able to get her daughter out of the pod—she still didn't know how to counteract Marie's mental locking ability. In the end, they'd had no choice but to bring her, something that continued to gall.

"*This* is what we're trying to save?" Marie asked with skepticism.

"I see you didn't grow out of that attitude," Roe said. He grunted as he pulled his ankle onto his knee. The rocket journey hadn't been kind on his aging body.

"What, while I was sleeping?" Marie rolled her eyes. Her knuckles turned white where she clutched the window frame.

"We're not trying to save this," Trent said softly. "We're trying to keep this from spreading to us." He shook his head slowly. "I'm so glad I was kidnapped from this place."

"Mommy, someone has been trying to unravel your code in the pirate network," Marie said.

Trent's gaze drifted to Marie's face. "Her range and ability keeps surprising me. Just amazing."

"It's not her range so much as the pirate intranet having a strong signal in this city. They've worked hard to boost it." Using the console, Millicent locked on to what her daughter had found. A grin tickled her lips; she knew exactly who was trying to break in. "She's wily. Looks like she picked up a thing or two from Toton's code. She's gotten better. Still not as good as me, though."

"She hasn't been analyzing it in a serene environment." Ryker leaned against the cockpit partition. "She's been fighting for her life, most likely."

"Who?" Roe asked.

"My sister. She's been trying to get into the pirate network." Millicent pulled up the firewall log as a list of all the things she needed to look into rolled through her mind. She glanced at Marie again, and sighed. *Why fight it?* "Marie, can you get an up-to-date overview of where the various conglomerates stand? Logs, hazard reports, social media—"

"Sure." Marie turned away from the window, pulled her legs into a crossed position on the seat, and closed her eyes. Using just her mind, she could go deep into the systems and find twice the amount of information Millicent could, in half the time. The older she got, the more she could do. It was staggering what she was capable of—what the human brain was capable of.

Trent put his chin on his fist and stared at Marie, clearly thinking the same thing and marveling.

"Toton hasn't gotten through in the seventeen months we've been on the rocket," Ryker said, reading off the console screen.

"They've tried, but no." Millicent hacked into Moxidone's decrepit intranet. Toton had ravaged it, breaking through the firewall and scrambling files. Millicent wouldn't be surprised if they'd also somehow erased backups. "Looks like they had more important things to do."

Gregon was next, and while the overall structure was just as shot and ragged, Millicent found wisps of a different sort of defense. A cyber wall of sorts that would take her ages to crack.

Pride welled up. Her sister had erected a small defense in the only way she knew how. She'd hidden her secrets well.

"There's a pattern," Marie said in a wispy voice. Her brow scrunched. "I can't quite . . . Mom, look at the screen."

Pages of data overtook Millicent's screen and started to scroll. Millicent took control, organizing the communications and security logs into sections before poring over the data.

"Looks like Moxidone and Gregon have been moving their high-level staffers from one safe haven to the next." Millicent flicked more data onto the screen. "People have still disappeared, though. Declared dead, it looks like."

She latched on to the pattern her daughter had spotted. Toton had followed the group of high-level staffers from place to place, tracking them relentlessly, until one of the staffers was sent off with a team of highly experienced security. Only then had the threat to the other "important people" dwindled to manageable defensive proportions.

Toton had changed their target. Instead of following the group, they had begun to follow the individual.

Millicent knew who it was before she read the name.

"Danissa Lance," her daughter said, as if reading her mind. "They tried to hide her identity but they are hacks, at best."

"Toton has realized Danissa would work perfectly in their machines." Millicent leaned against the craft wall.

"How do you know?" Ryker asked.

"Because they've followed her all over the city, or so these security logs say. Shit." A sick feeling churned in Millicent's gut. "The last is recent. They are down to a security team of two. Gregon hasn't sent reinforcements."

"Do you think we're too late?" Roe asked.

Millicent slowly shook her head. "There's no way to know. But we have to check it out." She searched the database for Danissa's last whereabouts. "We need to change our plans. She's on borrowed time. We have to find her before they do."

"Then we should split up." Ryker gently pushed Millicent away from the console. "We need as many eyes and ears as possible, and we need them now. I can arrange for other crafts so we can hit the various destinations at once."

"Remember that we need to see if the rumors about the gifted children are correct," Trent said. "Preferably sooner rather than later, because if some of them are anything like Marie, they can help."

"Once a lab rat, always a lab rat, huh, Trent?" Ryker said.

Trent's brow fell low over his eyes. "They're children. I'm thinking of the children!"

"Enough," Millicent said, moving back to the screen. "I have a last known location. It's on the other side of the city, upper level. Toton has the location, too. They have units there—"

"How do you know?" Roe finally rose to look at the console directly.

"Because I know how to get into their intranet, Roe," Millicent said with barely contained impatience. "What did you think I was doing the whole time I was analyzing Toton's code?"

"Farting around? How should I know. I thought that was code no one had ever seen before."

"It was. And while it is advanced, much more advanced than most people could understand on this planet, I am not most people. And with Danissa's help, I am confident I can take it down. But we're going to need an army to get close enough."

"We have a sizeable force with the Rebel Nation, and if we can enlist some clones, we will have our army. Roe, you take a team and get the clones—make sure they accept our offer of employment," Ryker said, assuming command. He took his position in the middle of the floor so the group of rebels toward the back of the craft could both see and hear him. "Spread them out into the designated locations until we're ready. I'm with Millicent. We're going into the belly of the beast to get the systems specialist. Trent, you're on lab duty. Get out as many of the kids as you can."

"Wait a minute—by myself?" Trent clutched his shirt.

"What about me, Daddy?" Marie asked, her eyes snapping open again.

"Trent, not just you. A team will go with you. Marie, sweetie, this is too dangerous. We need to put you in a secure location."

Marie's face closed down and her jaw set. It was exactly the expression she'd had before sneaking aboard the ship.

"Rethink that, Ryker," Millicent said in a low tone. She didn't want to undermine his authority, but if she didn't say something, the situation was liable to blow up in his face. Marie was too much like him for her own good, and she'd push against his authority with all she had. Millicent had seen it before. Often.

Ryker's jaw had exactly the same set to it as Marie's did. He stared at her. She glared back.

"She'd get out of the secure location and put herself at risk," Millicent pushed quietly.

"You will be grounded for the rest of your life when we get back to Paradise, young lady," Ryker said grudgingly. "You'll go with us *and do as we say*."

"Yes, Daddy." Marie gave him a sweet smile.

"Is that safe?" Trent asked.

"She's safer with me than anywhere else," Ryker barked. "Land this craft and let's get going. The clock is ticking. Soon Toton will realize there's a new enemy on scene."

"A new enemy, and three new incredibly competent staffers," Roe said, eyeing Millicent. "If you're right, and they are after your sister, you'll draw their forces like flies to shit."

Chapter 4

"We've got activity, cupcake," Ryker barked a couple hours later from the console. "Your alert is going off. Someone is trying to get through your firewall."

Millicent glanced up from the array of weaponry she'd spread out across the floor. Two of Ryker's handpicked rebel troopers leaned forward in their seats. The other seven sat idly, placid and patient. They were high-level security guys from Gregon and Moxidone whom Roe's people had easily snuck out of the system when all hell broke loose. None of them had wanted to go to Paradise. They'd all joined the rebel ranks to help free more of their brethren. Except for one—he was only interested in freeing a girl. Whatever worked.

Marie sat with her eyes closed and her legs crossed under her. "It's from the same building that we're going to. She's picking at the wrong points. She doesn't see the gaping hole."

"There is no gaping hole." Millicent sniffed, now wondering what her daughter saw that she had not . . .

"If you say so," Marie said in a singsong voice.

"I'm not looking forward to the teenage years," Millicent muttered.

"Do we let her in?" Marie asked.

"No." Millicent stood and took the console. "She might dismantle some of my work without meaning to. I can't risk making the intranet vulnerable. Any idea what she's after?"

"Help, most likely." Ryker shifted so he could lean into the cockpit. "Skies are clear of traffic. This city is in a bad state. The death toll must be three times what we were thinking."

"At least," Millicent said. "How much longer before we engage, and what do you need from me?"

"Fifteen minutes until showdown. I can see Toton's arsenal gathered on the side of the building in question." Ryker bent to look through the window. "They have quite a few forces, but I doubt they'll be expecting an attack. Not with the skies looking like they do."

Millicent took a deep breath. "I'm about to cross enemy lines again. If Toton didn't notice the first time I poked into their system, they'll probably notice this time. We're about to show our hand."

"What hand is that?" one of the rebel troopers asked.

"What side we're on. And that we're not only hostile, but a huge threat."

"What should I do, Mommy?" Marie asked, eyes still closed.

"Can you follow along with what I'm doing?" With a few quick strokes, Millicent let herself into the back door she'd created in Toton's intranet and quickly got to work.

"Yes. Mostly. There's a lot of disturbance."

Millicent frowned. She wasn't getting that from the console, but then, she had no idea how her daughter's mind worked.

"Any of those crafts on manual?" Ryker asked, attaching an electro-magnetic pulse device onto a large gun.

"No." Millicent ran through the information. "None. No sentient beings in the crafts, either, as far as I can tell. Unless Toton names its staffers using serial numbers."

"Then bring 'em down." Ryker braced near the door. "Let's go, men. Get armed and ready. This is when shit gets real."

"We don't dock first?" one of the guys asked, jumping up.

"What sort of a cushy job did you come from?" Ryker growled.

"Ryker doesn't like doing things the easy way." Millicent executed her various commands.

"This *is* the easy way, cupcake."

Millicent rolled her eyes, then started hunting for the devices that were deployed to this building's location. If she could cut their feed—

"Mommy! They're overriding your commands." Marie sat ramrod straight.

Millicent swore under her breath. "This will be the constant struggle against brain-powered machines."

"I'll take care of the crafts." Ryker leaned over and slapped the command to open the craft door. Wind whipped through, flinging Marie's hair around her head. He posed in the doorway with his gun held out before pulling the trigger. He shifted his stance, pulled the trigger again. Another shift, another squeeze of his finger.

"Marie, cut the controls on anything Daddy doesn't blow up," Millicent said, back to hunting for the various devices they'd be facing.

The first craft exploded, rolling a wave of heat and fire in their direction. Their craft only rocked, far enough away that the blast did no damage. The next went up, and then the next, pumping flames and debris into the sky before falling like stones.

"I'll do the last one, Daddy." Marie jumped up and ran to the opposite window. The farthest vessel, not affected by the violence of Ryker's device, started to shake in the air. One side dipped, then the other. "They're fighting me for control. Like wrestling. But it's rudiments."

"Rudimentary, you mean," Millicent said, pulling up all the many devices deployed to this area. "Wow. All this for one woman. She is a prize, and they know it."

"Jealous, princess?" Ryker grinned.

Millicent ignored him as a warning blast of code scrolled down. "Their craft losses have been recorded. The race is on, gentlemen. They'll send reinforcements, and soon. We need to get in and get out, or we'll be captured trying. They have way too many robots deployed for us to kill them all and walk away."

"Take that craft down, little lady," Ryker said to Marie urgently. "Let's get going."

"They've logged the details of this craft." Millicent had to raise her voice over the moving and shifting of the troopers preparing to disembark. "They have eyes in this area, it looks like. They'll blow it up if possible."

"I figured. We have another craft standing by." Ryker's arm flared with muscle as he leaned against the door.

"Where?" Millicent flicked all the coordinates she'd assembled toward her wrist screen, copying the data over.

"There you go, Daddy." Marie pushed her hands against the window. The distant enemy craft tilted violently, rocking back and forth, before it exploded.

"Holy shit," one of the troopers said, stooping down to look out the window. "*She* did that?"

"Ryker! They've got a lock on us!" Millicent twisted around, looking behind them through the windows. She didn't see a craft or anything resembling weaponry.

"What does that mean, Millie?"

"I have no idea." Back at the console, she finished her preparations. The craft drifted toward the building. "Marie, do you see where I parked all the coordinates for the Toton devices in the building?"

Marie tore her eyes away from the window and looked at the screen. She nodded.

"They are always moving. The map of the building isn't perfect, and neither are the movements of those devices. But they are all parked in that file, and I need you to keep your mind on them as much as possible, okay?"

Her brow scrunched. "I'll try."

"We'll do it together. I'll try, too." A warning blared. The craft started to beep.

"We've registered a missile lock," the pilot yelled back. "I have no idea from where!"

"Let's go, let's go, let's go!" Ryker slammed the console. The door opened, five feet from the edge of the dilapidated walkway that led into the floor's entrance seventy feet above ground level. Harsh wind whipped into the space, the environment prevalent within the ruined bay. "We don't have time to extend a platform. Jump it. Go!"

The beeping in the craft turned furious. "We've got three minutes!" the pilot yelled. "Hurry!"

"What about all the handheld weapons?" Millicent yelled, desperate.

"There's no time. Go, go, go!" Ryker slapped backs, half pushing his men out. They launched across the lessening distance and either got out of the way, or turned to help the next person out.

"Two minutes!" The pilot threw off his seat belt and hopped up.

"Take Marie!" Millicent yelled, shoving her at Ryker.

He scooped her up and jumped across, landing easily. With a last look at her precious weapons, she sprinted after him. Her feet touched down and she staggered forward, landing awkwardly. A large man grabbed her upper arm with a strong, firm grip and pulled her farther onto the walkway. "There you go, little lady. We gotcha."

The craft bumped off the bay lock and drifted away. The pilot waited for the last trooper to jump before throwing himself across the now-enlarging space. The roar of something flying via jets echoed off the buildings around them. The pilot landed at a backward slant on the very edge of the walkway. He windmilled his arms with wide eyes and a gaping mouth.

"Grab him!" someone shouted as someone else screamed, "Run!"

"Go, Ryker!" Millicent yelled, grabbing the front of the pilot's suit and yanking. He tipped toward the walkway. A small object trailing a white stream of smoke was sailing toward them.

"Run!" she yelled, turning and putting on a burst of speed. Ryker was right in front of her, carrying a terrified-looking Marie.

They raced into the building as the object made impact. An explosion slapped Millicent in the back and shoved her forward onto her face. Ryker staggered, but managed to stay upright with Marie, who was shielding her face with her arms.

Those strong hands found Millicent again, lifting her like she was a baby and carrying her farther into the building. Flames engulfed the craft moments before it sank away from the bay.

"That was a small-scale missile," Millicent said, looking over the wide shoulder of the man who had now helped her twice. "It had a tracking system and was designed specifically for enemy crafts. The nature of that weapon was to hit its mark while doing the least amount of damage to the property around it, be it a building or any surrounding crafts."

"Wow. That's pretty good. How do you know so much about that missile?" The man, a natural born and quite handsome, set her down. Marie was put next to her a moment later.

"Because I designed it. That was a Moxidone missile." She smoothed her hair back as the implications ran through her mind.

Ryker turned her around and touched a few points on her back that were probably scorched. "Any pain?" he asked.

"No." She dusted off her front. "No. I'm fine." Glancing around, she didn't see whom she was looking for—namely the man she had saved on the walkway, who apparently hadn't stayed safe for long—but noticed something else.

Her relief at surviving the blast was short-lived.

"Mommy," Marie said in a warning tone.

"I see it baby. Robot."

The man from before stepped in front of her, his broad back blocking out her view. Annoyed, she pushed at him, trying to get him to move. That worked about as well as it always did with Ryker. "Get out of the way. I need to see what we're up against."

"Dagger," Ryker barked.

Dagger took a step to the side before saying, "I see it. It's guarding the entryway."

Millicent glanced down at her wrist. "That's one of the spider models. Only one, probably relaying intel. Soft spot is—"

Dagger reached it in a rush of muscle and power. In a fluid movement clearly born of years of training and excellent breeding, he dodged one of its kicking legs, picked it up, flipped it over, and punched the soft spot on the underside. The legs spasmed before they folded in on themselves.

"A simple kick would've done," Millicent muttered, looking back at her screen.

"Do we bring this with us for observation?" he asked.

"No. No sense in carrying it. There'll be plenty more to grab along the way." Millicent turned to Marie. "But if one of those things comes near us, you get out of the way, okay? You hide off to the side and wait until Daddy and I take care of it."

"Okay." Hugging herself, Marie looked around. "Should I just hide behind the piles of garbage?"

"Hide wherever you can." Ryker dropped his hand to her shoulder, but his eyes kept scanning. "Make sure nothing can get you from behind. Put a wall to your back and make sure we're to your front, okay? Like we've practiced on Paradise."

"Yes, Daddy," she said in a tiny voice. The know-it-all attitude from times of safety was gone.

"Let's get moving." Ryker motioned everyone on. "There are bound to be more."

"Many more, yes." Millicent pulled Marie close. "I'm not going to be much good if I'm watching her." Anticipation made her heart flutter. Despite having lost a bunch of her handheld arsenal in the blast just now, she had weapons that could handle what they were walking into, but it had been a year and a half since they'd received the last thorough machinery report from Roe's people. Toton could've easily upped their game in that time.

"We got you." Dagger winked. "There ain't nothin' gettin' through us."

"Dagger just *sounds* like a Curve hugger, princess," Ryker said as the troopers fanned out around him. "He's actually two and three above. He was one of the New York security directors."

"She judging?" Dagger asked with a laugh.

"She's always judging, bro-yo."

"Oh lovely, you're using the slang now, too." Millicent tried to prevent a frown, since that would only lead to more teasing, regardless of the danger they were walking into.

"That's okay, I can cut it back for the boss. No problem." Dagger laughed and fell back, covering their rear.

"And we're moving," Ryker said. Millicent suspected it was for her benefit because the men around him kept position perfectly, maneuvering as one entity.

Ryker took out his specialized EMP gun, another item Millicent had designed.

"We have two hanging out ahead of us, one to either side." Millicent pointed for those who could see her.

"One above," Marie said in a small voice.

"Need distances, ladies," Ryker said. "Oh, there we go. I see the ones up ahead, two and ten. Keep an eye on your six, just in case."

"What unit of measurement are you using?" Millicent asked, looking up.

"Based on an old clock." His eyes kept scanning. "The ones with faces."

Millicent shook her head and pushed the explanation from her mind. She had no idea what they were talking about. Movement caught her eye. A rusty sort of metal skittered, upside down, away to the right.

"There's the other one," she said, pointing.

"Don't see it," one of the troopers said, looking up.

Two gunshots rang out. Then two more. "They aren't bulletproof, boys," Dagger said. "And this ain't your first picnic. Get 'em gone."

"Save this weapon, princess?" Ryker asked, hefting the EMP gun.

"Yes. If a high-caliber gun will take them down, use that. Save the EMP gun for when we're surrounded. Which will be sooner rather than later . . ."

"I got one." A trooper braced, sighted, and fired in rapid succession. A moment later, a spasming robot fell from the ceiling.

"Someone should've told me they could climb." Millicent looked harder at her screen. "What other advancements do they have that I don't know about?"

"Despite climbing, these things are weak." Ryker stalked forward, arms held up with his gun out, leading them across the devastated floor. "Compared to those smart doors I remember, they're useless."

"They're easy to make, cheap, and probably filled with a not-bright CPU." Millicent tried her best to detach herself from what those CPUs were likely made up of. "They can make a ton of them, send them out into the world, and make easy grabs. Now that they know a harder job is at foot, they might be readying something better as we speak. We need to pick up the pace."

As one, they heeded her words, walking through the level at nearly a jog. Marie actually did have to jog to keep up, wringing her hands in fear and looking from side to side. Millicent would bet she was constantly monitoring the robots' movements.

"Got something." Ryker held up a hand, and everyone but Millicent and Marie slowed. Millicent jerked to a stop, committing Ryker's silent order to memory for the next time.

Ryker toed a curled-up spider robot out of the way, passed another, and then kneeled next to a pool of blood. Millicent tapped one of the trooper men and thrust Marie at him. "Watch her for a moment."

"I don't think you should be—"

"Let her do her thing," Ryker said without looking up, silencing his man immediately. "She'd take you down without a struggle. She doesn't need to be coddled."

The trooper stepped away with Marie, helping the little girl crawl up a pile of debris off to the side, apparently so he wouldn't have to bend to grab her if things went south.

"If only you'd follow your own directive," Millicent mumbled as she advanced on a robot she hadn't seen before. No pictures or reports had come through about this particular model. "This is a transport system, it looks like." She kicked the thing to make sure it was a robot's equivalent of dead.

A shiver went through its strangely shaped frame, styled to look half human and half bug. It didn't reboot or wake up.

She bent over a damaged crater in the thing's back and then glanced at the other two CPUs that were still in place.

"Looks like our girl was injured." Ryker followed the droplets of blood around the robot.

"Marie, can you check to see if she's still trying to hack into the pirate network?" Millicent batted down the surge of anxiety that her sister had already been taken.

"So you said these things run off these metal globes?" one of the guys asked, looking at the CPU that had been torn off and thrown to the side.

"It is a computer, and yes, that CPU is integral. The computer can't run without it. The organic matter within the CPU dies very quickly after being separated from the body in a normal robot. Those globes are for storage, I think. This thing is a life-support system, for lack of a better analogy."

"And if it's not segregated?" another asked, holding his position and facing their rear.

"It has a while before it goes to sleep and never wakes up." Millicent grimaced. "I think. This is all theory."

"So . . . like . . . it's a human brain in there, right? It's a person?" one of the other guys said, distaste curving his lips downward.

"Yes. I have no idea if it retains its identity. Although, it wouldn't have much of an identity, anyway. Not if the person was taken from one of the conglomerates."

"Speak for yourself, princess," Ryker said, frowning at the ground. "I was all identity when I was in the conglomerate."

"You were an exception, yes," Millicent said dryly, making a few notes on her wrist screen. "For better or worse."

"She's still trying to get in, Mommy." Marie pulled at her earlobe, something she did when she was anxious. "But Toton is sending more crafts here. We don't have much time."

"Not much at all. Twenty minutes, *maybe*." A wave of adrenaline coursed through her body. "Let's go, Ryker. We'll aim for the area the robots are targeting. We don't have time to investigate."

Another tiny robot ran by the fortified office deep within the building. Danissa had taken Puda down as far as the elevator would go, which was to floor forty-three. The environment wasn't turned on, or maybe it wasn't working, so the stagnant air smelled putrid and slightly burned her throat.

She sat, holed up in an office blocked off from the main floor by an overturned table in front of the door. The robots, which were a stupider tech than the others, were tiny dronelike devices that used a brain-wave seeker. She'd long ago learned how to change the readings of her implant and mask her brain. But if the bigger machines or the heat-seeking robots came down, she was out of luck.

Shaking from hunger and fatigue both, she stared at the code on the screen. So intricate. There were only a few points that she could pick apart in the hopes of weaseling in. Millicent Foster had really upped her game in the last few years. She'd clearly learned the same new tricks from Toton as Danissa, but she'd then expanded on them and created a unique and interesting product.

Frustrated tears obscured her vision, and she wiped them away furiously. Puda's ragged breathing was worse now, and his head had begun to bleed again. She'd found another Medi-Kit on this floor, but even the fresh supplies were barely helping him cling to life.

"C'mon, Danissa," she whispered, her mind churning. "There must be a way in. *Must* be."

She'd already sent a plea for help to Gregon and Moxidone's security departments, but it had been intercepted by Toton, like all things sent through the internet these days. They had their hooks in everything, except her rooted, private network and Ms. Foster's pirate network. Those were the only available options for communication, and since the hard port in this building wasn't working, that left the pirate network.

The impenetrable pirate network.

Hopelessness tugging at her, Danissa analyzed the code on the dim screen. "Okay, what if I try . . ." The screen flickered.

Danissa yanked her hands away. "I didn't do anything yet," she said to Puda, even though he wasn't responsive. It made her feel like he could be. Like he was okay.

It flickered again, the information in front of her wobbling.

What if Toton had already cracked this code? She'd be stuck. That would be it.

The screen went white, and then the whole thing seemed to melt. A hazy picture of a blue ocean appeared. A large wave crashed down.

Danissa blinked in astonishment.

Light flickered outside the windows of the office.

Danissa stood, as if in a dream, her mouth dropping open. Outside, in the open space filled with rows of mostly intact work pods, all of the screens flickered to life. From dull gray, they turned crystal blue, cut through with the foamy white of a cresting wave.

"It couldn't be," she said in barely contained hope.

A message popped up on all the screens. "We are coming. Mommy said to just hold on. We will be there as soon as we can."

It was a message from Millicent Foster. It had to be. She'd always sent little taunting notes within Danissa's favorite image of a cresting wave. Her daughter was clearly with her.

Or was it a trick of Toton? They were known for hacking into systems and creating a very similar display. The message was a first, but she wouldn't put it past them.

The light from the screens illuminated the shadowy places. Danissa sucked in a breath. Robot bodies were crowded in all the corners. Movement flickered across the floor. The robots had found her.

Chapter 5

Trent clutched his gun in a shaking hand and tore his mind away from the danger Marie was in somewhere else in this Holy-forsaken city. He was used to looking after her. Even on Paradise, when a rampaging bull got out or something, he watched the kids while Ryker and Millicent baited the animal back into its pen. That's what he excelled at—nurturing. Educating. Patience. He wasn't a psycho like the other two.

He shouldn't be heading up an extraction, as they called it. With his lack of experience, his mission was doomed for failure.

"Okay, sir, we're ready." Rhett, one of the troopers who had been chosen to go with him, stood beside an open door in one of the many nondescript buildings in this part of the city. The upper levels had been blasted away, but this middle section was mostly untouched except for a few scars.

Trent looked back at the craft waiting in the sheltered bay, alone. No vessels drifted by within the travel way. The area looked deserted, more so than the rest of the city.

"We're sure they're in here?" Trent adjusted his fingers on the gun.

"Yes, sir. We got this information from a Gregon staffer."

"And Toton doesn't know about it?"

"No, sir. The information is behind an ironclad cyber barrier of some sort set up by the Foster sister."

"Danissa."

"What's that, sir?"

"Danissa is her name. And stop calling me sir." Trent took a deep breath and looked at the open door. Then back to the craft. "You should move that thing, right? So no one wonders why it's parked there?"

"Who is around to notice, sir?"

He had a point.

With the other members of the extraction team waiting for him, he turned sideways for reasons he couldn't explain and tried to drift through the open door as he'd seen Ryker do so many times before. An empty reception desk stood in the middle of the wide aisle, all the screens dark. Faint light from two rows of emergency strips glowed from the somewhat grungy floor, casting a horribly brownish-yellow glow. Corridors branched out to the sides, as empty as the space that lay before him.

Trent checked the coordinates that had been sent to his wrist screen. Millicent had rigged his implant to receive messages on a certain frequency. Or something. Truth be told, he wasn't really sure how it worked. "What this says is go straight . . ."

"Yes, sir. Follow the map."

Trent scowled in confusion. He didn't have a map. Just step-by-step directions. Millicent clearly didn't trust him.

Eerie silence preceded them down the desolate corridor. Occasionally, a scuff of one of their shoes echoed off the walls.

"Someone is here to monitor the children, right?" Trent asked despite the desire to remain as silent as possible. He flashed his light upward, looking for security cameras. They were there, staring down with their black eyes. No glowing lights on top of the units, though. Turned off. Much like the overhead lights.

"As far as I understand," Rhett said quietly. "It's like a bunker. Just the bare minimum."

Trent read his screen and turned right at the next corridor. "This is a maze. Ours was never this confusing."

"They moved the kids here specifically because it was a maze."

A heavy hand fell on Trent's shoulder, stopping him. Rhett put his finger to his lips and motioned for Trent to stay put. Trent wasn't going to argue.

Trying not to wring his hands, Trent watched as Rhett practically melted against the wall by the corner. He motioned to another trooper, who then flattened against the opposite wall.

Rhett nodded to the other trooper, who peered out into the corridor. A loud pop made Trent jump. Red fluid sprayed the dirty cream wall. The trooper slid to the ground. His head slapped off the floor.

"We've got fire," Rhett yelled.

"Obviously." Trent quickly dropped to the ground. Low was a good place to be. Enemies didn't expect people to attack on their bellies.

"Mirror." Rhett reached an open hand toward the other troopers. He was given a small mirror attached to an extendable pole. Body plastered to the side of the hallway, Rhett eased the mirror into the open space.

Another gun blast exploded the mirror into fragments.

"Sharpshooter," Rhett whispered.

"Another fairly obvious statement . . . ," Trent muttered.

Rhett looked at his wrist screen. Another trooper took out a small mobile screen, which meant she didn't have a working implant.

"We can try to go around," the mobile-screen gal said. "But I bet they'll have the hideout covered on all sides. I would."

"Do they have the manpower to keep everyone out?" Rhett asked.

"For Toton? Probably not. For us? I would imagine so."

Everyone looked down at Trent. He rolled to his side. "What?"

"You're in charge of this op. What's our next step?" Rhett asked impatiently.

Clearly Ryker hadn't relayed some very important information regarding Trent's skill set.

He sat up, since the situation seemed to demand it. "Well . . . Gregon and Moxidone are in cahoots now, right?"

"Sir?" Rhett's brow furrowed.

"Well, only Toton is the enemy, right? And the other two conglomerates, for now, are friends?"

"I'm not sure I follow—"

"Yes, sir," the female trooper said, lowering her mobile screen. "For the most part, they have banded together."

"Well, if Toton is their common enemy, then all we have to do is say that we're not Toton, right?"

Rhett shifted, his face still screwed up in confusion.

This must be how Millicent always feels, Trent thought, *when no one understands a word that comes out of her mouth.*

"Okay, well . . ." Not trusting his solution enough to actually stand and carry it out, he crawled toward the corner. He shook off the hammy hand of Rhett on his back, which slipped uncomfortably to his butt when he kept going forward.

"Get off—" Trent twisted enough to slap the hand away, and then got to his knees as he reached the corner. He edged his mouth closer to the corridor, though it probably wasn't necessary, and said, "We're human. I'm with Millicent Foster's crew. Ms. Foster and Mr. Gunner are back from Paradise. We're here to help. We want to get these kids to safety."

As his words died, silence floated down like ash.

"They don't trust us," Trent mumbled. Not that he blamed them.

Something nudged him. A thin extendable rod was placed into his hand, another mirror attached to the end.

Grimacing, he said, "I'm going to put a mirror into the corridor, just to see if you . . . are there." He steadied himself and made ready to stick the mirror out. A gunshot sounded and something knocked his boot. He jerked back. A chunk was taken out of the sole.

"What the hell?" he screamed, struggling away. "I'm friendly, damn it! I want to save the fucking children! If they are even *half* as gifted as Marie, like I've heard, and you've spent time *teaching* them a little something, they could help you out of this mess. But *no*, you go around shooting at the nice guys, for fuck's sake."

He threw down the mirror and fingered the chunk taken out of his boot. Another inch and it would've taken off his pinky toe. He tried very hard not to glance over at the limp body oozing blood, and failed. His stomach started to churn.

"How did you know Marie's name?" someone called from beyond the corner.

After clearing his throat in sudden, unexplained nervousness, Trent said, "Because I named her. Well . . . *I* didn't name her, but I went along with the name Millicent chose. It seemed fitting, if a bit unorthodox. It really is next to impossible to say no to Millicent. She's a bit . . . intense."

"There's no need to be so chatty about unimportant things, sir," Rhett whispered.

"You do you," Trent said as he wiped his forehead, then wiped his newly moist fingers across his suit. "Let me do me."

"What do you know about that girl-child Marie?" came a woman's voice.

Rhett rolled his hand in a circular motion, indicating that Trent should keep talking with them. Trent rolled his eyes. Clearly these people thought he was an idiot.

"I know everything about Marie. It was my concoction that made her extraordinary abilities possible. I have seen her every day of her life, both on this planet and on Paradise. I did the research that led to her parents' pairing. And I know that the woman who made this hiding place possible is a blood relation to Ms. Foster. As in, they had the same two parents. Very intelligent young ladies, to be sure. I thought Millicent was the more advanced of the two, but I actually think she's just the most diversely trained. I wonder if—"

Trent shook off Rhett's heavy hand, but didn't resume speaking.

"All right, then," a man said. "Send out a robot first."

All the troopers stared at Trent. He stared back. No one had said they were supposed to bring a robot!

"Do the rebels even *have* a robot?" Trent whispered.

"A few of Toton's, but we only use those to study." Rhett licked his thin lips. "Bluff."

"How? By walking out stiff-backed? They'll blow my head off!" Trent huffed before raising his voice to the others. "We don't have robots. Just people. As you saw a moment ago when you killed one of them."

Silence descended. Time stretched. Trent earned some pretty annoyed and menacing stares, but realistically, why not just tell the truth? It's not like they could conjure up a robot, and a lie would only result in more bodies. Those people had itchy and expert trigger fingers; they had the upper hand. In Trent's experience, that demanded respect. At the very least, wariness.

"Fine. Come out one at a time with your hands up."

Trent's eyes popped. They were letting them in!

"I don't want to go first," he said a moment later. He couldn't help it—he wasn't cut out for extreme situations.

"I'll go first," the female trooper said before tucking her mobile screen into a pocket and then patting the pocket closed. The defiant and annoyed look she shot at Trent fell on an indifferent attitude. He wasn't trying to be a hero. Smart people died less often for a reason.

She jammed the gun into her utility belt and raised her hands as she walked beyond the corner. Facing in the direction of the previous gunshots, she planted her feet and stared forward with a blank face.

"You reach for any of those weapons, and we'll shoot you," the male voice called.

"Big barricade blocking off the whole floor," the woman trooper murmured.

A gunshot blasted. A divot in the floor opened up right next to her boot. She didn't so much as flinch.

"She's tough," Trent said, waiting with a pounding heart.

"That'll be enough talking," the male voice called. "Bring out the rest. Let's see all of you."

One by one, the troopers walked beyond the corner and faced their attackers. Trent waited until the very end, really wanting to crawl out on his belly. He doubted it would help, though.

"Which one of you is the doctor?" the raised male voice said.

Not one of the troopers looked Trent's way, but they all waited, probably wondering if he would show at all.

"Here," Trent said, shaking all over. "Just back here."

"Come out."

"I don't really want to, in all honesty. How do I know you won't shoot me?"

"'Cause I said I wouldn't."

"No, you didn't . . ." Trent edged to the corner. He breathed deeply for a moment, squeezed his eyes shut, and then hopped out into the open. Whole body tense, fists balled, he stood his ground, waiting for the worst. A gun cocked.

Chapter 6

"That all of you?" the voice asked.

Trent peeled an eye open. As the woman trooper had said, a giant barricade hulked in the corridor, made up of everything one might find in a lab or office. Chair legs stuck out at odd angles; shards of screens littered the ground; sections of desks and work pods were piled up. It reached nearly to the ceiling.

A flicker of movement drew Trent's gaze to the upper left where a small cutout revealed a long black barrel. Beyond was a head and face mostly obscured by a woolly hat. A flicker on the other side told him there was at least one more person looking down on them.

Trent let his other eye drift open, though his body didn't quite relax as a result.

"You must be Trent McAllister." The head on the left shifted, indicating he was the speaker.

Not able to help it, Trent's back straightened in pride. "Why, yes I am! How wonderful that you've heard of me."

"Of course I've heard of you. You started the disgusting mutant human experimentation."

One of the troopers snickered.

"There is nothing mutant about what I did," Trent said in indignation. "All of the children were born naturally. The mothers were given a perfectly safe biological concoction with very mild side effects. Just a little extra queasiness. Certain food pouches could have had the same effect—"

"You may have started that way, but when you took the girl, they went in a different direction. They killed more kids than I've ever seen. Disgusting. You lab rats are always trying to see if you *can* do something, instead of asking if you really *should*."

Trent's heart twisted. He scrubbed his palm against his pant leg. "There is nothing wrong with Marie. Nothing at all. She's not a mutant. She's like any other kid, except extremely intelligent and—"

"Yeah, whatever. I should kill you right now."

"Please don't." Trent braced, about to jump back beyond the corner, but what he'd just heard about the kids kept him rooted to the spot. If there was a chance he could help them, he had to take it.

"We can't stay here now, anyhow," the woman's voice said from the other side of the barricade. "If *they* found us, it's only a matter of time before Toton does."

"We got the information from someone who recently left the conglomerate," Rhett said. "Toton won't get through the firewall."

"You really don't get it, do you?" the man behind the barricade said. "They surely know you're here right now. Your craft is probably bugged. Or maybe they'll capture someone who'll squeal. Maybe they'll be patrolling and see your vehicle in a place where no vehicles ever stop. Whatever it is, they'll know. Now or later, they'll figure it out. Ms. Lance hid this place from them, but that's no good if she didn't manage to hide it from all of you, hip to that? We're trekked. Now we gotta move a bunch of kids. In fact, I really should just shoot you. One less person to—"

"If you leave, you will get caught," Trent said in a rush. "But we can help. We're *here* to help. Millicent and Ryker got Marie off the planet. They are a deadly team. The rebels have a whole underground system set up on this planet, with safe houses and defense . . . I mean, Millicent designed a crap load of weapons to fortify it. She's the leading weapons designer in the world. They're going to rescue Ms. Lance right now. Literally, as I speak, they are rescuing her. We can keep you safe until we get the children off-planet and away from the conglomerates and Toton. I'm sure you can come, too, but you'll probably have to be a little nicer. And put the gun down . . ."

Trent's words drifted away. The tension pressed on him. If the surly guy opened fire, they'd have to dart back for cover, but one or two troopers would get picked off. Trent would be the first, of course. He'd serve as the indication things had gone sideways.

"What've we got to lose?" the woman said, standing up. A skinny thing with a gaunt face, she looked like she'd missed dozens of meals.

With a sigh, the man stood up as well, his appearance much the same. These people didn't have much in the way of supplies, that was obvious. They wouldn't have been able to hold out much longer.

"Can I see the children now?" Trent asked tentatively.

"Yeah. You got to climb over this wall, though. The easier ways in are on the other side of the floor, and you'd probably get shot because we can't leave our posts to walk all the way over there."

"Right . . ." Trent glanced behind him at Rhett before he started forward. "You guys don't have communication devices?"

"Got no implants." The man tapped his head. "Had to dismantle them to keep Toton from frying our brains. We weren't high up enough to get our implants fixed like our superiors."

"But . . . you still have—" Trent cut off because there was no point in reasoning with the man. While they did have the tech and sufficient power in the building to rig up something, they didn't have Millicent to do it, or even Ryker to guide them in a work-around. Trent had forgotten what it was like to live without top one-percenters around to make life easier.

"Hurry up," the woman said, watching Trent's arduous progress.

"Can't you lower a rope or something?" he asked in a collection of grunts. A chair leg stuck him in the side. He grimaced and then slipped on a loose flank of metal. Something sharp cut his arm. "This is ridiculous! It only keeps out humans. Robots could probably get right up this."

"Why'd you ask us to send out a robot?" asked Rhett, right below Trent.

"Stop it." Trent wiggled to dislodge the large hand that had covered his butt cheek. Rhett was trying to push him upward. "I don't need you touching that."

"If you'd sent out a robot, you would've shown your hand, wouldn't you have?" the man said. "We would have known you were Toton."

"But . . . not exactly . . ." Trent paused to rub his eye. "If we took over some of the robots, reprogrammed them, and started using them to save human lives, then we would have a robot. We lost one of our team, as you clearly saw . . . since you shot him. With a robot, we wouldn't have."

"If you had sent out a robot, we would've shot you when we saw you. Only Toton has robots."

"I feel like we're talking in circles—get . . . off!" Trent slapped Rhett's hand away. He heaved himself to the top of the pile. Breathing heavily, he said, "Oh good, you have stairs on this side."

Trent made it down to the floor without killing himself, which was miraculous. When everyone except the woman on the wall, who stayed at her post, was over the barricade, they started off down the corridor. The directions on Trent's wrist aligned with their progress. After a couple more turns, they came to a second barricade.

"Don't you be coming no closer, hear that true?" a woman called from the top. "I got a rocket launcher with your names on it."

"It's me, Gertie," the man called out. "These people are here with that rebel group. They're going to get us out of here."

"Sounds like a bunch of crap to me," Gertie said in a bold, crackly voice. "Look like security, they do. They ain't coming in here. Someone done sold out, that's what I'm thinkin'. You can bork out on your own, Kajel. You ain't takin' all of us with yous buggers."

"Is that Standard?" one of the troopers asked, eyeing a mobile screen.

"Just a bunch of slang," someone answered.

"This idiot started the breeding projects." Kajel hooked a thumb Trent's way. "Bred that kid, Marie."

"Actually, if you knew your history, the breeding projects started soon after the Enlightened Ages when we put a stop to the majority of natural births," Trent said in disapproval. "With Marie and the others, I merely enhanced the natural—"

"You're a damned fool is what you are." Gertie leaned over the wall to get a better look. Skin sagged on her face and around her jowls. She was old for someone so obviously low in the conglomerate hierarchy. Those without the creature comforts of plush living, or clones to switch out body parts, often succumbed to the harsh environment much sooner than those of higher-level status who had all those things. Unless she was actually a superior and chose to affect the slang so common among the lesser staffers, as Ryker was starting to do. "You opened a door for those resource-stealing, air-clogging sons of test tubes? Once they got a whiff of what could be done, they went crazy with it, they did. Created a bunch of monsters."

Ryker would have to strive harder to match Gertie's flair.

"I assure you, I—"

"Bah!" Gertie waved her hand through the air. "You're all the same, yous buggers. But anyway, how do I know it's really you, eh?"

"I'm well fed and healthy, for one." Trent spread his arms. "Off-planet will do that to you . . ."

"Showboatin' now? Cog swogger." Gertie lowered a large barrel that could only be the rocket launcher she'd warned them of.

The troopers tensed. Trent raised his hands. "I just meant that I've obviously been off-planet because I've been eating right. Otherwise I'd be skinnier. Like you." Trent cleared his throat. "If you pull that trigger, this whole place will fall on your head. Think that through."

"He knew the first one's name, knew the parents, and has a tendency to babble," Kajel said in a bored tone. Clearly this wasn't the first time Gertie had threatened to use her weapon. Thankfully, judging by the intact walls and floor, she hadn't yet made good on her threat.

"That right." Gertie lowered the weapon a fraction. "You do babble a lot. You did know her name."

"Not to undermine myself, but anyone could've just looked it up. It's in the conglomerate natural birth record—"

The hard elbow in Trent's back cut off his words.

"They wiped her record clean," Kajel said, starting toward the barricade. "Took her name out and gave her a number. Classified whatever compound you used to create her. Then started experimenting. Our Ms. Lance lifted the details so our labs could use it, but not the name. Ain't no one save a select few heard the kid's name."

"Then how did you know it?" Trent asked.

"Gertie, get out of the damn way, will ya?" Kajel said. "We don't got this kinda time. Suppose Toton saw these buggers land? We gotta pack it up."

"*I* knew the name," Gertie yelled down. "I was screwing one of the Moxidone lab rats when that whole thing was going on. Said the creator named her, and that ain't never been done before, you hear me, Hometown? That name stuck in my brain. Then she got taken by the creator and the natural dad, and the three of 'em up and disappeared. Well now, that got some people thinkin', yes it did. All them women wanting their babies—"

"Gertie, get out of the damn way, I said!" Kajel yelled.

"Fine, fine. But I still say this is a bad idea," she grumbled, disappearing from the top of the wall.

"That's it?" Trent asked incredulously. "All that and she just wanders away?"

"You got a problem with keeping your mouth shut, Hometown," the female trooper said. The rest of them snickered.

"What does *hometown* mean?" Trent asked. "I mean, besides the town in which one's home is located?"

"Get going." Trent felt a nudge much too low for his taste. Rhett was too grabby by half.

"Is there an easy way to . . . no. We're just climbing over this one, too, are we?" Trent hung his head for a moment before following Kajel up the pile, thankfully a smidgen easier to climb than the last.

On the other side, he sighed in satisfaction. It was a development facility like the one he'd had back in the conglomerate days. Memories of children laughing and toddling around made a smile crease his lips.

Gertie opened the glass door manually and then pushed at it to keep it open so he, Kajel, and the troopers could walk through. The room beyond was encircled with low cushioned benches, and faded and worn children's toys littered all the surfaces. Funny animals and matted, stuffed bears brought warmth to his heart.

"What phase are they in?" Kajel asked Gertie as he made his way across the room. He stepped on one of the bears.

"Watch out," Trent berated, moving the bear out of the way before turning back to everyone else. "Kids chew on things. Don't get your filthy shoes all over their toys."

"Oh yeah, he's Trent McAllister, all right. Drove all the staffers crazy with his constant rules." Gertie's lips pursed.

"It's logic and plain common sense," Trent spat, his mood turning sour. "Keep the children healthy, keep their minds active, and watch them flourish. Obviously it's the right way, given how excellently Marie and her siblings turned out. I'm now in charge of the birthing and child development station on—"

"I'm already sick of listening to the cog swogger." Gertie pushed past. "Through here. They should be just waking up from their naps."

"What's a cog swogger?" Trent asked Rhett.

"Dick wagger."

Trent scowled as they entered a smaller room with miniature work pods set up, all of the screens blank. Primitive writing tools lay scattered around, along with some material that had been scrawled on.

"This is where they're taught?" Trent asked in disbelief. "Are they below the Curve?"

"In the beginning, we tried to teach them their letters, but these kids . . ." Kajel waited by the next door. "They're different. They're not like normal kids. So we just try to keep them contained."

"What are we walking into?" one of the troopers asked, fingering the gun at his belt.

"*You* are not walking into anything." Trent held up his hand. "Stay out here. I'll go in."

"Suddenly found your balls, huh?" one of the troopers muttered.

"They are *children*, people!" Trent bellowed, unable to help it. "A lunatic old lady with a rocket launcher is terrifying. A child is—or *should* be—sweet and innocent. It's people like you who really bring the overall intelligence level to soggy depths, I will tell you. I have to remember to tell Millicent she was right all along."

"No way would I work with him, I'll say that much," Gertie said, shaking her head. "Good thing I was off in Gregon when he had his reign of terror."

"Oh, just shut up." Trent pushed past Kajel and then slowed at the sight of little beds and a couple of cribs. Ragged and torn, the bedclothes were stained and crusted, not cleaned often enough. Little arms lifted and wiped tired eyes. Small bodies shifted to look at him. As they did so, he caught sight of their badly sagging and thin mattresses, not much better than sleeping on the floor. Gaunt little faces broke his heart. They hadn't had enough sustenance, either, as small as they were.

This was war, he had to remind himself. The children were alive, and he was here in time to help them. He had to focus on the positive.

"Hello, everyone," he said in a chipper voice as he entered the packed room. "Did you have a nice nap?"

"Who the trek are you?" an older boy asked, sitting up. His black hair sprayed around his head. He was a few years older than Marie, by the look of him.

"Ah. I see they didn't watch their language around you. Hmm. What's your name?" Trent sat down on the floor with his legs crossed, a nonthreatening position.

"Why should I tell you?" The boy scowled.

"Mhm. Okay." Trent turned his attention to a little girl Marie's age, clutching a raggedy gray blanket. There was no telling what color it had been originally. "And how about you? Did you have a good nap?"

"Don't talk to him, Suzi," the boy said, standing up.

"You're not the boss, Terik!" Suzi yelled. She turned back to Trent, dirt splotching her angelic little face. "I'm Suzi and I hate napping. But they make us do it even if we're not tired. They say that napping means we won't be as hungry."

Rhett leaned in through the open door. "A black craft just slowly passed the bay. Let's get moving."

The danger he'd managed to forget at the sight of the children drifted back, pressing on him. He threw a nod over his shoulder to keep the riled-up trooper at bay before turning back to the children. It was important to establish a pathway of trust, especially in this setting. Otherwise, the children might balk at any orders they were given, putting the whole group in danger. "My name is—"

"*Now*, Hometown," Rhett barked.

"That glance was intended as silent communication," Trent said through clenched teeth. "Give me a second to get everyone mobile." He turned back to the children. "As I said, my name is Trent. I used to work with children like you when I was on Earth."

"What do you mean, when you *were* on Earth?" Terik asked, stopping a little boy as he jumped off his bed and ran toward the door, all energy and movement.

Sensing that he had to gain the trust of Terik in order to have any sway with the group at large, Trent shifted his focus and body both. "I was kidnapped from the lab I worked in by the parents of one of the children. You see, they wanted to take their child off this planet so they could all have a better life. And we do have a better life in our new home. You will, too."

"So why'd you come back?"

"I'm so glad you asked—"

"We don't have time for this," Rhett said in a dangerous tone.

"We heard that this planet was in a lot of trouble," Trent continued, standing. Heaviness pressed down on his chest—the urgency to leave was at war with his need to appear calm and nurturing. "We wanted to help. And most importantly, we wanted to free the children. *You.*"

"I'm hungry," the little boy said.

"We've got lots of food pouches on the craft." Trent smiled. "And on Paradise, we grow our own food! So we always have plenty to eat. You'll love it there. But first we have to—"

A soft buzz in Trent's head made him reach toward the spot behind his ear where his implant was located. That was a warning from the craft. "But now we have to hurry because the bad people have found our hovercraft, and they might want to do us harm. All of us."

"I know who Toton is. And they aren't any worse than the other conglomerates, who just blow up buildings regardless of who's in them," Terik said.

"Will they catch us, Mr. Trent?" Suzi asked with large round eyes.

The little boy Terik had stopped broke free and did a strange little dance before grabbing his crotch.

"No one is going to hurt you, Suzi." Terik grabbed the little boy's shoulder. "I'll protect you."

"Oh, hmm. Interesting." Despite the danger eating away at them, Trent couldn't help staring at Terik for a moment. "The protection complex. I wonder what their breeding goal was with you."

"Let's go," Rhett barked. "We're out of time."

"We're leaving?" asked one of the children, a little girl of about four.

"I say good riddance." Suzi's face screwed up. "I hate it here. I liked the other place better."

"Where are you taking us?" Terik asked, lifting a toddler out of one of the cribs. The other was vacant. Only five children occupied this whole complex, it seemed. So many security precautions for so few . . .

Gregon really wanted to keep these children safe. The rumors about them being different had to be true. The question was: What made them different?

"To a safe place." Trent glanced at his screen. "Oh no. The black craft is back, and it's hovering just outside of the bay." He glanced up at Rhett. "It's stopped. What does that mean? Can we get out?"

So much for that calm and nurturing demeanor.

"It's just the one." Rhett adjusted his utility belt. "We can blast it out of the sky."

"How many crafts can we fight and still have a chance at survival?" Trent asked, shooing the little boy in front of him before helping Suzi zip up her suit.

"Three, max. And that's if they don't have any surprises Ms. Foster didn't plan for."

"Do we have enough room for everyone?" Trent grabbed the younger boy's hand. The child ripped away and then kicked Trent in the shin. "Ouch! Why did you do that?"

"He always does that," Terik said, taking the four-year-old girl's hand.

"With the two coming in from the barricades on the other side, and the one we left on the way in, we'll barely have room." Rhett spat onto the lab floor, which was uncalled for. "But we'll make do. Let's go."

Trent quickly bent, bringing his face eye level with the younger boy. "Please don't do that. It's not very nice. Now, we have to—"

He barely saw the little hand before it slapped him across the face.

"Good *night*!" Trent jerked away.

"Here." Terik handed off the toddler, but not before blasting Trent with a commanding stare that most men three times his age couldn't have duplicated. "If you try to harm any of us kids, I will kill you."

"I think you'll need to start training with Ryker, A-SAP." Trent hoisted up the toddler, thankfully placid, as Terik grabbed the little boy.

"Are you trying to get us killed?" Rhett seethed. "Let's go!"

Adrenaline fluttered in Trent's stomach. "I wasn't the one who left the craft out there for the world to see," he muttered.

They pushed through the doors and hustled out. None of the five children so much as glanced at the adults they passed. Instead, they kept their heads down or straight ahead, watching where they were going. They'd largely been left to their own devices, Trent surmised. They were being kept, but they were not being raised.

At least we got here in time. Focus on the positive.

"I flat out told you they would know," Kajel was saying as Trent emerged into the corridor with the children. "Didn't I say? Now we're trekked."

Trekked, Trent thought. *Terik . . .*

It was an interesting similarity in naming. It made Trent wonder . . . He really wanted access to the breeding files.

"Wait! Toad Man!" The energetic little boy yanked out of Terik's hands and turned back the way they had come.

"His stuffed animal. We have to get it." Terik calmly grabbed the boy.

"No way. We need to move." Rhett motioned everyone onward. The troopers filed in immediately, followed more slowly by the facility staffers.

"I think it would be smoother if we just went back for it really quick," Trent said, stopping. "Otherwise he'll certainly be a problem to maneuver."

"We gotta keep going." Rhett roughly grabbed Terik and jerked him forward.

"Hey!" Trent was pointing a gun at Rhett's face before he even realized he'd snatched it off his utility belt. Ryker had rubbed off on him. "Do not manhandle the children—"

Fire burst to life along Rhett's legs, reaching toward his belt like a live thing.

The trooper looked down with widening eyes, shock bleeding through anger. "What the—"

Terik, face calm, yanked out of the trooper's grip.

The other troopers all froze with wide eyes.

"Damn you, you little resource raper!" Kajel rushed forward, his hand lifted out to strike.

"No!" Trent swung the gun Kajel's way, suddenly realizing that he was drawing a very clear line at that moment. Soon it might be him and a bunch of children against a small army of armed adults. There was nothing for it, though. Striking children in anger was not done. Not on his watch. "Back off."

"I ain't afraid of no small-minded hip chucker." Gertie swung her arm to finish Kajel's intent.

Trent braced, ready to fire a warning shot, when suddenly Kajel, Gertie, and Rhett flew backward. They rammed against the wall, bounced off, and were then lifted into the air by unseen hands and slammed down on their backs. Their heads thunked off the ground.

"Holy . . ." Trent stared, out of breath though he hadn't moved. The three moaned. "Holy . . ."

The fire along Rhett's legs sputtered out. One minute it was burning full force, eating holes into his fire-retardant suit, and the next it was simply gone.

Wide-eyed, Trent turned his head slowly to stare at the children. He couldn't form words.

"Them two ain't worth taking," Gertie spat before rolling onto her side. She coughed. "Disgusting wastes of space. Monsters!"

"What the fuck just happened?" Rhett asked, getting to his feet. The rest of the troopers had their guns out and were looking around wildly, clearly with no idea whom the enemy was or what they'd do once they found out.

"Was that . . ." Trent cocked his head, black craft forgotten, staring at a nonplussed Terik. "Did you do that?"

"Toad Man!" the little boy yelled. He jammed his balled fists toward the ground in anger.

The glass doors behind them shattered. The adults jumped. The troopers peeled away to the sides, probably looking for cover. A moment later, a dingy stuffed toad flew through the air until it hovered in front of the violent boy. He snatched it up. "Toad Man."

"What do you say?" Trent said with a slack jaw, on autopilot.

"Thank you," the boy muttered, swishing his hips from side to side.

"An abomination, that's what them is." Gertie climbed to her feet and spat bloody mucous at the ground near Terik. "Shoulda been recycled with the rest of the retards."

"Screw you, old woman!" Terik sneered.

"That is a disgusting thing to anyone, much less children," Trent said to Gertie, grabbing Suzi and pulling her close. It was clear from the children's placid reactions, however, that worse had been said to them—and often.

They are still alive. I can still help.

Dozens of questions were suddenly burning through him, but there was no time, so Trent gently nudged Suzi forward. "Let's go. We need to make it to headquarters, and then life will get better for you children. I promise. We just have to get past Toton."

They started walking forward as a group, with Trent near the front. Someone in the back whispered in a shaky voice, "Did they do that?"

"Seems like it," someone else answered. "That's weird. It isn't natural."

Trent shook his head. "You aren't natural, either." He glanced back, hitting everyone with his hardened gaze. "We were all born in a lab. So before you throw stones, think about that. The only differences between you and these children are they are smarter, and they have awesome natural abilities this world has never seen. They are furthering evolution whereas the rest of us are just running in place. Open your minds."

"Big talk for someone that don't know what evil he's shepherding," Gertie said, keeping pace with him.

"What I don't know is why they gave a rocket launcher to someone who is obviously insane. That's what I don't know." Trent shook his head and took Suzi's hand. She was walking so close she was bumping up against him.

They turned the corner and continued through the darkened, empty corridors, the lighting stripes on the floor guiding their way. Footsteps and breathing pushed against the silence. Trent's curiosity flared within the deadness.

"While we have a second," he said conversationally, his lifetime of training getting the better of him. "What is it that makes you children special? Can you really move items telekinetically?"

"Don't tell him, Suzi," the other little girl said. "He'll just think we're weird like everyone else does."

"He said we have awesome abilities," Suzi replied.

"That's right, Suzi. I think you are fascinating and special. All children have gifts; don't get me wrong. Especially children above the Curve. But you—or some of you?" He waited for elaboration on who had enhanced abilities. No one spoke up, not even the adults. "You are one tier more advanced than that. It really is an exciting situation for all of us. We are literally seeing the progression of evolution before our eyes."

"Does that guy ever shut up?" someone said in the back.

Trent pressed his lips together.

"I'm smart, too, but no one seems to care about that," Terik said quietly.

"On the contrary, I am keenly interested in *how* intelligent," Trent replied. He couldn't help himself. This felt like the realization of his life's work. How could he *not* be excited? "Did they test you against the Curve?"

"Yeah. I'm four and three above, so they said. They were all excited until I accidentally lit something on fire. I barely remember doing it. Then their tune changed real quick."

"I'm three and some four," Suzi said. "But mostly just three. Terik is smarter. But I can control my power better. Once I have access to it, that is. That part is still hard."

Gertie huffed in derision.

"Do any of the little ones have special abilities?" Trent asked, thinking that a direct question might get some answers. "Or heightened intelligence?"

"They may test high, but they ain't smart," Kajel scoffed as they came upon the large barricade they'd crossed earlier.

"They need to be taught—oh, just never mind." Trent waved the rebuttal away. "I'm not usually an asshole, but you need to be sent to the front lines of this war. There. I said it."

"Get the children over." Rhett stopped at the base of the barricade and motioned everyone up. He brushed his fingers against his implant. "We got more trouble coming. It doesn't take Toton long to swarm."

"Here." A gruff-looking male trooper stepped closer and reached down for the energetic little boy. "Fancy a ride, little man?" he said, his harsh voice softened.

"I'll help." The female trooper smiled at Suzi. "Hi, smart girl. Can I help you?"

"Now that's more like it," Trent said as Suzi shyly took her hand. "At least some members of the group have sense."

On the other side, where they were joined by the staffers who'd protected the other barricades, Rhett paused. "Shots fired!" He stared at his wrist screen and swore. "We'll be fighting our way out of here."

Without a command, the group sped up, hurrying down the corridor. Suzi's hand found Trent's, trembling. Or was it Trent who was trembling? It was hard to tell.

Trent's wrist screen lit up with a warning. When he got to the large entranceway to the floor, able to stare through the glass to the bay beyond, he knew why.

Four black vehicles hovered around the bay openings, waiting like sharks in Paradise's salt lake. Two bodies were sprawled on the ground outside the rebel craft. Blood pooled in the places where their heads should've been.

Someone retched. Trent's stomach swam.

"They shot through the bay. We won't even make it to the craft," someone whispered.

"There are too many." Kajel shook his head. "They'll come in after us!"

"How are we going to get out of here?"

Terik stepped away from everyone else, his gaze pinging between the waiting craft and the bodies on the ground beside it. "Suzi, get everyone ready," he said in a haunting voice. "We can handle this."

Chapter 7

"This floor is teeming with them," Millicent whispered as they waited in the stairwell with half the troopers. Marie huddled in close beside her. The other half had taken the elevator, just in case one way didn't pan out. It wasn't a surprise to anyone that Ryker had chosen the stairs for his family—the elevator had the most probability of failure.

"How many would you guess?" Ryker asked as he crouched by the door, EMP gun in hand.

Millicent bit her lip. "Hundreds. They clearly realize that Danissa is the most valuable player in this war."

"That's because they don't know you're planet-side."

"No. It's because they don't know Marie is." Millicent felt the familiar pang of agony in her gut. If she had been a mom who spanked, she would have turned her daughter's butt a fierce shade of red for forcing her way into this journey.

A comforting hand rubbed her back. Ryker's confidence and strength bled through the touch. "We'll all make it out of this, Millie. We are prepared for the worst. This isn't it by far."

A sob welled up—instinctive fear for her child. She forced it back down. This was not the place to lose her cool. Instead, she nodded and blinked the moisture out of her eyes, annoyed that her three births had turned her into a sobbing mess. Biology was a real asshole.

"Here's what we need to do," she said, back on track. Barely. "We'll take out the first wave of critters with this." She held up the Deadener, a sleek little orb fashioned from the same metal as the CPU casings. "It'll electronically sever the brain unit from the motherboard. The system will be nonoperational, but the brain will not die. As soon as the Deadener stops working, the connection will restart, and the critters will be back in business."

"How long will it last?" Ryker asked.

"In testing, it lasted five hours. But gravity and time are different on Earth than on Paradise due to the gravitational—" Millicent registered Ryker's clenched jaw and the impatient shifting of the troopers. This wasn't the time for a science lecture. "It'll probably last a little longer if the environment doesn't corrode it, but it's tough to say."

"It'll last long enough for us to kick the little fuck—excuse my language—spiders in the nuts." The trooper rolled his shoulders and then his neck, glancing at Marie.

"Exactly." Millicent glanced at her wrist screen before zooming out to get a better view of the floor as a whole. "I only have one Deadener, and that will reach a radius of ten feet, so twenty feet diameter in a nearly perfect circle. Again, that may change in this environment. Don't waste time trying to kill them all. Marie and I will take care of most of that. Just run past them and kill however many you can."

"I don't want her touching—"

"Ryker, you can use the EMP gun on the second wave of robots"— Millicent raised her tone to drown him out—"which will allow me to move the Deadener close to Danissa's location. Hopefully the elevator crew will have caught up by then."

"And if you can't get the Deadener into a useful position?" Ryker asked with a severe tone and flashing eyes.

In other words: "If it's too dangerous, you better keep to safety and leave us to handle it, or there will be hell to pay." But she had paid hell plenty of times—this would be no different. There was no sense telling him that, though. He'd only push his point. "Then we improvise. I'm sending the coordinates of Danissa's probable location. To those who can receive it, obviously. The rest will just have to figure it out. Shouldn't be hard. Their host is converging on one spot. She is likely in that spot. Any questions?"

"No, ma'am," many of them said.

Ryker nodded and started gesturing—pointing and flicking his fingers, flashing numbers, and waving his arms. His vocal language was grunts, mostly. Millicent had no idea what directions he was giving, only that he *was* giving them. The men shifted and braced themselves for action, some bringing out guns, some switching to knives—all their bodies coiling into attack readiness.

"You better not be undermining my plan," she said for his ears alone.

"I will not lose you or Marie, Millie, no matter what perfect strategy is involved. Your ruling has been usurped by the king."

"All hail," someone said.

"Kings got their heads cut off in times of old," she retorted, getting ready. "I'd be careful if I were you. I might take an active interest in history."

"I love your violent foreplay." Ryker glanced at the troops. "Here we go."

He ripped open the door from the stairwell and quickly stepped aside, leaving a gaping entry for Millicent. She filled it immediately and rolled the Deadener in front of her. In the ball's wake, scurrying robots slowed, jerked, and then their legs curled up under them. They sat immobile.

"Kick their faces, or stomp on their—" Millicent cut off as Ryker flicked a robot up with his toe and, while it was still turning over, kicked it. A sizzle and spark accompanied its crash to the ground twenty feet away. "Or do that."

She reached the first robot and stomped on the CPU, dislodging it from the base enough to hear a strange sort of mechanical whine. A shiver arrested her. It was just the mechanics, she knew, but it sounded a little like a robot scream.

Time to harden up and use her training, or she'd end up in one of those CPUs.

Picking up the pace, she stomped on another as all the troopers started flicking and kicking, only some of them able to properly take out the robots, and none so masterful as Ryker.

"Moving on to the next phase." Ryker left the circle of stilled robots. He aimed his gun at the moving, scurrying swarm of insects beyond the Deadener's range.

Millicent's skin crawled. She slapped at a tickle on her arm, feeling imaginary legs crawling up under her suit. "They had to pick the most vile animals as models for their robots . . ."

"Not animals, ma'am. Insects," a trooper said as he ran by.

"Yes, I—" Millicent rolled her eyes and pulled Marie close. "C'mon baby, we need to follow Daddy now."

"There are more on the way," Marie said with wide eyes, taking in the teeming space in front of them, festering with the insect robots. "There are too many."

"They are a stupid sort of robot, sweetie," Millicent said, not able to soften her battle-ready voice. "They are here to collect a prize, not do battle. Danissa must not have shown any sort of serious resistance in the past. But Daddy and I do resistance best. We'll be fine."

But the sheer number of spiders in front of them put lead in Millicent's stomach. Toton wanted Danissa something fierce, and they'd sent quite a collection unit to grab her.

"Let's go, baby, we're falling behind." Millicent grabbed the Deadener and ran forward, staying to the middle of the path, making way through the EMP-downed robots. They wouldn't be getting back up—that was the beauty of that gun. Too bad it didn't last longer or maintain a larger charge.

A robot scurried out from the side. Its leg swung out, aiming for Marie's thigh. Millicent swung her daughter around behind her and dropped the Deadener.

Five-shot.

The gun filled her hand as the robot swiped again. She dodged, yanked Marie with her, and fired into the creature's face area. It readied another leg, but Millicent fired again. Smoke curled up before the robot started to jitter. It would die a moment later, Millicent knew. She didn't wait around to watch.

"C'mon, baby. Hurry!"

"I thought they were dead," Marie said in a panic-stricken voice, clutching on to Millicent's thigh, slowing her down.

Millicent snatched up the Deadener and forced it into Marie's hands. "Figure out why that stopped working, baby."

Another robot rushed in from the front, swiping with two feet. And another from the side.

"Crap." Millicent turned, fired. Turned back and fired again. She stepped forward to kick a shaking wounded robot in the vulnerable area on its underside. She wrapped her fingers around Marie's arm and ran, dragging the little girl behind her.

"Mommy!"

A robot ran behind them, trying to get at Marie. Another came from the front. "Ryker!" Millicent yelled as she kicked the one in front of her, sustaining a slash in the process, before swinging around to shoot the one behind. Its sharp claw glanced Marie's ankle before it went down. She clutched her little girl tightly, no idea where to stash her or turn her to keep her out of harm's way.

"I gotcha!" Dagger, the leader of the team that had gone into the elevator, ran up out of nowhere, followed by his group of troopers.

"Here we go." He scooped up Marie and swung her around onto his broad back. "Hang on tight, little lady. Don't fall off now, ya hear?"

"Let's go, let's go, let's go," another trooper said, firing down at two robots running out of the darkness.

"You got any light in your bag of tricks?" a trooper asked as he swung his foot back before delivering an intense kick. A robot went flying. "It'd be nice to see into these shadows."

"Where'd you guys come from?" Millicent's heart was pounding in her ears.

"Ran into a wall of desks." Dagger jogged forward. "Looked like it was made recently. These robots aren't as dumb as you say. They're trying to keep our mark on this floor. Trap her."

"Danissa must've come down on the elevator, then." Millicent checked her wrist as the troops surrounded her. "A smart robot would've also blocked the stairs."

"Touché."

"Okay," Millicent said, recovering her focus. "Straight forward and then curve left—"

"Millicent!" Ryker emerged from the gloom, his men fanned out behind him.

"I got 'em. We're good, sir," Dagger said. "I'll keep the baby. She's as light as they come. But Sinner's right—a light would sure be nice."

Sinner? Someone with an active sense of humor had named these guys.

"Marie, can you activate the screens again?" Millicent said as she reached Ryker.

His gaze coated her body, lingering on the scrape on her leg before rising to meet her eyes. "You good, princess?"

"Now that Marie is taken care of, I'm good. I was having trouble playing hero."

He flashed a grin that didn't reach his eyes. "Leave the hero business to the big dogs, cupcake. You handle the nerd stuff."

"Cute." She pointed at a diagonal right. "We're headed that way, ultimately."

Cracked or faded screens flickered before a cresting wave filled them. Light shone down on the critters, which were skittering into a sort of cluster ahead of them.

"How about that Deadener?" Ryker asked, staring ahead.

"Cut out. I don't know why. Marie is hopefully working on it." Millicent glanced back at her daughter, who was trying to hang on to Dagger and look at the orb at the same time.

"I don't know, Mommy," Marie's little voice said. "The program is fine, I think. I don't know why it's not working."

"You focus on that, Millie." Ryker flashed his hand signs. Why he couldn't just speak so they were all on the same page, she did not know. Dagger transferred Marie to a smaller guy, who then drifted into the middle of the new configuration of battle-hardened men. Millicent was handed the Deadener and then nudged into the middle with Marie. "That thing might make the difference between completing this mission and running like hell. There are too many."

"Too stupid to do it on their own, so send a bunch," Millicent mumbled, looking down at her device. Small lines of corrosion already marred the sleek metal. A sort of grunge coated one of the sensors.

"That's why they've covered the CPU with a harder material," Millicent said to herself. "The other metal corrodes too quickly."

A hand plucked at her sleeve. Everyone started running as a blast sounded ahead of her. Ryker had used the EMP gun again. Another blast in another direction. At this rate, he would drain the weapon faster than they could get out of there.

The men around her surged and retreated, taking out anything the gun missed. But no matter how many they took out, more robots still emerged from the flickering light.

Millicent scrubbed the rest of the sensors on the Deadener and cleaned off the surface. "Earth is nothing like Paradise, and it's showing in the durability of the tech." She scraped goo out of a crack with her fingernail. Like a shock wave, robots paused and shook around them. "It's working."

"That's my girl. Now let's get this done before it borks out again." Ryker motioned her forward and they all ran, staying to the middle of the debris to keep it easy, firing at stalled robots along the way.

Somewhere in the distance, a strange thrushing sound permeated the whine of robots.

"Anyone got a visual?" Ryker called as they rounded a corner.

A sea of flickering screens showed a semicircle of robots, the light glittering on their metal bodies.

"I got nothing," someone called from the back.

"Nothing here, sir," from the right.

"Just spiders," Dagger said from the left.

Straight ahead, a table was on its side, wedged into the doorway of an office. Standing behind it, a long pole in hand and a cloud of hair frizzed around her head, was the woman who had caused so much annoyance in Millicent's old life. Her blood. Her sister.

She was besieged by robots, and only her feeble attempts with that pole were keeping them from pushing that table aside and forcing their way in. Judging by the focused surge forward, the battle wouldn't last much longer. Thank Holy that Millicent and crew had arrived in time.

The robots around them spasmed. And then climbed to their feet.

"Shit!" Millicent swore, looking down at the orb. "It cut out again."

"Prepare to be swarmed," Ryker yelled.

Chapter 8

Fear choking her, Danissa blinked away the sweat dripping into her eyes and tightened her grip on her pole. A spider bumped the table, knocking it toward her. She swatted down with all her might, *thwapping* it in the back. The bulbous body dented a tiny bit. The critter jerked, as if it felt the impact.

Danissa hit it again, grunting with the effort. This time a large section caved in. The robot spasmed and curled up, continuing to shake. Two more scurried up to take its place.

Breathing heavily, she looked around wildly for something that might help her. But nothing in the office could be pulled away to fortify the table. She sagged, nearly out of energy. The pole was too light and the robots too many.

Two huge men with thick arms materialized out of the darkness. Behind them, other large men fanned out, their movements lithe and graceful. They looked to be higher-level security, much like the ones who had fought and died for her to get at the hard ports.

A gap opened in the middle of their group. Danissa saw a man with two little arms wrapped around his neck. To his side ran a woman, currently looking down at something in her hands and not paying attention to the fighting going on around her.

"Oh thank Holy," Danissa said, tears coming to her eyes. "They're here, Puda. They've come."

Trying not to focus on that silence behind her, she smacked her pole down on one of the new spiders even as the other bumped up against the table. She staggered back at exactly the wrong moment. It bumped again and the table fell toward her.

"No!" she yelled, slamming her body against the hard surface. The robot bumped back, but its leg had already made it through, aimed at her hip. She'd survived until the rescue only to miss the mark by ten seconds.

"Gotcha!"

A loud thunk and the spider went sailing away. One of the large men kicked another spider, sending it flying. He glanced at her, winked, of all things, and then turned his back on her. "Feisty fuckers, eh? I got you, lady. Just hang tight. The best of the best are here to save the day."

"You're an even bigger showboat than Ryker." The woman who'd been in the middle of the group stopped beside him, working at a small metal orb in her hands.

"Hat trick," the large man said before kicking another robot.

"What?" The woman glanced up from the orb in irritation.

"Here, take the child in there with you." The man handed the little girl over the barrier, and suddenly Danissa found herself holding a fearful-looking child as two people bickered in front of the office, all while they were swarmed with spider robots.

"Have I died and this is my punishment for not picking a deity to praise?" Danissa asked in confusion.

The woman with the orb looked into the office, straight at her face. "I'm Millicent Foster. That's my daughter. You harm her, and I'll kill you. You got that?"

Danissa blinked. This woman, whom she'd competed against for years before Millicent escaped off-planet, and whom she'd never met face-to-face, was much harder than Danissa had ever been. No wonder she'd made it from Earth with her child.

"You got that?" Millicent pushed.

"She's in shock," the man said. "She'll be fine. I'm watching her. Get that thing working."

"She'll be okay." Danissa licked her dry lips. Her arms constricted without thinking. She loosened her grip in case it hurt the child. "I've got her."

Only then did the woman look back down at her hands.

A blast sounded to their left. A group of robots stilled and curled up. On the right, men were kicking, shooting, and hacking their way through the horde.

"Really need that sphere operational, Ms. Foster," the man said.

"Nagging won't help my productivity, Mr. Dagger," she retorted.

Another blast, followed by a second section of robots curling up.

"What is that?" Danissa asked.

"Just one of the things you're going to help me perfect," Millicent said without looking up.

"I'm out, princess," a deep voice bellowed from somewhere outside the office. "Cluster together. Fall back."

"This should work." Millicent ran forward. In a circular area around her, the robots ceased activity. Men drew near to her.

"Dagger, take my daughter from the stranger and have her fall in," a deep voice said. Danissa couldn't see the speaker, but his voice was hard and commanding. He'd led men before. *Thank Holy.* "We're getting out of here as fast as possible."

"Wait!" Danissa yelled earnestly as the man next to her reached for the child. "Puda. There is a downed man in here. I need to take him out."

The man next to her—Dagger—hesitated. A man with jet-black hair in a loose bun on his head stalked into view, all muscle and brawn. Without a word, he reached for the child. For Puda's sake, Danissa wanted to hold on to her. They would be forced to help him if she held the child hostage. But that hard, flat stare, burning with intelligence and violence, had her handing over the little girl before she knew what she was doing.

"Dagger, get the fallen. We need to move." The large man turned away with the child clutching his shoulders in an extremely familiar way.

"Is that . . . Gunner?" Danissa said in disbelief. He'd been a legend when he'd worked for Moxidone, the best they had and the most lethal.

"Who else did you think would be traveling with Ms. and baby Foster?" Dagger asked with a grin. "Now let's go. We need to get out of here while Ms. Foster's device still works."

Hand to her head, Danissa backed away from the table to let Dagger knock it down and enter the office, which was suddenly a lot smaller. "This is surreal."

"You got that right, pretty lady. This the guy?" Dagger bent to Puda. He placed two thumbs on Puda's neck before bracing his hands on his knees. "Is giving him a proper send-off worth risking all our lives?"

"No, he's okay. He's unconscious, but he's alive." She took a ragged breath. "He is. I checked before the robots started to advance. He'll be okay. I gave him more Cure-all."

"What's going on?" Gunner called in.

Dagger's handsome face tilted upward. His dark eyes met hers, as if he were reading her. Judging.

"He'll be okay." Had that sob come from her? She couldn't tell. All she could feel was pain. Horrible, body-consuming agony at the gravity in this man's gaze. At the truth he was too kind to speak out loud.

"Okay." He hauled up her best friend and longtime lover and threw Puda over his wide shoulder. Without another word, he turned and started jogging toward the group.

"I don't know how much longer this thing is going to last," Millicent said in clipped words. "The EMP gun is out of charge. We need to do this at high speed."

"I'm your mayfly." Dagger glanced back as he fell in with the others. He nodded in approval when Danissa jogged up and stopped beside him. "Stay close and you'll be okay, you hear? I'll get you outta here."

"You've got that quote wrong," Gunner said, handing his daughter off to the smallest of the staffers. His hands and fingers danced, and then everyone except the two women started jogging. At Millicent's scoff, Danissa figured she didn't understand the silent security communication, either. "I saw the original vid," Gunner added. "The remake changed that line."

"You didn't see the original," Millicent said. "You saw a remake of the original. Which was probably a remake. No one can think up new ideas anymore. Save your ammo, everyone. If this thing goes out," she said, hefting the little globe, "you're going to need it."

"The point is, I saw a way older one than he did," Gunner said.

"What's the line, then?" Dagger asked. He kicked a robot. It did a huge arc through the air and landed fifteen feet away.

"I'm your huckle-homie." Gunner kicked a robot. It went a little farther. He grinned at Dagger.

"What the hell is a huckle-homie?"

"Like a friend, I think. *Homie.* Old-school slang."

"But huckle?"

"I don't know, bro-yo. It's an old vid."

"We're down!" Millicent shouted. She bent to the orb in her hand.

"Peel off. Stick the others in the alcove while we give Millie more time," Gunner barked. "Please tell me I am correct in assuming that thing is fixable, cupcake."

"Don't know," she said. "Give me a moment."

"That's all you might have."

The smallest man turned toward the alcove with the girl. He climbed over a pile of debris.

Cold dripped down Danissa's middle. "No!" she cried, shoving Dagger out of the way and grabbing at the man. "Bombs. There could be—"

Snap.

Danissa clutched at him in panic. He looked down at his foot in confusion, not moving.

Something heavy hit her, knocking her to the side. Her feet flew up and her back slapped the ground. Before she could roll away, a solid object landed on her, stealing her breath. A loud explosion blasted heat, scalding her arm and washing across the soles of her boots. Wall spat out, rolling toward her face. She tried to turn away, but her head was wedged between a man's muscular chest—the thing that had landed on her—and the floor. Squeezing her eyes shut, she waited for cement and plaster to strike her.

But the blow she expected never came. The man on top of her shifted. He grunted, probably because the debris he was shielding her from was raining down on top of him.

Silence filled the room except for a light ringing in her ears.

"You okay, pretty lady?" came a deep and scratchy voice.

She had no idea.

"Danissa?" he asked again, shifting, probably to look at her face.

She peeled her eyes open as he moved away the large piece of wall. He'd stopped it right before it hit her nose. *That was nice of him.*

"The little girl," she said, dazed. Unable to breathe.

"She's okay. Gunner got her. What about you?" He peeled off her. She felt gentle prods and squeezes to her extremities. "Anything hurt?"

"No." She allowed him to pull her up. The ringing persisted no matter how many times she shook her head.

He ran a single finger down the side of her arm. Shivers erupted. "That hurt?" he asked.

"Feels . . . cold," she said, confused. "Wait." She looked down at her blackened suit, scorched from the blast. "No, I'm fine. Sorry. I had weird shivers just then. But I'm okay. Puda?"

Her gaze fell on him then, lying on the ground in a heap. Dagger had dropped him to grab her. He'd gotten blasted by the fire, too. Part

89

of his face was scorched, though his suit had held up. His eyebrows were burned away, and some of his hair. He lay perfectly still. His chest didn't rise and fall.

Barely able to breathe, Danissa turned her face away and squeezed her eyes shut, the truth hot and sharp in her gut. She wanted to give in to the blackness that threatened to consume her. The guilt, the sorrow. But he wouldn't want her to die here, with him. He'd want her to live.

A hand covered her shoulder. "You okay?" Dagger asked softly.

A sob wracked her. She dug her nails into her palms and clamped down, fighting against the rising tide. The pain wobbled, threatening to take over, but she held firm. This wasn't the time to let go. Not here, where death always lay around the next corner.

"Yes," she whispered, forcing her eyes open. She took in the rest of the scene, desperate to get her logical mind firing to drown out the sea of emotion.

The alcove had been blown to hell. With it, the man who hadn't moved in time. His reactions hadn't been as fast as Dagger's or Gunner's. Gunner was off to the side, his back a mess of burned suit and blackened and bloody skin. Another man was already sticking him with Cure-all or some other medical necessity. The little girl was sobbing in Millicent's arms, being clutched like she was a priceless bottle of water.

Two other men were getting treatment, though their burns weren't as bad.

"How did he survive that?" Danissa asked, staring in shock at Gunner's back. "How did he even get there in time?"

"He's bred for it." Dagger lifted an elbow so he could look at his side. "He trained for it. And he heals fast. I got lucky—I got the same healing gene. Still hurts like a hornet's tit, though."

"Don't it ever," Gunner said.

Robots were scattered about them, their legs curled under. They hadn't been touched by the blast itself, but they'd somehow been affected all the same.

A lightbulb came on. "That's why Moxidone hid all those bombs inside the buildings," Danissa said. "Something about them takes out the robots."

"They could've gone about it a million different ways." Millicent's every word was laced with anger. "A million different ways. All without harming humans. What fucking useless—" She ground her teeth.

"You didn't design that?" Gunner asked Millicent.

"A device with that long of a delay between detonation and blast? No. What's the point? You either want to blow someone up, or you don't."

"They probably set it with a delay to give any humans the chance to get outta Hollywood," Dagger said.

"Got that saying wrong, too." Gunner shook his head. "It's get outta Rango."

"Where's Rango?" Dagger asked.

"Somewhere in the prehistoric Earth desert, I think."

"If they did set it up that way, then some Curve hugger programmed it." Millicent scowled. "It's not a long enough delay for most people to get cover, and I doubt robots can set them off, so why have them up there?" She shook her head. "None of that makes sense. I think Moxidone had an ulterior motive."

"Or they're just lost without you." Gunner grinned with tight eyes. Danissa had the distinct impression he was trying to cover up his pain. Or maybe ignore it. It didn't appear to be working very well.

"They were definitely lost without you," Danissa said in a wispy voice.

"C'mon," Millicent said. "My device, which won't kill people, is probably working. We need to go."

"Probably?" someone asked.

"Can I get a shot of Fire-soothe for the road? My shi—stuff hurts," Dagger said, turning toward the others.

Danissa sucked a breath. Red and blistered skin shone through his seared suit. Blood oozed in places. With his lightning-fast reaction time, he could've easily gotten clear and saved himself a world of hurt. Her assigned security would've hesitated. Instead, he had knowingly dived into the fire to pull out a perfect stranger.

"Who are you people?" she asked slowly.

"Best of the best, at your service," Gunner said, taking something out of his utility belt.

"Blowhards, mostly." Millicent hugged her daughter tightly as Gunner stuck Dagger with the Fire-soothe. "But fast healers, thank the Divine."

"All right. Let's get moving." Gunner stepped away from Dagger.

"That stuff doesn't make it hurt any less," Dagger growled. "I got cheated."

"You look tougher when you suck it up, short stack." Gunner slapped the other man on the back.

Dagger gritted his teeth and tilted his head slowly. Fire danced in his eyes. "You'll live to regret that."

"That's the plan. Let's go. The princess is getting agitated. Something about her machine not living up to expectations and putting us all in jeopardy." Gunner took his daughter back from a scowling Millicent and kissed the little girl's head. "All right, sweet pea?"

"No, Daddy. That was scary."

"We're almost there, baby. Almost there." Gunner hugged her. "I'll carry you for now, okay?"

"Touch Daddy's back, Marie, he likes that," Dagger called.

"Don't listen to Curve huggers, honey, they speak nonsense."

"What about Puda?" Danissa asked, staying by his side. She couldn't leave him. Not after all they'd been through together.

"Don't you worry, pretty lady. I got him." Dagger bent.

"I got it, bro-yo." One of the other staffers put his hand on Dagger's shoulder and took his place. "We don't need you passing out from the pain."

Dagger shot a glance back at Danissa before stepping away. "He'll be in good hands with Sinner, all right?"

She nodded meekly, her brain still trying to shut down. Her emotions threatening to take over.

After a while, Dagger said, "I thought Danissa was supposed to be just as . . . precise as our Foster?" Danissa heard the lightness in his voice. The teasing.

Was he trying to lift her spirits? While in the middle of a battle zone with death hiding over every pile of debris?

"Precise . . ." Millicent squinted at him. "Is that your way of saying uptight?"

"Yes it is, ma'am. It sure is, you caught me." Dagger put his hand on his heart. "Danissa seems downright pleasant, though."

He *was* trying to lift her spirits while in the middle of hell. Danger apparently had no effect on the man.

Millicent minutely shook her head, working at her device again. "She's in shock." Her hands lowered and her head came up. She motioned everyone forward. "Wait until she's back in her element. You won't be able to stand her."

Danissa could hear the others laugh but couldn't understand the sentiment in her state of numbness. She just wanted to get free and see to Puda. That was all.

"Did they put those bombs everywhere?" someone asked.

"Yes," Danissa answered automatically. "Best to stay in well-traversed areas. Don't step on debris. Don't go too far off the path."

"We got lucky, then," someone muttered.

"Very," someone else answered.

"A lot of people have already died by those bombs," she said in a monotone. "The bodies were cleaned up . . . by someone. I don't know who. Or why. But quite a few people, mostly staffers, have tripped those bombs."

"Are there bombs in the Moxidone buildings?" Millicent asked. Her voice barely carried over the swish of fabric and the heavy tread of the injured.

"I don't know. I've never been in a Moxidone building. I mean . . . you know . . . since all this started. The conglomerates are largely working together but are still mostly separated as far as the staffers go."

Millicent didn't respond, or if she did, it wasn't loud enough for Danissa to hear. While normally Danissa would want all available information to make a sound judgment on the happenings of the world around her, at that moment, she was thankful for the silence.

"I'll go first," Gunner said as they reached the stairwell. He stood the little girl next to Millicent.

"How many floors up?" Millicent asked, stepping out of his way, but not so far as to touch the remains of a crumbled work pod behind her.

"Five. I hadn't realized we'd be down this low when I set up the rendezvous." He opened the door quickly before stepping through with his gun pointed. A moment later he backed out. "Going down would've been easier than walking up."

"Astute," Millicent said.

"I'm a master of strategy, cupcake. Take a lesson."

Someone huffed out another gruff laugh. And then people were moving, taking a cue from some unspoken signal. Two men pushed past Gunner and into the stairwell, taking up position with their guns. Gunner guided Millicent in next and lifted his daughter.

"Your turn, pretty lady," Dagger said, holding his arm out behind Danissa and walking by her side, corralling her into the stairwell. She couldn't tell if he thought she was fragile, or unhinged enough to sprint away in an attempt to find a bomb and end her suffering.

"Stop calling me *pretty lady*," she said as she filed into the stairwell. She'd rather seem like an asshole than a weakling. Maybe it would even help her get through this.

"Will do, Miss Lady."

Her breath came in fast pants as they raced up the stairs, practically running. With each floor, they hesitated to check the way ahead. Before they started forward again, the man at the back would pass up some sort of hand sign that she eventually realized was *all clear*.

When they reached the intended floor, they stood against the wall and looked up as the two leads braced themselves by the door to the landing.

"I see a few robots meandering in the open space," Millicent whispered as she stared down at her wrist. "There are a great many hovering around the elevators—on all the floors, not just this one. If we stay away from the elevators, and don't make too much noise, we should be okay. In theory."

"How can they get in the elevators?" someone asked in a hush.

"I have no idea," Millicent said with a furrowed brow. She looked at Gunner. "There must be someone or something on the premises that can reach the button. Or that can hack into the building loop, but I've seen no indication of that."

"Let's talk about it later." Gunner looked at the stairwell door. "How's that device of yours working?"

"I cleaned the sensors again. Hopefully it'll work fine. Worse case, you'll get more target practice."

"I love that you're always thinking of me." Gunner's grin didn't reach his eyes. "Use your silencers, everyone. Take note that it will cut the power of your gun in half."

"Just gotta use a bigger gun, then," Dagger said, taking a small metal circle out of his utility belt. He affixed it to the side of his gun barrel.

"I thought silencers went on the end," Danissa said in confusion.

Dagger winked at her. "We got the best weapons maker in the world on our side. In *two* worlds, actually. That woman up there is a superhero."

"What's a superhero?"

"Like . . . the flying guy who wears tights and a cape."

"Sounds like a tart," someone muttered.

"Let's go," Gunner said, putting the child down next to Millicent before jogging up the stairs.

Millicent followed, slower now that Marie clung to her.

"Here." Danissa reached out her hand. "I'll stick with her. I don't even have a gun."

"Then get a gun," Millicent said.

"Why? So I can shoot someone's toe off as I fumble? I'm not as skilled as you with weapons—"

"Yet—"

"—so I'd be better off taking the child."

"Her name is Marie."

"Whatever," Danissa said, unable to help her snotty tone. Despite everything that had changed, their long-standing rivalry had invaded the conversation.

Millicent hesitated for a moment before taking the few steps that separated her from Danissa. "Stay with her, Marie. Stay within the circle of security."

"Okay," the little girl said in a tiny, fear-filled voice. Why they'd brought a young child with them to battle, Danissa had no idea. It was ludicrous.

Together, they reached the door to the landing, where Gunner stood waiting. As Millicent jogged through, he stepped forward suddenly so his size bore down on Danissa.

"That is my daughter you're watching, Danissa Lance."

His rough tone and the glint of menace in his eyes sent dread creeping down her spine. "I've got her."

He stared for a moment longer before taking Danissa by the arm.

"Deadener is active," Millicent whispered when they met just off to the side.

"Then let's get to the craft as quickly and quietly as possible." Gunner ushered Danissa through the door and waited for the others to exit the stairs.

A moment later, Dagger was by her side, hurrying her through the quiet floor. "Let's go, Miss Lady. I've got your back. You just keep that little girl safe, and we'll get out of here without a hassle."

Two by two, they jogged across the empty floor. Blank screens stared at them as they passed, haunting in the scant illumination from the light globes a few of the men held. Vacated work pods stood silent, some crumbled from a bomb that had exploded. Broken glass littered the aisles.

"Here we go," Dagger said, motioning for Danissa to veer left.

Up ahead, hazy gray light drifted in through the windows, most of which were intact. Those that weren't, however, let in the harmful rain at a slant to pound the thin carpet and the cracked cement tiles.

The men made a straight line to one of the broken windows. A moment later, the sound of a craft vibrated through the floor.

"What are we doing?" Danissa asked through the sudden noise. She glanced behind her. Movement caught her eye a ways back. The robots would hear the racket and come to investigate.

"We're making our getaway." Gunner jogged toward the window. He bent to look through the jagged hole in the glass, and then thrust out his arm. He extended a metal pole, an inch thick, from his sleeve and used it to bash out the remaining glass.

"But why not use a door?" Danissa glanced up at the glowing exit sign. "There are a bunch of landing bays on this side of the building . . ."

"Don't question him," Millicent said as she took Marie. "His logic never makes any sense. You'll just get annoyed."

"Doors are anticipated." Gunner reached through the window and motioned the craft closer. He watched the base before holding up a fist to stop its progress. The craft's doors slid open and a platform extended out.

"We got company," someone shouted.

"But big windows work just as well. Let's get you girls in." Gunner waved her forward. "There is no way they can anticipate all the bays. Or back doors. Or . . . hell, a freight bay would work, and some of them are pretty well hidden."

"Like I said, you'll just get annoyed." With a small smile, Millicent guided Marie onto the thin platform. "Best not to look down," she hollered as she lithely ran across after her daughter. It was obvious she'd made dozens of those kinds of crossings.

"Send the rope, Millie," Gunner said.

"That device is faltering," someone called. "Them damn critters are advancing on us."

"Shoot 'em, bro-yo!" Dagger yelled. No sound came when he pulled the trigger, but it took four bullets to down the first spider. "Damn it all." He stripped off the silencer and stuffed it back into his utility belt. "More power!"

The rest did the same and opened fire.

"Let's go, let's go, let's go!" Gunner yelled.

Danissa felt a hand grab her and yank her toward the door.

"What about Puda?" she yelled as a rope was secured around her middle.

"We'll get him. Start walking. If you fall, the rope will catch you. Go!" Gunner didn't shove her, but he didn't have to. Something about the man's various *looks* got the job done just fine. Before she could argue, she was walking onto a thin platform forty-something floors above ground level, in biting rain and freezing temperatures. Her balance wavered. Her foot slipped. She teetered seconds before hands grabbed her. Millicent pulled her into the safety of the craft.

"You got it. Harden up, Lance. We have a ways to go." Millicent patted her on the shoulder, readied the rope again, and swung it across.

"How are you so good at all of this?" Danissa asked, out of breath. Fear crusted her voice, and she'd bet her face was bleach white. She'd never been in a situation like this in her life. Until today, the guards had always been there to protect her.

"I had very different training than you did, and I pushed hard to learn to fight. You don't work with weapons and ignore all the things that could kill you."

"But you're so well suited for systems."

"Turns out, I'm great at both. Maybe you are, too. We'll see."

Danissa could only shake her head as a man carried Puda into the craft. He didn't even need the rope—he didn't wobble once.

"Get us ready to go," Gunner yelled as he boarded. "I'm sure their people are already trying to find this craft. Let's disappear."

"They'll find you," Danissa said, helping to situate Puda. "They always do."

Chapter 9

"All right gang, here we go." Roe took a gun out of his utility belt and glanced around the craft. Eager young guys and gals wearing their combat suits hung on his every word and action. They were ready to storm the gates and free the clones.

The craft docked and the door lock disengaged. As it slid open, someone asked, "Should we go out first, sir? To make sure the coast is clear?"

"Son, I'm old, not useless." He stepped out onto the exposed walkway before pulling his hood further over his head. Face shielded from the harsh elements and driving rain, he glanced from one side to the other. Dim light from hanging posts barely showered the cracked and buckling walkway. Nothing waited to the sides, and no flickers of movement announced looters or robbers in the shadows. "This is quite a change."

"There aren't a lot of people roaming around, anymore," someone said from within the craft. "One conglomerate or another got rid of most of the riffraff, whether they meant to or not."

"That helps the overpopulation problem, I guess." Roe motioned everyone out and walked to the side entrance of the building. Once there, someone stepped out of a shadow a dozen or so feet away, a knife in a shaky hand.

Roe grimaced and lifted his gun to point at the skeletal face. "You can fuck off, or I can kill you and end your misery. Up to you, buddy."

The man hesitated. His hand lowered. He kept walking toward Roe.

"See ya in the afterlife, then." Roe fired without flinching and then turned back to the others. "And let that be a lesson. If someone wants a mercy kill, including me, give it to them. There are worse things than dying, and that includes being taken by Toton."

"Yes, sir," the troops chorused.

"Holy Hades on a picnic, you lot are way too anxious. Here, get out of the way." Roe shoved one kid to the side and shook his head as he looked at the keypad on the door. It needed a code, which Roe had. He squinted at his portable screen and then pushed it farther away from his face. Giving up, he handed it to the woman next to him. "Can you read that?"

"Yes, sir." She took the screen and gave him the first series of numbers. With each entry, the display changed. Sometimes the numbers got smaller, and sometimes they shimmied, but they always changed location on the screen. After a failed attempt, followed by a restart, he huffed. "This is for the birds."

"What's a bird, sir?" someone asked.

"Where are you going?" someone else wanted to know.

Muttering, Roe made his way to the craft and pulled up the outside console. "Stand back, everyone."

The group split down the middle, still much too close to the door.

"I said stand back, damn it. Get out of the way." Roe waved his arm, more effectively scattering them this time. He pulled up the weapons panel, chose something that was sure to work, and hit "Execute." Two barrels inched out from the front of the craft.

"Sir, Mr. Gunner said—"

"Gunner does things his way, and I do things mine. Here we go." He aimed the guns, not easy with the walkway there, and then hit "Fire."

A blast had the troops staggering away. Roe fell onto his butt. The craft didn't so much as bump back. "That woman sure knows her weapons."

He got up slowly, paused so a piece of building could roll past, and resumed his place. Instead of a door, there was now a sawtooth hole in the wall. A corridor on the other side had a ragged hole through it as well, and a gaping door knocked on its hinges beyond.

A cluster of terrified faces stared out of the forced entryway.

"These people aren't real bright." Roe stepped forward, his mood darkening from the rampant lack of logic he saw before him. "The normal reaction is to run *away* from someone exploding a hole in the side of your house."

"This is the clone facility, sir. This isn't actually their—"

"Now I see why Gunner stuck me with you lot."

The clones cleared a moment before a conglomerate security staffer slipped out of the ruined inner door.

"We don't mean any—" Before he could say "harm," the staffer raised his gun and curled his finger around the trigger. Roe reacted, firing his gun before he could earn a hole in his chest.

The staffer jerked as he shot. The bullet smacked into the ceiling above Roe. Dust showered down.

"Fast thinking, sir," one of the young troopers said. Roe felt a pat on his shoulder.

"Keep touching me, and you're next." The hand fell away.

He stalked forward as the clones' faces once again filled the gap. "Spread out. Secure this facility. Offer the conglomerate staff the option to leave quietly or join up with Gunner and Ms. Foster. Use their last names. If they still try to kill you, kill them first."

The troopers filed past him as a security staffer slipped out of the opening. The first trooper reached him at a run. He knocked the staffer's gun away, sending it skittering across the floor, and then punched the man in the face.

"Do you want to join with us, leave quietly, or die?" the trooper asked.

The staffer sank to his knees, bent his face to the ground, and covered his head.

"Whatever works," Roe said, shaking his head. He ducked into the clone facility, where he was greeted with soft-yellow walls and brightly colored art. "Well, isn't this lovely."

The clones' faces were indistinctive, similar in appearance to any lab born, but their bodies were fit and muscular, perfectly in shape and well proportioned. "I think you all are going to have a leg up on getting dates on Paradise, I'll say that much. The women will go bonkers."

"We've got comms," someone yelled over the loud speaker.

That was fast. These young troops were efficient. Or maybe that was just their age. Very energetic.

"Follow me," Roe said, motioning to the clones who'd gathered around him. They came without further prompting. Without questioning. "I guess when you're going to die soon anyway, you don't fear strangers."

"A few security staffers are holed up in the eatery," someone called out.

"Give them the offer through the door," Roe said. "If they don't take it, blast them out. Is someone checking for Toton's forces?"

"Yes, sir."

Roe sauntered into the exercise facility, which was still half full. "Holy Masses, you're still at it even while you're under siege. That's either dedication or stupidity, and I'm not sure which." He flicked the screen on the wall, couldn't figure out how to turn all the exercise systems off, and then shot it.

"What happened, sir?" one of the troopers called out over the loudspeaker. Someone else ran in.

Roe wanted to call him over, but he had no idea what any of these kids' names were. While he should learn them, or at least one or two of them, it was really below his level of interest.

"Do you need help, sir?" the kid asked.

"Yeah. Turn these things off." He gestured toward the running mats, which still had people on them despite the fact that he'd shot a round at the wall.

That was either a really great sign or an extremely bad one.

"Yes, sir." The kid took to a different console. A moment later, all activity in the room ceased. Still no one spoke or asked what was going on. They were like robots, only they didn't have one ounce of tech in them. It just went to show that the human mind could be programmed with conditioning like any computer could be programmed with code.

"All right, listen—" Roe paused as another group of people were ushered in. Many had scared expressions, but a few looked angry. "Ah. So here are the survivalists. I wondered." He made a mental note of the angry ones. They'd be the most useful. "Right, okay. My name is Roe, and I represent—"

"A few more, sir."

"Just bring them in quietly, for the love of Holy!" He shifted and redirected his attention to the waiting people. "As I was saying, I represent a faction of people who have rebelled against the conglomerates' control. This started before Toton declared war. But we've decided we want more. We want to put this world back the way it was. At least as far as the ruling system goes. The people are supposed to be in charge, by the way, since only those with history books would actually remember that. To give power back to the people, we need to cut the legs out of Toton and the other conglomerates. Who's with us?"

A few of the newcomers looked around in confusion. The ones who were still standing on their running mats stared placidly.

"Holy shit, this is something else." Roe ran his fingers through his hair. "Okay, look. You can either stay here and get turned into hamburger meat—"

"They don't know what that is, sir . . ."

Roe thinned his lips to keep from shooting his helpers. "You can either stay here and be killed for your parts, or you can come with us. If you come with us, you can choose to help us save this world, and possibly die in the process, or go to a safe house to eventually be transported to Paradise, another planet. The choice is yours. So. If you want to go with us, form a cluster over there . . ." Roe pointed to the right. "And if you want to stay, form a cluster over there . . ."

Everyone looked around. Many blinked. Someone looked at the stilled running mat at his feet.

"Should we just kidnap them, sir? We don't have much time to get to the other facilities."

Roe stared at the most placid human beings he'd ever encountered in his life. "Well, fuck it. They're going to die anyway, right? Might as well give them a bit more time to think." Roe started back toward the holes he'd made in their facility. "Let's get them loaded up in the carriers. Call the rebel headquarters and let them know we're going to need a lot more carriers as we make our rounds, and a lot more dedicated space for the former clones."

As he moved down the hall, he peered in the rooms. Someone was still in one of them, reading.

"And check all the rooms. The cleaning stalls, too. These people aren't normal."

"Well, no, sir. They're clones. So—"

"Stop helping," Roe said, waving the persistent trooper away. "Go do something. And stop referring to these people as clones. They were made in the lab just like you were. Probably." Roe glimpsed three people in one of the rooms, naked and writhing. "C'mon, you three. You can have sex in the carrier. I doubt any of this lot will care. Hell," he said, continuing on. "Maybe they'll join in and give an expression or two. That would be better than all these bland faces I keep seeing."

"Sir," one of the troopers said as Roe reached the new door he'd fashioned with the heavy artillery. "We've seen no activity from Toton. Their communications have noted the disturbance down here, but it didn't get escalated into the more secure areas of their net. They aren't interested."

"You guys hacked into their internet? Does Millie know that?"

"The baby Foster got us in, sir. From wherever she is. She sectioned us off into certain areas that wouldn't disturb them . . . I think."

"The baby *Foster*, huh?" Roe huffed out a laugh. "That'll piss Gunner off. You don't sound sure, though." Roe ducked through the door and immediately raised his gun. Nothing waited on the walkway except bad weather and a dead body.

"I'm getting the information secondhand. That kid is a genius. She easily rivals Ms. Foster and she's only a kid."

Roe huffed again and climbed into the craft. "And that'll piss Millicent off. You guys are going to create some hostile enemies." He sat and leaned back. He wasn't as adept at traveling as he used to be. He wasn't old enough to feel like he did. To be this tired. "Fine. So they have eyes and ears in this part of the city, but they don't care about harvesting the clones for their machines." Roe thought back to the mostly blank faces and placid mannerisms. "I think I can guess why. Let's keep to the schedule, but if Toton has eyes and ears out, I don't want to lead them straight to our shelter. Take the clones—people—to another location and squat there until I can talk to Millie or Gunner. If Toton doesn't want them, we're not in any hurry to take them home."

"Do you know what Toton does want, sir?" the kid asked.

Roe took a deep breath. "I think it's less of *what* they want, and more *who* they want."

Chapter 10

Millicent glanced away from the craft's console to look at Danissa. Her sister sat next to the man they'd carried out of the building, silently holding his hand as sorrow coated her face. Clearly they'd been close. She'd dragged him down a lot of floors and holed up in that office with him, holding on to the hope that he would live. Now he was gone.

A shiver passed through Millicent as she shifted her gaze to Ryker. His tight eyes indicated he was in pain, but he'd push through. He'd been injured worse before. On his lap sat Marie, who was hugging him tightly.

Millicent would lose her mind if either of them died. If Danissa felt even a fraction of that soul-sucking love for this man, it was amazing that she was holding it together.

Although, what choice did she have? This was Earth. People either hardened up or they let death take them.

She tried not to think of a third outcome, which had to do with Toton.

"Any indication they're following us back to headquarters?" she asked Ryker.

He and Dagger glanced up, the two sitting side by side, equally in pain and equally trying to ignore it.

Ryker flicked his hand and Dagger stood smoothly. "I'll just grab a look-see, will I?" Dagger crossed to the cockpit.

"How are you holding up, Millie?" Ryker asked softly.

It was amazing. There was half a large craft between them, ensuring he had to use the full volume of his voice, and still he made those words sound intimate, as if he'd whispered them in her ear.

She shivered for an entirely different reason. "Small injuries, nothing to worry about."

"Did you eat?" he asked.

"I grabbed a food pouch after we pulled away from the building. I gave one to Marie, too. I never realized how disgusting those were."

"You hadn't had real food before Paradise, so how could you have known?"

She glanced out the window at the clear skies, completely devoid of city traffic. "I could've never imagined this, either. It's so . . ."

"Dead," Ryker said, looking out the window across from him. The trooper in front of it raised his eyebrows, clearly wondering if Ryker was looking at him.

"Literally dead, or is everyone in hiding?" Millicent muttered.

"Literally," Danissa said from her seat. "This city is a shell. It was a madhouse—the constant battles in the beginning, the higher-ups hiding, the lower-level staffers killing each other, people disappearing . . ."

"I got word from Roe." Ryker looked at his wrist screen. "He successfully transferred the first facility of clones. Toton noted the disturbance in that area, but he has reason to believe they won't interfere."

"Interesting." Millicent leaned against the wall in fatigue. "I wonder if that was a part of the city they usually watch, or if there's something special about those clones . . ."

"They watch the city," Danissa said, staring blankly. "They followed me from place to place. They always knew where we landed not long after we landed there. Places we hadn't planned to go, and still they were right behind us. They have eyes everywhere."

Ryker transferred Marie to the seat and stood. He stalked down the center of the aisle toward Millicent, and feet either pulled back or got stepped on. "Then we'll have to blind them."

"Our scanners are reading various outgoing feeds," Dagger said, leaning on the panel just outside the cockpit. "They all take the same amount of bandwidth, and not much at that. But"—he looked at Millicent with a twinkle in his eyes—"you probably knew that."

"My guess is they're video uplinks." Millicent selfishly wished Danissa would snap out of it. Toton probably wasn't watching the *whole* city, in which case the places they were monitoring needed to be mapped and analyzed for weaknesses. That would take time, and if Danissa helped, it would go much quicker. "They're compressed, but they're low quality. They probably take the identification numbers off the passing vessels and run them, trying to keep track of who's moving around. Those most likely get stored until they hit on a flagged vessel, which this is not."

"I thought you said they'd be trying to find this craft since the other was blown up?" asked Sinner, a lean young man who pined after a woman who was being safeguarded with the higher-level Gregon staffers. Going by the gossip, she didn't know he existed. Millicent bet that would change when Sinner showed up out of the blue and rescued her in the way only these guys knew how.

"I took care of that flag." Millicent glanced at the screen that would flash red should any of her alerts go active. It was a miracle none were going off at the moment. She had an awful lot of them set up. "If they flag us again, it will immediately be unflagged. What I'd like to know, however, is if we are physically being followed."

Dagger wore a huge smile. He crossed the space with his infallible swagger, clearly a uniform of security directors since Ryker always wore the same one, and leaned his hand against the wall next to the console. He smiled down at her. "Look at us go! Feels good to have the most valuable player in this game. Whoooowee! Super Foster."

"She's going to need a little more room, bro-yo," Ryker said in a warning tone.

Dagger's hands flew up and he took a decisive step back. "I hear that, Ranger Danger. I sure do. That was my bad. She's pretty and smart—hard to resist stepping close."

"Try."

"Yes, sir, I absolutely will." Dagger started to laugh, not at all afraid of Ryker's menacing tone. "Yes, sir. I know where you're coming from."

"You men act like a bunch of apes." Millicent shook her head. "Their communication can't be great with those spider robots." She bit her lip, thinking out loud. "They knew where we exited. If they could relay exact coordinates, or even vehicle type, someone would already be on our tail. We don't have to be flagged to be followed. Probably."

Dagger's smile melted away and his eyes stopped glimmering. "I didn't see anyone. But they could be keeping their distance. Getting analysis."

"True." She blew out a breath. "That's what I would do. We need more information, I just don't know how to get it."

"How are you planning to take them down?" Dagger's voice was laced with aggression now. He flipped moods quickly. "How do we end their reign?"

"We have to technically cut the legs out from under them." She lifted her hand to stave off more questions. "All I have are ideas at the present. No solid plans."

"I ain't gonna push, pretty lady. I'll let you keep your secrets." Dagger walked past her.

"Don't call me *pretty lady*."

"What is the problem with pretty ladies not wanting to be called pretty ladies? I don't get it."

"They're prickly," Ryker said. A few men chuckled.

"We're not prickly—we know that when you make comments like that, you're thinking with your dick. Being that no intelligence whatsoever resides in your dick, and, indeed, you actually become stupider whenever you use it, you and those comments are annoying at best, and dangerous at worst. Best to verbally cut it out at the root so we don't progress to having to physically cut *it* off at the root."

"Yikes." Dagger grabbed his crotch. "Point made."

"Fine. Keep your eyes on the sky."

"I'm on it. I'm no Gunner, but I've got this security detail handled."

Millicent rolled her eyes. "Thanks."

Dagger had only taken a few steps away when he slowed, his smile melting. His eyes had landed on Danissa, and his gaze was rooted to her face. An expression crossed his visage that Millicent recognized easily. Longing. Her sister had made some sort of impression on the muscular man.

Millicent remembered her own courtship dance with Ryker. He'd pursued her for over two years, and even though they'd spent much of that time apart, Ryker's feelings had never altered or subsided. He'd admitted in a quiet moment on Paradise that soon after he'd seen her, that was it. His heart had been taken, and he would've waited forever for her to come around.

Of course, he'd been positive that she would. The man's ego was mighty.

Now, looking at Dagger, Millicent saw that same deep softness in his eyes. The desire not born of lust, but of something deeper.

Dagger's gaze flicked to Danissa holding Puda's lifeless hand. He glanced away and braced his hands on his hips. Shortly thereafter, he fully turned away to look out the window. Millicent could tell he was staring at nothing. He was probably fighting the urges he felt.

A strange surge of butterflies filled her stomach. It was like watching one of those romance vids. She was enraptured with what would happen next.

Dagger blew out a breath, minutely shook his head, and then, in a purposeful sort of way, turned toward Danissa and took the open seat opposite Puda. He sat still for a moment, staring at nothing. Then, in a quiet voice, asked, "Are you okay?"

Danissa blinked lethargically. Her head turned slowly until she was staring at him full in the face. "Dagger, right?"

"Kace, actually. Kace Dagger."

She nodded and looked straight ahead again. Her thumb moved slowly over the skin of Puda's hand. "Thank you. For saving me. I'm not sure I thanked you for that."

"No thanks necessary. It was my pleasure." He rested his hands on his knees and leaned back, seemingly to get comfortable, but with his back not yet healed, he must've been anything but. Clearly he was trying to put Danissa at ease with his presence.

Smart move, Millicent thought.

"He'd followed me from place to place," Danissa said, staring vaguely. "I thought he would make it."

Dagger nodded slightly. "It's hard to lose a loved one."

"Yes. He was my best friend. And my lover." Tears dripped down Danissa's cheeks. "Some called him my pet, but he wasn't. I truly enjoyed his company."

"And I'm sure being with you gave him the happiest moments of his life. He died protecting you. Any man would think that was the highest honor."

"I'm not so sure." Tears tracked down her cheeks. She wiped them away forcefully. "Sorry. I don't usually fall apart."

"It's okay to feel the pain. To let your emotion bubble out. It's healthy." Dagger's hand drifted toward her thigh, but he paused in the air. Instead, he covered her forearm, a place that implied emotional support instead of intimacy.

Good guy.

Some of the conglomerates' directors of security had gone badly wrong, like Mr. Hunt, whom Ryker had killed before they left Earth. That man had been so dangerous and twisted, he hadn't been allowed in close proximity to important people without supervision. But some of the breeding went perfectly, as Ryker had shown. It looked like Dagger's creators had also hit the nail on the head.

Millicent wondered if Danissa was in the protection bubble Trent was always railing on about. If Dagger would tear apart the Earth to make sure she was safe.

Another thought rolled through her mind, one that was useful to their situation and not born of a good romance vid. She glanced at her wrist screen. "Ryker, have you heard from Trent?"

In the back of the craft, where all the weapons were stowed, Ryker glanced at his wrist screen. "A handful of minutes ago, I got a blank transmission. Nothing since."

"Before that?"

"He found the children safely despite interference from some insane protectors with rocket launchers."

Her sister and Dagger immediately forgotten, Millicent turned back to the console. "I don't recall any of the other protectors having such extreme weaponry."

"They also weren't hidden away, and their whereabouts weren't protected behind an ironclad wall of coding, right?" Ryker looked at Danissa, who was back to staring blankly. Her mind had shut down, probably from shock. "Those kids must be different than the others. The rumors must be correct."

Millicent thought back on the rumors Trent had talked about. "Special. Like Marie, you think?"

Ryker shrugged. "Trent is often . . . optimistic. I doubt they are as good as Marie. Or as balanced. I haven't heard great things about what came out of the experiments."

Millicent waved the thought away. "Whenever the word *experiment* is tossed around, people get nervous. If they're protected, there's a reason why."

"But is that a reason for us to take them to Paradise, or a reason to leave them behind? I will not jeopardize the safety of the colony."

"Then you might not want to take those kids," Dagger said in a low tone. He glanced at Danissa. Still unresponsive. "I've heard the rumors, too. The term that is thrown around most commonly is *monster*. From what I've heard, something went badly wrong with those kids."

"If their protectors are still alive, let alone willing to use an extreme weapon to protect them, then they can't be that dangerous," Millicent said.

"Are you sure?" Dagger asked. "Why else would they be hidden under lock and key?"

"From Toton, I imagine. If they are special in some way, clearly Toton could use them against us. Hopefully Trent keeps them safe." But as Millicent turned back to her console, suddenly she wasn't so sure. What could those kids do that would cause people to label them monsters? And whatever it was, would they do it to Trent at their first glimpse of freedom?

Chapter 11

"Get those kids out of the way," Rhett growled as Terik stood in the middle of the corridor, staring out at the enemy crafts beyond. The older children had stepped away from the group as well, taking his lead.

"No," Trent heard himself say, not knowing what they were doing exactly, but confident they'd work better as a unit. These kids had become a family in face of the horrible environment and constant hostility they faced—they could probably work together better than anyone on the planet. "No. Let's wait and see where we fit into their group."

"Where *we* fit into *their* group?" Rhett spat, aggression clear in every syllable.

"Trust me," Trent breathed, watching strain enter Terik's face.

"Trust *you*?" Rhett said in disbelief.

"This repeating thing isn't getting you anywhere." He waved Rhett back. "This is how it has always been with Marie. A strong, intelligent leader—like Millicent—can direct her, but someone who doesn't know her capabilities needs to wait and see how to help. We know nothing about what these kids can do, and despite the age gap, we're not as smart as them—we have to wait and see. Where they show weakness, we have to fill in with strength. Hopefully."

"Hometown is the sort of cracked that can't be fixed, and he's going to get us all borked out of existence!" Gertie hollered.

"I really do hate that woman," Trent muttered. "Where do you need us?" he asked Terik.

His question was met with silence as Terik walked forward with a sort of swagger that niggled at Trent. It reminded him of someone, but he couldn't place whom.

"We're here to save him, not send him to slaughter." Rhett lifted his gun, watching Terik walk closer to the glass doors separating the interior of the building from the bay filled with the deadly enemy.

"Let him go," Kajel said. "He's the worst of the group. A real—"

"Holy help me, I will send you out to act as a human shield; don't think I won't." Trent shot Kajel a fierce scowl, then swung the same look toward Gertie. "I'll throw you out on your head if you say another word."

Gertie's lips thinned.

"He's focusing," Suzi said, edging toward Terik. "He's starting it. He always starts it. It helps me rally my . . . power."

One of the guards hissed. Apparently that was a taboo word in their world of small-minded idiots.

"Getting what started?" Trent asked in a hush, moving forward with her. The black crafts waited, definitely able to see them at this point, but not yet acting. What were they waiting for?

The volume of the scene turned down. Trent focused on his breathing and registered the minute shifting of the troopers, showing their anxiety and fear. In contrast, the children waited patiently, their eyes on Terik, like they were waiting for their battle commander to give them a directive. They had always been at war, and now they would fully experience it.

Shivers of anticipation ran across Trent's skin as he analyzed the kids. Children had so many tells—one didn't need to hear them speak in order to know what they were planning.

Terik's left shoulder ticked upward. His hands clenched and unclenched. Sweat dribbled down his temple. He was working hard without moving, his focus intense and labor arduous.

"Suzi," Terik said in a wispy voice. "Get ready."

Another wave of shivers washed over Trent. A weight settled on his chest, half fear of what was coming, half excitement. Were these kids really that dangerous? Could they throw only a man, or could they dominate larger objects?

Another thought occurred to him as the little boy danced toward the opposite wall: What if they lost control?

"This is bullshit," Rhett cursed. "If we stand here staring at the enemy any longer, we won't be able to get out at all."

"Suzi . . ." Terik's voice drifted away.

Suzi lowered her head and went completely still.

"Zanda," Terik said. His hands clenched and unclenched again. His shoulder ticked.

The four-year-old girl, clutching a ratty stuffed animal to her middle, scrunched up her brow.

The windows in the black crafts shattered simultaneously, the shards bursting outward. A noticeable crack crept along the closest craft's door. It started to shake, rocking and tilting like a ship on high seas teamed with the movements of a salt shaker, and the others followed.

"Devil's play," Gertie muttered.

"I've never wanted to punch someone so badly in my life," Trent said, moving forward so he was near the children. If Toton opened fire, he needed to drag them away.

The little boy did a shimmy and punched his Toad Man in the face. "Guns, Tek. Guns coming."

"What kind, Billy?" Terik asked, his face contorting with strain.

"Big. Big ones." The little boy, Billy, slammed Toad Man against the wall. "Under black things."

"Suzi?" Terik asked.

"It's *hard*!" she whined, slumping her shoulders. "There are a lot of them."

"Focus on the first one," Trent said, kneeling down beside her. "Just focus on the one closest to us. One at a time."

Billy punched Toad Man in the face again. "Guns coming, Tek. AHHH!" He jumped and then stomped both feet on the ground.

"How long?" Terik asked, completely in control and unfazed by Billy's random violence.

"Open fire on those vessels," Trent yelled at the troopers.

The girl trooper ran forward. She fell to her knees and slid across the tile while jerking her hands out. Her body stopped in the middle of the corridor as long, sleek barrels emerged from her suit and clicked into each hand. Small, fast blasts erupted out of her guns, shattering the glass door of the building and peppering the sides of the enemy crafts. The corridor filled with noise and firepower as another trooper joined her, his guns similar to hers.

"Where's that rocket launcher?" Rhett yelled over the din.

"I done left it. Didn't know yous buggers couldn't handle yourselves!"

Terik clenched and unclenched his fists again, staring out the window in consternation.

"How long, Terik?" Trent asked. He wanted to run. To grab the kids and get the hell out of there. "How long before whatever you're working on happens? How much time do you need?"

"Almost . . . Just . . ." Fists clenched. And unclenched.

A flap opened on the bottom of the closest craft. Four metal barrels pushed out, unimpeded by the shaking of the vessel or the small holes opening up along its side. The craft was probably run by robots that were not afraid to die.

"Those are really big guns," Trent said in sudden panic. "We need to get out of here. We need to run!"

"Suzi!" Terik yelled.

The girl bowed in on herself. All the crafts stopped moving. For a moment, everything paused, except for the guns. An electronic whine accompanied all four barrels on the closest craft as they slid forward. The black voids in the round barrels stared at them, taunting. Promising death.

"Hurry!" Terik said.

Billy started to scream. The guns shimmied to a stop.

It was too late.

"I'm ready." Suzi said, her voice drifting into the sudden panic-filled silence.

One of the guns fired. The barrel coughed out flames.

"Get down!" someone screamed.

The front face of the building beside the door blew up. Fragments of wall flew across the area around them. Some smashed into the corridor entrance and ricocheted off, striking the female trooper. She collapsed to the ground.

"We have to get—"

Before Trent could finish the sentence or grab any of the children, the closest black craft jerked upward in the air, as if a giant held it in its clutches. Another gun blasted. It struck the upper portion of the building, raining down debris. The craft flipped over and then smashed down onto a neighboring vessel. The roofs of both flattened as the metal smushed together.

"Got it," Terik said with a sigh.

Flames burst from all five crafts simultaneously, blowing out through their middles. Billows of smoke poured out the bottoms, followed immediately by more flames. The crafts didn't explode; it was more like they just burned from the inside.

The first pair of vessels fell from the sky like rocks.

Fragments of what Trent could only assume were pieces of building rained down into the bay, smashing onto the concrete leading to their craft.

"That was from their shot hitting the higher floors of this building," one of the troopers said with what, until moments before, had clearly been a slack jaw.

"Real genius, yeah. Way to state the obvious, numb nuts," Gertie said.

The flaps on the remaining three vessels dropped open. Guns started to push out from the sides as flames engulfed the crafts.

"Should we shoot?" someone asked in a shaking voice.

"Suzi—"

One vessel was flung away. Rolling end over end, it smashed against the building across the travel way. Glass and concrete spattered the air before it all fell.

The remaining crafts, now balls of flame, sank in the sky. First one, and then the other, dipped below the bay. Soon they'd be plummeting, Trent had no doubt.

Breathing hard, Terik slumped. Trent rushed forward to catch him, but the boy rolled his shoulders, futilely trying to get out of his grasp.

"Okay," Trent said, light-headed. His ears rang in the intense quiet that followed the short battle. He couldn't seem to stop blinking. "Let's get to the craft, shall we?" He patted the kid, either comforting or trying to get him moving, Trent wasn't sure which.

"Get off," Terik said, rolling his shoulders again.

"I'm not done wrapping my head around all this," Trent said.

"And you never will," came Gertie's croak. She would not let it go.

"We need to get going." Rhett scowled at Terik, and then spread the dark look to the other children. "We don't know when more are going to come."

They had just saved him, but Rhett's fear of what these children could do was already turning into mistrust. *Typical,* Trent thought. *Small-minded.*

He straightened up, tamping down his awe at what he'd seen, his misery for what these kids had endured, and his terror of what else awaited them in this dangerous world. None of that would serve him well now. If he'd learned anything from Ryker and Millicent, it was to focus on surviving and kicking ass while you were in the belly of the beast.

This was certainly the belly. Maybe even the back end.

"We shouldn't take the normal route back," Trent said, walking forward on wobbly legs. "Someone get Billy. Don't let him run off."

Billy had danced toward the wall and was kicking it. "Watching, Tek. They watching us. On little screens. Watching us walk out to the gray thing."

"In other crafts, or . . . ," Terik asked.

"I'll scout it out," one of the larger troopers said.

"Send Gertie," Trent heard himself say. That woman brought out the mean in him.

They all drifted closer to the ruined door as a lone trooper walked to the craft. Once there, he looked skyward. Apparently seeing nothing, he turned in a circle. When nothing happened, he checked out the craft, stepping over a dead body to do so. The doors slid open and he walked inside. Still nothing happened.

"Is that a go-ahead?" one of the kids' caretakers asked.

"It's going to blow up," someone said.

"What the—" Trent turned back to see who'd said it.

A thin trooper shrugged. "What? He's all by himself, the danger seems to have dissipated, but suddenly, and out of the blue, the whole thing blows up. That's logic."

"You watch too many vids, bro-yo." The guy next to the speaker nudged him.

"You're all cracked," Gertie pronounced.

"Like you're one to throw stones about being crazy," Trent muttered. She had a point, though.

The man emerged from the craft and turned away from them, staring at the buildings around the bay.

"They probably have cameras in those buildings," Trent whispered. He wasn't sure why he was trying to be quiet. Another thought occurred to him. "Maybe they aren't interested in this facility if they have the ability to watch it and haven't invaded."

"How would they even know it was occupied?" Kajel asked, inching forward to get a better look.

Annoyance stole over Trent. "Off the top of my head, I'd say by the random crafts parked in the bay to distribute supplies . . ."

"We didn't get no supplies. They created a distraction, and we got dropped off on an upper-level floor in the middle of the mayhem. Lost two kids and a staffer in the process. Before they left, they gave us a bunch of food and told us how to ration. Toton blew that upper level to hell, or we would've gotten more food out of there. We still had another year of food pouches. They wasn't great, though. Getting sour."

"Another *year*?" someone asked.

"Who knows." Kajel shrugged. "We been here a year already. It's war. Wars last, this one especially." He shrugged again.

"I realize that you do, in fact, love the children," Trent said in a soft voice, knowing that the kids were listening. He didn't want to upset anyone by giving voice to what everyone surely felt. There was no telling what Terik would do. "But the close quarters have certainly put everyone on their toes. That's obvious. So why stay here?"

"Didn't you hear me?" Kajel asked with a nasty scowl. "No coming, no going. I said as much in there." He jerked his head in the direction they'd come. "The dead bodies said as much out there." He jerked his head toward the outside. "The enemy has eyes everywhere. Looks like their response time is ten times quicker what it used to be, too. Even if I wanted to end it all and head on up to Holy Guenes early, none of the other guards would have let me. Once the enemy killed me, they'd roll through and take out everyone else. They don't want people in these buildings. Nah. No leaving."

"You hate the job. Why sign up for it?" the large trooper asked. "And don't tell me you liked it at first. These kids aren't kids in your eyes. They're freaks."

Rhett stalked forward. "Looks like we're clear. Give me ten to ready the systems."

"I'll tell yous buggers why *I* volunteered," Gertie said. "My old job was in the labs. I liked creatin' the little buggers. Cute things, most. After Toton took over and we was all dodgin' for our lives, this thing came up. But that air-cloggin' conglomerate didn't say *nothing* about watching freaks. I volunteered for this because I thought they was kids, not monsters!"

"I will punch you in the mouth if you don't shut up," Trent said as his temper surged. "I don't care that you're old. I will punch you."

A couple of troopers barked out laughter.

"I'd like to see you try, Hometown." Gertie smirked.

"What is taking them so long?" someone mumbled.

Trent turned to Terik. "So you can create fire, is that right?" He heard a shuffling. He held out his finger. "If anyone says anything negative about these children again, even just *one* thing, I will shoot them. You might think I'm kidding, but I'm not. I've had it with you people. One more thing, and I'll shoot you and blame it on Toton. Are we clear?"

A scoff and silence was good enough.

He turned his focus back to a smirking Terik, whom he realized was a little younger than the age Marie would've been had she stayed on Earth, and hadn't been in suspension during the flights. Terik must've been born shortly after the conglomerate realized they'd lost Marie. Or maybe directly after Gregon had stolen the files regarding Marie.

"That's some ability," Trent said, letting his hand drift to his gun. He really hoped he didn't have to go through with shooting someone.

"I don't get you, bro-yo," Terik said with a puzzled look. "Are you for real?"

Trent opened his mouth to formulate a response when one of the troopers said, "*Fin*ally, trek." The troopers started forward.

"See? Didn't blow up," another trooper said to the vid watcher. "You're an idiot."

"Figures. I joined the Rebel Nation, and my life *still* isn't anything like a vid. They never send me with the important missions, that's why."

Rhett gestured everyone toward the craft, impatience lining his movements. "Let's go. Headquarters says there was a notice posted on Toton's intranet. They'll probably be coming by to check this place out before long."

"Okay, we got everyone?" Trent asked.

Billy ran at Trent before punching him in the leg.

"Good*ness*! Why does he do that?" Trent stepped away. "Ouch. He's got a hard punch."

"He's always been like that. I think he's stronger than other kids his age. Come here, Mira." Terik picked up the toddler. She wrapped her arms around his neck.

"You're telling me. That'll give me a bruise." Trent rubbed the offending spot.

"Are you coming, or what?" Rhett yelled at them as everyone else hovered just inside the doors, waiting.

"I meant, I think in addition to his premonition ability, he has super strength. Or will." Terik reached down for Billy's waving arm. "C'mon, Billy, we have to go."

Billy danced away. He threw Toad Man into the air and then kicked him. The poor stuffed animal bounced off the wall and plunked onto the ground. Billy cackled.

"Grab that kid!" Rhett hollered at the waiting troopers.

"Billy has a hard time with focus," Suzi said, running to grab him.

"He's just a little boy." Trent noticed the troopers' annoyed expressions as Suzi wrapped her arms around Billy's upper body and tried to drag him toward the exit.

Billy shot his arms up, easily breaking the hold of a kid twice his size and age. Terik might've been right about that super strength. "Toad Man!" Billy shouted. "Run, Toad Man! Bang!"

Terik's head whipped around.

A black vessel rose up behind the bay. Its bared guns pointed at the building.

"RUN!" Trent screamed, grabbing Suzi and Billy and sprinting toward the nearest corner.

Blasting guns lit up their world. Large chunks of ceiling fell like deadly rain. The walls puckered and exploded, blasting the people standing next to them.

Trent didn't look back. He didn't look up. He held the children in his arms and ran for all he was worth. Something hot sliced through his leg. A dull object punched his back, making him stagger. He hit the wall and then pushed away, urging his legs to move faster. The spot he'd touched on the wall exploded behind him. Someone yelled. The air clogged with dust and smoke.

"Run, Trent!" Suzi said in his ear, a small voice filled with fear. "Keep going!"

Ignoring the pain vibrating through his back and the sharp agony on his leg, he pushed even faster. Gave everything he had. Only hoping for survival.

A zip of fire passed him. It barreled into the wall just in front of him and exploded. Huge pieces flew out toward him. There was nowhere for him to go. Something struck his head and all went black.

Chapter 12

"We clear to go in?" Ryker asked after about an hour of circling through the city. Only once had it seemed like someone was tailing them, based on something the operator had glimpsed while going around a bend. But they'd found a secluded place to camp, and they hadn't seen anything or anyone moving through the open travel way. Most likely, the operator's eyes had been playing tricks on him, fueled by fear.

They got the all clear, and the vessel lowered through the sky, aiming for the headquarters near ground level.

Millicent rubbed her eyes and looked out the window, still standing at the console. Marie lay to her immediate right, taking up two seats and kicking Sinner, who was seated next to her, in her sleep. The grayish-brown air turned slowly to muddy black as they descended.

"The feeds have all been disabled on this side of the city," a trooper said. He turned in his seat to look out the window. "But they keep cropping back up."

"So they obviously know the annoying humans are hunkering in this area," Millicent said as she analyzed Toton's firewall. Someone was patching it up from their earlier entry. Toton was playing defense. There was no finesse in their rebuilding. Millicent would be able to tear it down in a matter of minutes, Marie in even less time. The problem would be in hacking through the next layer, and the next after that. Millicent hadn't ventured far enough in to see what sorts of defenses they had, or if they had traps. She wanted Danissa's help for that, and her sister was currently sleeping with her head on Dagger's muscular shoulder. Sleeping on that hard surface was a testament to her utter exhaustion.

"We routinely take out their camera feeds all over the city," a man with bushy hair on his upper lip said. "Moxidone does, too, but with explosives. So there is no reason to assume—"

"There is every reason to assume," Millicent cut in. "They will know the difference between the weapons I used today and the weapons I designed before leaving this planet, which is most likely what Moxidone is still using. They'll know something is going on in this area."

"So why haven't they moved in?" the man asked, immediately defensive.

"That is another question for the list."

"Your designs are genius," Dagger said, staring at Millicent. "If they've been after Danissa—don't look at me like that, she said I could call her by her real name if I wanted." Millicent gave a noncommittal shrug. "As I said, your designs are genius. You'd be a prize to capture. So why haven't they been trying to find you?"

"They'd think I was here. Which leads us back to the question of why they haven't yet invaded the rebel headquarters." Millicent stared out at the darkening environment. "Or, at least, tried."

"Hold on, this will get bumpy," came a voice over the loudspeaker.

In confusion, Millicent gripped the bar on the side of the console.

"Grab the child," Dagger said, a command in his voice. He was looking at Sinner.

"Why?" Millicent asked. "What's going to—"

The lights blinked off. The console sputtered and the screen went blank. The noise from the engine ceased as people finished buckling themselves in.

"Hold on, cupcake, we're falling," Ryker said from the rear, gripping a seat.

"We set up EMPs all around the headquarters." The wind rushing past them made Dagger hard to hear. He wrapped his arm around Danissa, glancing at the dead man next to her. "With this entrance, you have to hit it just right so you don't hit buildings before the craft's systems turn back on. It's the only way for a vessel to get safely in. And safety is relative, of course."

"And you figured this out, how?" Millicent asked, slamming against the wall as the craft tilted. The whole thing shook.

"With their dicks," Ryker said with glee in his voice. That meant this was dangerous.

"Yes, you'd have to be stupid to think this is a good solution." Millicent pursed her lips. "I am not pleased that my child is involved in this."

"Only way in." Dagger grabbed the dead guy to keep him on the seat and leaned into Danissa for the same reason. "Probably should've woken her up."

"She's not going to be thrilled when that beau of hers slaps the ground with his face," one of the troopers said.

"Thanks for helping, slack ass," Dagger growled.

The guy shrugged. "She's got to come to grips with that dude being dead sooner or later. You're just putting off the inevitable, big daddy."

"I hate your guys' slang," Millicent muttered as the craft kept tilting, now at about a forty-five degree angle. "This is not good." Marie was starting to wake up, but Sinner had a tight hold on her. "Should we jump?"

"Almost there, bossy lady." Dagger grinned, his arms and legs bulging with muscle to keep his two charges on their seats. How Danissa hadn't woken up was beyond Millicent.

"Using your head for that nickname, huh?" Ryker asked with a laugh.

"You know it. She can't chastise me for that one."

"I'll give you a bossy lady," Millicent said as the motor roared to life. Lights blinked on. The vessel surged, swinging her around and slamming her shoulder into the door. Ryker reached over to steady her.

"A little late on that one, mister hero," she wheezed as the vessel righted, swinging her the other way. The dead man slid off the seat and flopped onto the floor. Dagger grabbed Danissa with both arms, his whole body flexing.

"I like to give you a little independence." Ryker laughed.

"Keep laughing. See how that works out for you." Millicent's knuckles were white around the metal railing attached to the side of the craft.

"Made it," Dagger said, reaching toward the crumpled body.

Millicent looked away. She didn't need the reminder of how fragile life was. Or that there was a dead body responding to gravity the way a live one would. Something about that was creepy.

"Can someone set this guy right so she doesn't wake up and start screaming?" Dagger asked.

"I got it." A younger guy unhooked and then fell out of his seat. He hit the aisle face-first. With a red face and amidst raucous laughter, he struggled up against the swoop of the craft and helped rearrange the body.

Through the gloom, Millicent could see lights randomly placed on the outside of buildings, like a landing strip. Wherever the glow touched a wall, a red circle with a line through it advertised what this place was.

"I want those rebel insignias painted over," Ryker said in a harsh tone. "The lights have to stay, but change them to a sort of rustic yellow. Anything that looks new or updated needs to get rusted out or beat on. We're all but advertising ourselves."

"Yes, sir," men barked, though the confusion was plain on their faces. They thought their EMP defense was good enough. It was naive thinking, and Ryker had seen through it immediately.

Farther down, at about level ten in the city, the environment was so oppressive it coated the glass. The craft shuddered as it docked in a well-maintained bay. Overhead, there was an electric whine as a cover slid into place, shielding them from the rain or anything falling from above.

"I assume this craft will be moved once we are let out?" Ryker asked.

"Yes, sir," Dagger barked.

He scooped up Marie and stopped near Millicent. "We don't have a lot of time. It must've taken time and manpower to set this place up. It's stable in a world that is extremely unstable. Toton will know it exists. They'd have to, with all their surveillance. You need to figure out why they haven't invaded already. Move that up on the list of priorities."

"I will." She glanced at Danissa for the umpteenth time. "Without help, though, I'll need to sleep for a few hours. Or I could take an upper . . ."

"No uppers unless we have no other choice. We'll settle you in for some rest. We all need it. Then we have to hit it hard. We need a plan and we need to get said plan under way. Time was running out before we landed on this planet."

"Yep."

Ryker lifted her chin as the door opened and slid his lips across hers. Even after so many years together, tingles spread across her skin at the contact. "Maybe we'll sleep together for a while," he said. "I could use some time with you, pretty lady."

She couldn't help the embarrassment heating her face. It felt like everyone around them could see the rush of desire flood her body. That was the thing about lust—the surrounding circumstances didn't matter; when Ryker was involved, her desire was as ardent as it was immediate.

"Fine," she said, giving him a little shove. "Just . . . get moving. We have a million things to do and war to wage."

Ryker's wrist lit up. Shifting Marie on his hip, he looked at it as he exited the craft. Millicent followed, leaving the others in the vessel to get organized and file out. "Roe checked in," Ryker said. "He's bringing in a lot of clones, but doesn't think they'll be as useful as he'd hoped."

"Damn," Millicent said, standing in front of the building's grand entrance. She shook her head, looking at the glass doors that could easily be blown to hell. Behind that, a walkway, filled with quickly striding people with stern faces and somewhere to be, passed in front of a guard station. Everyone was completely defenseless from the bay. "Who set this up for Roe, and why weren't we consulted?"

Ryker looked up from his screen. His brow furrowed as he took in the glass doors.

An entry pad glowed beside the door. Millicent tapped it with a knuckle to bring up a prompt. All it took was a few moments of analysis to be certain she could hack her way in. She didn't get the chance, however.

Ryker put Marie next to Millicent before stalking up to the glass double doors. He slammed his boot against the glass. One of the doors cracked, knocked off its hinges. A spiderweb of fissure lines spread from point of contact. He hit it again, and this time the whole thing crumbled, the glass shatterproof but no less broken. It tinkled across the ground at their feet.

The people on the walkway flinched, stopped in their tracks, and looked at the doors with wide eyes. The guards at that station stood around with equally wide eyes. No one made a move to intercept the man now striding into their midst.

"If I had used a gun or an explosive, you'd all be dead," Ryker said in a loud, hard voice. His gaze took in everyone on the walkway. "I just broke in with my *foot*. Ms. Foster could've let herself in quietly. I doubt you would've noticed before she killed you all."

The troopers from the craft gathered at the doorway, their faces grim. Even Dagger, carrying a lethargic Danissa, had a stone face and somber eyes. If anyone had forgotten who Mr. Gunner was in a past life, they were no longer under any misconception. He'd been a security director for a reason. He'd been the best. Clearly he still was.

"Toton may have some stupid tech running around, robots that look like spiders and humanoid cockroaches," he continued. "But I am positive they have other tech we *haven't* seen yet. I know this because I saw some of that tech firsthand the last time I was on Earth. The more advanced the apparatus, the less they want to risk it in our corrosive environment. When a stupid robot does the job, they'll keep using that. But the stupid robots stopped working today. We made sure of that. Ms. Foster will *keep* making sure of that. Do you know what this means?"

The sound of rain hammering on the metal overhang filled the silence that followed his words. A larger crowd had gathered, all staring at Ryker with slightly widened eyes and thinned lips. No one answered.

"It means that we just upped the stakes," Ryker continued. "We'd better be ready for Toton to rise to the occasion. I have no idea why they haven't taken this place out yet, but there is a reason for it. They know about us. We've been more than a thorn in their side. Besides them, we have the most advanced tech on the planet. Being that they were chasing Ms. Foster's sister all over the city, they'll want whoever designed . . ." He cut off. His gaze hit Millicent's with the force of a bomb. "Shit. They were waiting for you."

"What?" she said, stepping closer.

"They never bothered with the rocket. They didn't mind that we were taking people off-planet." He shifted as menace crept into his gaze. The troopers shifted with him, probably seeing what he did, or maybe sensing the sudden feeling of violence wash over the mood in the room. "Each time that rocket came back, or after one of my updates, a slew of new tech came with it. The network got better, more advanced. I'm sure the defenses did. Each time Toton established something new in this world, the next update or rocket saw that thing disabled or tracked. That, or we sent programs via the long-term zip communications, also traceable with advanced tech—which even Moxidone and Gregon have. Toton knew you were off-planet, they must've. They've left our transportation alone because why not? They figured you'd come back if they waited with enough patience. You did."

"If she didn't?" someone asked.

Still staring at Millicent, Ryker said, "They were after Danissa, who thinks so similarly to you. If that worked out as well as we all know it would've, then they would've gone after the other brilliant mind—you. We were right in coming here to crush this threat."

"They'll want you, too, Gunner," Dagger said.

Ryker shook his head slowly, his gaze rooted to Millicent's. A possessive gleam lit his gaze. "Not like her. Not like her sister. Their brains work a certain way that jives with systems. And these ladies are trained. Genius. They can beat Toton codes and redesign them to make them better. Millicent and Danissa would make the best super-computers man has ever known, smarter than any human. Ten times more powerful."

Millicent shivered. But it wasn't cold that dripped down her spine. It was fire. Her fists curled and she felt a strange grin tickle her lips.

She was responding to the challenge.

"I am already ten times more powerful, and after I get a few hours' sleep, I'll prove it." She turned to Dagger. "I need to see my room, and I need you to do whatever you can to get Danissa back online. She fell asleep on your shoulder, so she must trust you. Work with that."

"I don't think that's what that meant . . ." Dagger said in confusion.

"Touching to Millicent means intimacy," Ryker said. His teasing tone didn't reach his hard eyes.

"Whatever." Millicent motioned for him to get going. "I'll need a tranquilizer. My brain just kicked into overdrive, but I'm at red. I need to sleep to be at my best, so I'll need chemicals to get me there."

"I'm going to put in a few hours of work now, princess," Ryker said, not following behind her, "to make sure they don't kill us in our sleep."

Millicent nodded as she picked up her heavy daughter and followed Dagger. All the things she had to do rolled through her head, and one thing crystalized—she needed to figure out where Toton rooted their network, and blow it to hell. This wasn't a hacking job, this was a physically destructive job. From there, they could take over and bring it all down.

The memory of that smart door resurfaced. She knew from experience that Toton viciously protected what they valued. Millicent bet that there was nothing they valued more than their network root.

Chapter 13

All Trent could hear was breathing. He lay on his side with his face pressed against the cool tile of the corridor. Something large and jagged sat ten centimeters from his nose, give or take. A small hand slapped his head.

"Billy! Don't do that!"

A little girl's voice. Suzi?

Trent brought his hand up to move the thing in front of his face and groaned as pain flared through his back and side.

"Are you okay, Trent?" Suzi asked.

Blood was smeared across his hand. He pushed what felt like part of the wall away and then struggled into a seated position. He groaned again.

"You'd think he was dying, from all the sounds." Terik stood off to the side holding Mira. Small cuts and scrapes marred his face and neck, and a flap of skin was sticking out from the side of his hand.

"How are we alive?" Trent asked with a strangely constricted throat as he surveyed the crater in the wall and the rubble spewed all around them.

"Suzi kept the big pieces from hitting us," Terik said, stepping forward to kick another piece of wall down the corridor. It didn't make it far with all the debris in the way. "And Zanda made the pieces softer. They crumbled easily. Kinda."

"Are you okay, Trent?" Suzi asked again.

"I'm fine, Suzi," Trent lied. He fingered his head and winced when he hit a sensitive spot. His fingers came away glistening with blood.

"I misjudged the size of our bubble," Suzi said in a gush of words. "I thought I had it, but it happened really quickly, and there were a lot of pieces, and they were flying really fast, and—"

"We *got* it, Suzi." Terik kicked another piece of wall. Holding Toad Man by the foot, Billy joined in with a lot more gusto.

Blinking a few times to clear the sandy quality from his eyes, Trent looked toward the front of the building and stared. Huge amounts of debris were piled in the corridors. The walls appeared to have been blown in, and the ceiling had rained down. Light blared from high in the front, indicating a chunk of the building was blown off and now letting in the daylight. It was safe to assume the bay landing had suffered and their craft was destroyed.

The strips of lighting along the sides of the floor ran to the devastation and then faltered, flickering yellow across the jagged rocks littering the ground. That was the only movement. No sound greeted them from within the ruin.

"Did anyone else make it?" Trent asked in a daze. Panic fizzled through him. "The children. Did all of the children make it?" He did a quick count of the bodies clustered around him, sitting up or standing, all alive. "Why aren't they crying?"

"They've seen this before. They're desensitized." Terik looked down at the youngest's face. "Even Mira. She was born into it."

It was a horrible reality, but it helped them in the current situation. Maybe it would keep them alive. Maybe it already had.

"Okay. Well." Trent struggled to his feet and then patted himself down. A few places were definitely bleeding, but his injuries didn't seem life threatening. Walking would hurt, but he had very little in the way of medical supplies on his utility belt—best to save those. "Anyone hurt?"

"I checked them all while you were unconscious." Terik traced the jagged edges of the crater with his fingertips. "I'm the worst off, but I'm okay. Billy has a couple bruises from when you fell and basically tossed him, but he doesn't seem worried about it. We're all okay." Terik cut off like he was waiting for something.

"I couldn't help dropping him, in case your stare is accusatory." Trent looked down the way, collecting his thoughts.

"You saved Suzi and Billy," Terik said. "Instead of just running, you grabbed them. Why?"

"Don't ask stupid questions." Trent really should've been trying for gentle and soft, but he wasn't thinking all that clearly. He'd thought he was going to die. *Would've*, if not for Suzi. "They saved me, actually. Did you look for survivors?"

"If you didn't grab them, they wouldn't have made it. You run really fast."

"I've had a lot of practice. Survivors?"

"We didn't look. We waited here for you." Terik put down the two-year-old, who immediately started to cry. He picked her back up. "Do we need to bother?"

"Well . . . we can't just *leave* them."

"Why not?"

Trent stared off into the distance, struggling for an answer. His thoughts were languid and distorted, slow to form. He exhaled into the silent corridor. "We need to check for survivors. It's the right thing to do. Lord help me if Gertie is trapped under a beam."

"Why is that?" Terik started forward.

Trent dug into his utility belt, looking for a light orb. "Because I'll have to make the choice to either save her or put her out of her misery, and I'm not sure I can remain unbiased."

Terik sniffed in what sounded like a laugh. Trent didn't bother to mention that he was serious.

"Dang it." Trent gave up the search. "I can't find a light."

"We don't need one."

"Why?"

A moment later, blue flames licked up the wall and raced toward the debris. It crawled over the piles and illuminated the uneven pieces crowding the corridor. "And if that's not enough, I can see in the dark."

"You can manipulate fire out of thin air, *and* you can see in the darkness?" Trent asked, shocked. "That is some advancement in evolution. I had no idea humans were capable of that."

"Neither did anyone else. All of us are kind of a shock. With each new kid they made, it was always a waiting game to see if they were . . . different in any way. Not just smart, but altered. I mean, besides the obvious deformities, which were then killed right away. There were a lot of those."

"You were *born*, not made. And you aren't different and altered, you are enhanced and advanced. Start using the proper terminology about yourself, and hopefully others will use it, too." Trent moved forward slowly. He didn't plan to mention it out loud, but he was worried about what they'd find. The only reason they were alive was because of Suzi and Zanda, so Trent didn't have high hopes for the others, especially given the amount of rubble back the way they'd come. Which meant there would probably be blood and twisted bodies.

Trent hated seeing blood and twisted bodies.

Terik must've thought the same thing, because he said, "Suzi, you stay back with the rest. I'll call if I need you, and holler if Billy comes out with something."

"Okay, Terik." Suzi took the baby and then stared after them with big eyes. Billy kicked another piece of wall.

"Were any children born the natural way in the genetics projects?" Trent asked as they stepped carefully among the rocks. He looked up. Gaping holes where the tile had fallen away showed beams in the ceiling.

"A couple, but they didn't have the . . . advancements we did, so the conglomerates stopped natural births and just focused on lab births."

Trent shook his head. His toe kicked something soft. He grimaced and pointed downward, not wanting to look.

"Head's smashed in," Terik said, devoid of inflection.

"Let's talk about why you aren't worried about death when we get out of all this, shall we?" Trent swallowed down bile.

"I've seen a lot of death. They aren't my family, so I don't care."

"You get placed with families now?"

"We got put with other kids and sneering adults. I chose my family, and they chose me."

"Ah. Yes." Trent saw a leg sticking out at an unnatural angle. Another limb was severed altogether, and still smoking. "This might be a futile effort."

"Suzi put a lot of effort in, and she wouldn't have been enough without Zanda. The two of them work well together."

"Can you see down there?" Trent pointed farther ahead.

"Blood. Parts of building and people both—they didn't run as fast as you did. You didn't even weigh the option of fighting back, you just took off."

"Yeah. I value my life."

"Me, too. I was right behind you. The others were idiots."

"Don't talk about the dead that way. That is, if you're sure they're all . . ."

"Sure? No. But if they aren't dead, they are dying. We have limited medical supplies, and we can't sit here and wait for rescue. Toton will send in the spiders next. They always send in spiders. So unless you have superhuman strength and want to carry a few people, what good can we do?"

Trent shook his head, hating that he was basically being led by a ten-year-old. But everything Terik said was spot-on.

He bowed in defeat before switching gears. If he had learned any-thing from getting off Earth, it was to always have a plan, and to always be willing to improvise if that plan was blown to hell. "We need to come up with a plan."

"We?"

"You think I'm going to leave it up to a ten-year-old? You're out of your mind. I'm the adult here, I get a say."

They walked back to the others. "I meant, you're allowing *me* to have a voice?"

"Oh." Trent shrugged and picked up Mira. "I'd rather you not kill me in my sleep. I'm also hoping you know your way around this floor if not this building. We need to find another way out so we can get picked up. Preferably, we need to skirt their eyes and ears."

"You're in luck, Trent. I *do* know my way around this floor, and partially around this building. But I've never gone anywhere I could be seen."

"First, we'll grab all the food pouches we can carry, sour or not, plus any other supplies you guys had that we might need. While you compile everything, I'll send a message to Ryker about what happened. After that, we need to hurry up off this floor. If Toton sends robots to make sure there aren't survivors, I want to be long gone."

As they set out, Terik said, "I wouldn't have killed you in your sleep."

"Well, that's reassuring at least."

"If you'd endangered my family, I would've done it face-to-face."

Roe stepped out of the craft and heaved a sigh. In all the years he'd served as the leader of the rebel group, he'd never gotten into his head-quarters via what felt like attempted suicide by the pilot.

The rain hammered the cover over the walkway as he caught sight of the broken front door. "What happened here?" he asked the chirpy trooper who would not leave his side.

"No idea, sir."

"How about you go get me an answer rather than celebrating your ignorance?"

"Yes, sir. Sorry, sir." He jogged forward.

Once Roe was inside, he paused, no idea where to go. Passersby walked around him without a word. The kid at the front desk stared, waiting for him to approach.

The door had been kicked in and unfamiliar faces were in their midst, yet no one appeared to be paying attention. They were as bad as the clones. These people were just *asking* to be killed.

Roe took out his gun and fired three shots, directed outside. Someone screamed, hands covered heads, and everyone bent to the ground.

"Now I've got your attention, huh?" He zeroed in on a lady with a tight bun. "Do you know who I am?"

She straightened up slowly and put her hands out to show she wasn't armed. "No."

"What do you think this is, a robbery?" Roe stalked toward the desk as more of those chirpy troopers caught up to him.

"What happened?" one of them asked.

"This place is waiting to be taken over, that's what." Roe stopped in front of the desk as a large presence seething with danger arrived on scene. Before he turned around to meet it, he stared down the nitwit at the desk. "You are very lucky he showed up."

The kid gulped.

"Roe," Ryker said as Roe turned around. Ryker stood there with weariness dragging down his features, blood spattering one of his legs, and a charred suit curling around the sides of his torso.

"Had a bad day?" Roe asked.

"Walk with me." Ryker motioned him on.

Roe matched his speed as they took a thruway deeper into the building. Walls had been freshly painted cream, they even held artwork, and lights were bright. "This place looks like a damn corporation."

"A corporation with terrible security," Ryker growled. They turned left and stepped into a room alive with flashing screens and whirling tech. People worked on code or programs. Maps covered an entire wall.

"Latest tech?" Roe asked, sizing up this room and comparing it with the one he'd created in the old headquarters. It was much more state-of-the-art, not to mention way cleaner. Still smelled like shit, though.

"I wouldn't know. Listen, this place is a defensive nightmare. There is very little security, as you saw. They are mostly relying on those EMPs a handful of levels up. I think you know how easy it would be to circumvent that. Ground security is a joke. I'm not staying here longer than a couple days. If we don't have a plan by then, I'm changing locations with my family."

"Well, shit, I don't want to stay behind and die. I'll go, too. Do you think it'll come to that, though? You can't bring it around?"

Roe listened while Ryker told him of his suspicions regarding why Toton hadn't attacked thus far, and why they had left the rockets alone. Cold dripped down Roe's middle, a feeling he hadn't experienced in a very long time. Roe's gut said Ryker was right on.

"So what's our next step?" Roe asked.

"Millie is sleeping. I'm giving her another couple hours. When she wakes up, she'll hit this room hard. We need the best and the brightest in here with her, helping. Hopefully her sister will be firing on all cylinders by then—"

"You got her?"

"Yeah, but she lost someone she cared about and shut down."

"She'll be back up." Roe eyed someone hurrying by. Anxiety lined the man's face. "She was trained like we were. She'll push it all down and do her job."

"That's what I'm counting on. So as soon as Millie is awake, we're going to . . ." Ryker's brow furrowed as he studied his wrist.

Then he was all action.

"Pull up the last location of Trent McAllister's craft," he barked, walking up to a middle-aged man standing in front of a console.

The man looked over his shoulder and flinched. Apparently Ryker had already made his mark on the people in this room. "Y-yes, sir."

"What's happening?" Roe asked.

"Trent's team was taken out. He and the children are alive. Everyone else is toast."

"What's toast?" a seated girl asked.

"What happened?" Roe pushed a young guy out of the way and took over his console, ignoring the "Hey!"

"Toton. The kids are all gifted, like Marie, and they took down a few of Toton's crafts, or so I gather." Ryker looked down at his wrist screen. "He's half babbling, or else the program isn't catching his words properly, but it sounds like a craft came out of nowhere and opened fire. He's only alive because he ran first and fast, and because of the kids. Or *a* kid, I can't tell. Doesn't say how. He's holed up in the middle of the building. They are looking to move as soon as they get supplies. He's going to try to get somewhere safe so we can pick them up."

"Out of that whole crew, a lab rat and a bunch of kids survived." Roe shook his head as he pulled up images from a couple of their positioned cameras. "I can barely make out this one. Looks like the whole face of that floor took heavy firepower."

Ryker looked over with tight eyes. "Is Toton threatened by those kids, or is this their classic defense strategy? We don't know enough about the sit—"

The screens flickered. Two people pulled their hands away from consoles or screens and looked around. The screens flickered again before dimming. This time they went black.

"What is this?" Ryker asked.

"What's happening?" a man exclaimed.

"Not again." A woman pushed away from the screens.

White code rolled through the black screens.

"We saw this when Toton first made their presence known," another woman murmured, continuing to work the console despite the fact that nothing was happening. "They've hacked into our systems. This is the beginning."

"The beginning of what? We need details," Roe yelled.

"Someone wake up Ms. Lance and Ms. Foster," Ryker barked. "And get some grade-one, quality uppers. They're going to need them."

Chapter 14

Millicent clawed to consciousness as a hand shook her body. Blinking her eyes open, she saw the hazy form of a woman by her bed. She rubbed her eyes and sat up. "I think I need a few more hours."

It was then she noticed the blinking purple on her wrist screen, her warning that her firewall had been breached. "Shit! What's happening?"

"Gunner said to wake you. It's Toton," the woman said in panic-stricken tones. "It's like when they took over the conglomerates' information. They're doing it here."

"Get Marie. Get Danissa. Where is a console?"

"This way, Ms. Foster. Someone is waking Ms. Lance. I can have someone wake up Marie, as well."

"Do it. We'll need them all. Are we in danger physically?"

"Not yet, ma'am, but Gunner said he isn't confident in the security here."

"Why would he be? It's a mess." Millicent hastened into her suit and thought about waking Marie, who was in the adjacent room, herself. She quickly discounted the idea. She'd just scare her daughter, and that would hinder Marie's ability. "Have the person who wakes Marie do it slowly. Easy-like. Treat all of this like a game."

"Yes, ma'am. I'll do it after I drop you off."

They only made it a few feet down the corridor before the sound of hurried steps behind them made Millicent glance back. Danissa, with a pale face and wide eyes, was rushing through the corridor. She saw Millicent and a wash of relief crossed her face. It hardened up immediately. Thank Holy.

"I've been through this a few times," Danissa said as she caught up. "Enough to know that you aren't going fast enough. Hurry!"

"What are they doing?" Millicent ran behind her sister. "And where are we going?"

"Hang left," the rebel woman yelled, now trailing them.

"They hack into the system, run through the files, lock everyone out, and download whatever they need. Then they screw up the system as best they can. At first that was it. Radio silence for a year or more. But in the last few years, they did all that, left, and you thought you had a second to breathe. That's when their spiders would roll through."

"Hang right, just through there!" the woman instructed. "I'll go get Marie."

"How do they lock everyone out?" Millicent jogged into the control room.

"Trent's team was taken out and he's been marooned with some gifted children," Ryker said as she shoved her way in front of a console. Danissa did the same. Neither of them noticed the infuriated squawks from the misplaced persons.

"*What?*" Millicent asked, turning away from the console.

"Focus!" Danissa snapped. "We don't have time."

"I'll work on him. You work on this." Ryker pointed to a flickering screen.

"I can go for him as soon as you get his location." Roe's voice drifted over the din.

"The lock they place is easy to get around," Danissa said in a loud, clear voice, cutting through all other noise. "Ms. Foster, follow along. You'll pick it up quickly. Unless you're off your game."

"I'm not off anything." Millicent felt the fire of competition roar through her blood. She watched her sister's keystrokes, processing how her code interacted with the locking program. Just when Danissa was about to break out of it, though, Millicent barked, "Stop!"

Danissa paused with a scoff. "You have two seconds."

"I wonder if we can follow this back . . ." Millicent traced the origin of the hack and met a ramshackle firewall. Within moments, she had made her way through and was rummaging around in their cupboards. "What are you after?" she asked softly.

"I can work around you," Danissa said. "Burrow in and I'll crack off this lock and disable their attempts to copy our information. We don't have much time."

"What are they copying?" Millicent asked, but nodded when Danissa looked over for her assent.

"Holy shit," someone gasped as the sisters worked. "Who are these women?"

"The stupid of that question literally smells bad," Roe growled. "Who do you think they are?" He huffed in annoyance. "Ryker, you got some information or what? I need to go blow something up. I'm still not right from that rocket ride."

"People. They're after people," Danissa said, shaking her head. "They're trying to download our records about them. They did this with Gregon and Moxidone."

"I'd heard that. Let them. They'll get a nasty surprise."

"What kind of surprise?"

"One that disables their systems. What else are they after? They're hunting for our access keys. I don't even know what that is. But they're searching for it."

"My superiors implanted the use of access keys." From Danissa's tone, it was clear she was rolling her eyes. "It was an extra step for added security, or so Gregon thought. Waste of time. It took me longer to set up the whole thing than it did for them to break through."

"Uh-huh. Well, let them keep searching." Millicent shook her head and backed away from the console for a second. "Stop." She said it loudly enough for everyone to hear.

"What?" Danissa asked, still plugging away. The whole room had gone still around them. Everyone stared at their screens with wide, disbelieving eyes.

"Stop."

Danissa looked over, confusion evident.

"What are we doing?" Millicent asked, gesturing at the screen.

Danissa's brow lowered even more. "It sounds like you're requesting a very obvious answer, which means I am missing your real meaning . . ."

"How nice that someone realizes that." Millicent couldn't hold back a smile, and then a bigger smile when Danissa's lips twitched in response. It was nice to speak to someone on the exact same level, with very similar training.

"They're trying to get in." Millicent motioned at the screens. "So what?"

"All your files can be accessed through here . . . right?" Danissa asked.

"This is a *pirate* network. Things are bought and sold by dubious characters with fake identities. The rebels have collected their defense information on it, but any idiot can get around that." Millicent ignored a scoff. "If they try to shut down our communications, we'll just override. So rather than waste time preventing them from chasing shadows, let's find their ground wires and figure out how to snip them."

"What's a ground wire?" Roe asked.

"It's a hard port." Danissa lowered her hands. "The foundation of their network. They'll have the backup server on it, but it'll be nearly impossible to get to it. We'd have to travel all over the world to destroy them all."

"Wrong again." Millicent laughed. "Look." She cleared a screen and pulled up a world map. She added blue dots that identified the active Toton presence. "They are all over the world, yes, but their communication directives seem to stem mostly from Los Angeles. Their hub is here, I'm sure of it—the supercomputer that controls their overall efforts. They keep updating their tech, so they must have a concentrated area to design and test it, and considering everything we've seen, I bet this is it. In the future, who knows, but for right now, they have yet to truly expand their headquarters. I really think cutting out the hub will cripple them globally. At least for a time. Hopefully long enough for our forces to strike and do lasting damage."

Danissa blew out a breath. "It's the best plan I've heard thus far. But given the people I have been working with, that isn't saying much. So what do you think?"

Marie walked in rubbing her eyes. She sidled over to Ryker and wrapped her arms around his waist. "I'm tired."

"I know, pumpkin." Ryker bent to rub her back.

"Do you want to play a game, Marie?" Millicent asked.

"No."

Millicent thinned her lips. That wasn't the response she'd hoped for.

"I will," Danissa said.

"Okay. Then the first one that breaks through Toton's various walls, locks them out, and exposes all their secrets, wins!"

"Oh! That *is* a real game. You're on!" Danissa leaned over her console.

Another flash of excitement rolled through Millicent. She'd only said that to get her daughter going, but Danissa was already working. Millicent bent to her own console as she heard, "I want to play!"

"Here, baby. Sit here and see if you can beat Mommy and Aunt Danissa."

"Aunt?" Danissa said in a vague voice. It was clear she was focused elsewhere, and didn't register the real meaning. She had no idea they were blood relatives. Millicent was a little hesitant to explain it, for reasons she couldn't understand.

"I need the coordinates of whatever place we will need to break into," Ryker said.

Millicent took a quick break to pull them up and flick them to another screen. "That's my best guess so far."

"I second that assumption," Danissa said.

"But that's . . ." Roe's comment drifted away.

"Right next to Trent's location," Ryker said. "Those kids were in Toton's backyard the whole time. Now we know why Toton opened fire. This just got a lot more interesting."

"Obviously I'm going to try not to be seen," Trent muttered at his wrist. It flickered and went out before coming on again a moment later.

"That's Toton." Terik pointed at Trent's wrist before handing over a canvas sack filled with medical supplies. "I remember that happened to the screens in the lab right before everyone lost their minds."

"What lab? Oh, where you were born?"

"Raised. I was never given over to the Milestone department. They kept me in the lab. They constantly did tests as soon as I showed what I could do." He hefted his own sack before wheeling over a sort of cart. "We can take this for Mira. I made it a while ago. We'll have to haul it up the barricades, but it'll be worth it. She gets heavy."

Trent stared incredulously at the boy for a moment. He could not believe Terik was only ten years old. They'd been back at the children's former living space for about an hour, and while Trent had impressed upon them that they'd be picked up soon, despite telling them to grab all the food, Terik had insisted they take enough supplies for a few days, if not longer. More clothing, additional blankets, and small comfort items for the children. "Planning ahead," he kept saying. "Just in case."

He'd collected all the right medical supplies without supervision, and knew which food pouches to take and which were rancid. Clothes were packed, the kids were fed—he was like their parent. He looked after them just like they were his own. Despite being an adult who'd looked after little ones all his life, Trent would be hard pressed to outdo this boy.

It blew his mind.

"Why didn't you pack anything when we were leaving for the craft?" Trent asked as they got under way.

"Didn't have time, did I? That lead trooper had a short fuse and he wasn't too keen on you. What little power you had was about to be stripped away."

"He was fine with me." Trent scowled, but then he found himself studying the boy's face again. "You remind me of someone. Do you know your parentage?"

"I'm a bunch of genes mixed together with a squirt of chemicals. I don't have parentage."

"You most certainly do. That particular mix of genes came from somewhere."

"My mommy was a unicorn," Zanda said.

"She's fascinated with animals from prehistoric Earth," Terik said.

"A unicorn wasn't . . ." Trent let it drop. There was nearly no point in killing the girl's dreams. "Where are we headed?"

"I know a lookout. It'll give you an idea of where you are so you can tell your friends how to find us."

"They can track my coordinates."

"Not for long. Toton will tear down their communications. We'll be on our own."

"You think you know everything, but trust me, you have no idea. When you meet my friends, you'll no longer be the smartest person in the room. Nor the most stubborn. Nor the most insanely protective. Billy won't even be the most violent, and that is saying something, let me tell you. You're a big fish in a little pond right now, but soon, you'll be scrambling to learn what goes on around you."

"What does 'big fish in a little pond' mean?"

"Never mind. How far?"

It turned out to be quite far. They heaved the rolling cart over the barricade Trent hadn't used before, then had to take trips to bring the kids over, since most of the little ones couldn't make it on their own. After that, they climbed another barricade and then squeezed through a charred kid-sized hole in a door that had been welded shut. Trent nearly didn't fit. It took Terik pulling and the two older girls pushing to get his middle through.

Once that was done, they had to carry the cart up five flights before they emerged through an open door to total ruin.

Breathing heavily, Trent forgot to be dismayed that Terik and the kids had all made this journey on several occasions, somehow getting past their caretakers to do so. Eyes wide and out of words, he looked at the devastation. The work pods and screens had been reduced to piles of debris spread across the floor. Most of the ceiling tiles were missing, leaving gaping black holes. To top it off, it looked like someone had come through and set off small explosives. The light from the windows fell across patches of char along the walls. Metal was twisted and bent, crusted black in many places.

"Did you do this?" Trent asked, breaking the hush that had fallen over the group.

"Of course not," Terik said, lifting Mira out of the cart. "We would have been noticed if I'd set fire to this place."

"Then what happened?"

"The other floors are like this, too. The ones above us. These buildings used to be Moxidone offices, I think. Toton did this to force them out."

"Robots, or . . ."

"I don't know. I wasn't here. I just heard some of the adults talking about it. Staffers were in here working. Toton fried their systems, and a few days later they came through and blasted them out. It was one of the first acts of war, I hear."

"Holy shit—excuse my language. Why didn't the lower floors get this treatment? Why didn't they burn you guys out?"

"We were moved in after the whole place was vacated."

Terik led them as Trent felt a little hand curl into his. Zanda looked up at him with big brown eyes.

"Are you okay?" he asked. She nodded solemnly.

Not sure what that interaction meant, he followed the others around the corner and then into a corridor. "Will we get there anytime today?"

"Almost there," Terik answered from a ways in front.

"And what did you mean, you'd be noticed? Does Toton still come around?"

"You'll see." The words floated down the empty hallway, almost like a taunt.

A few minutes later, Trent *did* see. His stomach twisted and somersaulted at the same time. He turned to the side and retched. Thankfully, his stomach was empty.

"I thought you guys knew when you first showed up. Yeah. It's something." Terik settled into an alcove that was mostly protected, though the windows were obscured from the harsh environment blasting through the openings along the destroyed side of the building.

Across a huge but dead travel way, the top half of the closest building was lined with bays on each floor. Within each bay was one or more of the black crafts that had opened fire on them earlier. Lining walkways and skittering up and down the outsides of the building were moving objects that looked like insects. The place was teeming with them, almost like a hive. And not just the spiders Trent had seen in pictures. Strange creatures with bulbous middles and long legs, large and small, moved in dizzying ways. Some staggered or wavered like drunks. A couple of the creatures crawling up the reflective windows randomly fell off, hit the bay, and tumbled out into the open air. Occasionally, Trent saw a long thing with no arms or legs slide across the ground. There were metal spheres attached to its back.

Spheres like the one Millicent had experimented with on Paradise.

"What is that place?" Trent asked through a tight throat.

"Toton," Terik whispered. The hush seemed unnatural with so much movement happening across the chasm. "The only crafts that fly through there are Toton's. The only ones I've ever seen, anyway."

"Are there always that many robots?"

"There are more now, but there have always been a lot. More of them used to fall off the side of the building. When they first started climbing like that, it looked like rain coming off. They had to erect a net to catch them all. It's like they're getting smarter."

"How long have you been coming up here?" Trent asked.

"Almost since we were moved to this lab. I started exploring right away, and once I saw all that, I made sure to check in regularly. It's close, so it wasn't a big problem. Getting to the lower levels was a lot harder."

Trent shook his head as another wave of bile rose in his throat. All those robots . . .

"There is no way we can be rescued from this side of the building." Trent's words felt hollow.

"No, I don't think so. And unless they are really quick, the other side won't be great, either."

"This has turned into a really bad day." Trent ran his fingers through his hair.

"Welcome to my life. Here, let's check out the other places I've found. You can see different parts of Toton."

It wasn't an appealing offer, but Trent knew he should find out everything he could about the enemy. If he didn't make it back from this venture, he could at least relay to Ryker what he'd found. Maybe it would help.

"I will not end up in one of those robots," Trent muttered to himself. They sounded like famous last words.

Chapter 15

"What do we have?" Millicent asked as she stalked into a large room filled with holograms of the building where Trent and the kids were holed up.

"Trent has been sending us detailed descriptions." Ryker didn't look away from the hologram he was studying. "The upper levels are . . . not available to us."

"How are we going to get him out of there?"

"We're not. He's going to meet us in the lower levels."

"I'm sorry, *what?*" Millicent leaned against the table and shoved Ryker's shoulder to get him to look at her. "He has a bunch of children."

"Five children. One who can see in the darkness and somehow create fire. One who—"

"I don't care what they can do. They are *children*. Some of them are young children, at that. We can't take them into the battle zone."

"We won't be taking them. They'll be meeting us—"

"Holy help me, Ryker, if you don't stop talking nonsense, I am going to stick something sharp in your eye."

His grin didn't reach his eyes. "One of the kids, the oldest, knows of a tunnel that leads from the building they're in to Toton's building. We looked into it. It was a sort of thoroughfare from one building to the other. A smaller building sandwiched in between two larger build-ings. The nearest we could figure, someone attempted to collapse it. It's mostly still standing, though I don't know how. So what the kid is saying, in essence, is that there's a direct route through all that rubble to Toton's lower level. We'd still be a handful of floors up, maybe more. The building they're in was thirty floors high before someone blew it to hell. But if the kid's correct, then we have a silent, hopefully unmoni-tored way into Toton's building. Probably the *only* unmonitored way into the building."

"That kid was way up in the upper-middle floors. How could he have known what went on way down there?"

"Danissa checked the records. The lab logged a death report on the oldest, who they said disappeared from the care room for a week. Later, someone attempted to delete the report, but he or she wasn't competent. It was one of four death reports for that kid in the last year. The truancy issues were three times that for the two oldest. A younger boy had the lion's share of reports, the last a blatant appeal to get rid of him. He's violent, apparently."

"These kids sound like a nightmare."

"I was a nightmare. Look how I turned out."

"Yes. Thank you for proving my point." Millicent wiped her hand over her face. "How are we going to get there without raising any alarms?"

"Black out the city."

Millicent stared at Ryker's electric-blue eyes, waiting for more. He stared back, not offering an explanation.

She lifted her eyebrows.

He continued to stare.

If he wouldn't easily dodge it, she would've punched him. "Do you not realize that my staring at you is a silent question of *how*?"

"I do. It is a judgy silent question, at that." He shifted ever so slightly, meaning he felt a tiny inkling of doubt. That was a cause for concern, as the man standing in front of her rarely experienced that emotion. "I don't know. That's your job. The big dog plans. The peons figure shit out. Go get with Danissa and figure shit out." This time his grin did reach his eyes. He took her hand gently, no longer joking. "I have no idea how to get there without them seeing or knowing. Trent suspects that they have cameras everywhere in the area—video, I would imagine. Obviously we can cut the feeds, but they'll quickly put two and two together."

"What we need . . ." Millicent bit her lip, her mind whirling. "Is to be invisible. The answer isn't to cut out their feed, but to make it so their feed doesn't see our crafts."

"Can you do something?" Ryker asked, stroking his thumb along her skin.

"How much time?"

"Trent and the children have provisions for a while. It's this place I'm concerned about. How's the pirate network?"

"They backed off after that second surprise virus." Millicent couldn't help a smile. "I barricaded that one in. All the time and effort they spent getting to it, and *oops*. Their systems are limping along. We are so far up their butt, they probably aren't sitting right. We're copying everything we need, like how they're taking over the food plants, their defense around Moxidone's rocket, their intel on the conglomerates—everything."

"How can we keep the information safe? Can't they just hack in again?"

She huffed. "We're putting it on external hard drives, obviously."

"I need you to stop hanging out with your sister—you're starting to get the idea that everyone is as smart as you. Fine. Physical drives. And where do we keep those so the enemy doesn't recover them?"

"I'm just a peon, remember? I leave those tough decisions for the big dog." She ran her finger through his messy black hair before planting a kiss on his full lips. "I'll talk to Danissa about getting to that building incognito. Hopefully we can figure something out between the two of us."

"Thanks, love."

"Now you need to get some sleep. Otherwise you'll be no good to us."

He started to shake his head, but stopped as the tranquilizer needle slid into his arm. Dagger, who'd snuck up, had injected the fluid.

Ryker gave her a small smile. "You hate not getting your way, don't you, princess?"

Dagger stepped out from behind him and pulled the tranquilizer away. "Sorry, sir, but it's my shift and you're cramping my style. Calling me princess is going a bit too far, though . . ."

"You're so tired you didn't even notice him creeping up on you." Millicent pulled Ryker's arm. "Get some sleep. Let Dagger take over. Hopefully I'll have a solution by the time you're awake."

"Love you." Ryker said to Millicent and punched Dagger in the chest as he passed.

"Love you, too, sir." Dagger said. "Night-night." He wiped his chest, clearly trying to rub away the pain, judging by the grimace and tightness of his eyes. "Okay. Let's get cracking."

"This isn't much of a solution," Danissa said as she stared at the long flat device made of smooth, shiny metal. The spheres the humanoid cockroach had been carrying had been made of a similar metal. "This is the thing they use to mess with our minds?"

Danissa watched as Millicent smoothed her hair back and then glanced at her wrist, where a counter flashed 4:57. Gunner had been asleep for nearly five hours so far. With Millicent leading the charge, they had hidden booby traps all over Toton's net, set a timing code to execute Millicent's somewhat genius prison programs on the top staffers of both Moxidone and Gregon—in the hopes that everything else would go as planned—and fixed or enhanced the various weaponry

Millicent had designed. With Danissa helping and Marie doing things Danissa hadn't even known were possible, they were flying.

Problem was, it still might not be enough.

"Yes. It quickly and painfully debilitates humans," Millicent said, finally answering her question. "I think that was the reason for their quick and easy victory in the beginning. Simple to work around, as you figured out."

"One of the reasons for their victory, anyway." Danissa ran her finger along the smooth metal. "You're sure we don't have anything like this in the metal plants? Making something from scratch would probably be easier than trying to alter this."

"This metal doesn't come from Earth. Paradise has it in large quantities, so I was able to experiment with its properties. That'll help us here."

"I've never been good at the hardware. Only software."

"You're smart and you can learn. Time to get good. Now, I've already altered the output of this thing. It isn't geared to human brain waves anymore. Unfortunately, it isn't geared to much of anything. I'm trying to get it to emit a sort of frequency that will confuse the video surveillance enough to where we can run—"

"Mommy! Mommy!" Marie fell off her stool and scrambled to her feet.

A distant explosion made the floor rumble and screens quiver.

"Already?" Millicent gasped, grabbing the device and standing. Her hip bumped the table and knocked a screen to the floor. It shattered as another explosion shook the room.

"What the hell is happening?" someone shrieked. Others screamed. People looked around, wide-eyed.

"Pull up our feeds!" Danissa yelled, already on her feet and taking charge of the situation. She'd been through this so many times, the commands were second nature. "Cover these walls with our exterior eyes and ears. We need to see what's going on. And for the sake of Divinity, someone wake up Gunner!"

"Where we at, pretty lady?" Dagger said as he jogged over.

Danissa didn't scoff at his choice of name. She needed him thinking and acting with his dick right now, since it was directly tied to his testosterone. She was the brains—he had to be the brawn.

"They are blasting their way in. They have some heavy artillery."

"So do we," Millicent said, working at the console. "Marie, create hell in their systems. Don't set off the viruses and Trojans, but scramble their communications and the uplinks from their crafts. Blind their headquarters."

"Update me," Gunner said, jogging in. He pulled his suit over one arm and stuffed his other hand through the armhole.

"Work faster, people!" Danissa yelled. To Gunner, she said, "We've got nothing to update you with so far. Stand by."

Images popped up one by one. Black crafts idled just above the EMP areas, blasting holes in the building. It was clear they didn't know the exact location of the EMPs, but it was equally clear they knew the EMPs existed—and at approximately the correct height.

"Clear everyone away from the main entrance," Gunner yelled. "We're going to have heavy debris raining down."

Light flared from the bottom of one of the crafts. Another explosion shook the building. Flames coughed out into the sky, distorting the camera for a moment.

"I have rockets trained on the first craft," Millicent said in a calm, focused voice. This wasn't her first time in combat, either. "Do I fire now, or wait until I get them all lined up?"

"Fire," Gunner said, stalking over to an open console. "Do we have any crafts rigged with heavy artillery ready to go?"

"Yes, sir," Dagger said, standing near the door. "We built them to Ms. Foster's specifications. They are in bays four, five, and eight."

"Pull up a map of the area," Danissa said, pointing at a mousy woman on her right. The woman nodded and did as she was told. "Mark those bays and mark the locations of the known enemy crafts."

"Danissa, take this on the move," Gunner said in a voice full of command. "We're going to use this distraction to get behind enemy lines. Let's get to the crafts."

Cold bled through her. Images of Puda's slack white face filled her mind. Memories of explosions, of body parts, and of all her near-death experiences across the city rooted her feet to the spot. It felt like they were kicking her out of the safety of the fold—just like the conglomerate had. They were thrusting her into the waiting arms of the enemy, and this time, there wouldn't be anyone to come to her aid.

"Hey." Shivers coated her body as that strong, firm hand landed on her shoulder. "You've got the best of the best in your corner, Danissa," Dagger said softly, for her ears alone. "We've got your back. I won't let anything happen to you, got it? We'll take out those killers, and then you can come back here and give your man a proper farewell. Stay strong for him."

She placed her palm to her chest, where a heavy weight had settled.

"Take three deep breaths," Dagger said calmly. "Three deep breaths, and then we spring into action. One . . ."

Danissa sank into his words and his confidence. Grounded by his dark, dynamic eyes, she took a deep breath, and let it fill her lungs.

"Breathe it out. And take another one. Good work. One more . . ."

She blew out the third breath and nodded.

"Let's go!" Dagger yelled at her.

Startled out of the relaxing exercise, she snatched up two mobile screens and a hologram unit without thinking, and was running beside Millicent before she had registered what was happening.

"Their training is very effective," Millicent said in a conversational tone.

"Aren't you terrified?"

"I'm leaving my child behind in safety, so no." She paused a moment, then said, "Don't think about danger. It doesn't help. Think of the outcome. Think of how to make that outcome happen."

"What's the outcome?"

They turned a corner as another explosion rocked the building.

"A better life. Green fields. Those waves you love so much, but in real life. Children's laughter. People you care about. Or just peace and quiet with no superiors. There is a future for you, but you have to be tough enough to take it. It won't be handed to you. You have to *take it*!"

"Take a right, ladies, and put some hop into that step," Dagger said, easily catching up to them.

"Do you have the same genetic makeup as Ryker?" Millicent asked.

"I have no idea what you are talking about," Dagger answered. "Just through here."

"Trent has ruined me," Millicent muttered.

"In you get." Dagger palmed an archaic security pad and motioned them through. "You go first. Check for monsters in there, would ya? I don't like monsters jumping out at me. They plague my closet and under my bed."

"What is he talking about?" Danissa said as she followed Millicent into the craft. Seats lined the sides of the vessel and curved around toward the cockpit. There were storage bays along the back, next to a locker that hopefully contained extra suits and spare parts.

"They get amped up for battles." Millicent took a station at the console by the craft door. She gestured toward the back. "There should be another console back there. Maybe two, if they did as I instructed."

"We did indeed, bossy lady," Dagger said, practically bobbing by the door. A rumble hinted at an explosion.

"We have three targets lined up," Millicent said. "Danissa . . ."

Danissa positioned herself by one of the consoles, and no sooner had she started it up than a map flashed in front of her, code scrolling along the side.

"I need help," Millicent said. "I see three more crafts. Their shots are slow to come, which means they are either having trouble aiming, or they're giving it a second after each shot to gauge the impact. Pinpoint them with this . . ." A tracking program loaded onto Danissa's screen. "Then we can target them."

"You do some things very well," Danissa said, quickly deconstructing Millicent's program and rebuilding it with passable code. "And some things you really suck at. Here. Use this in the future. It'll save you time."

She flicked the program to Millicent's screen before implementing it on her end. "Find the rest with that, and I'll create a heat-seeking program that can target them all at about the same time."

"Oh great, two annoyingly smart women playing 'my program is bigger than yours.'" Roe clicked on a heavy utility belt as he sauntered into the craft. "At least men have actual dicks to measure. It puts an end to the endless one-upmanship."

"Don't walk into a gunfight with a knife, bro-yo," Dagger said from the doorway.

"I ain't afraid of them." Roe took a seat like it was a lovely and relaxing day.

"What do you want?" Dagger asked someone outside of the craft.

"Let them on," Roe called. "They are the surliest of the former clones I picked up today. No implants, though, and they have no idea how to work a console."

"Can they read?" Millicent asked as the building rumbled. The craft shook, the metal of the docking groaning.

"Yep. They can read, run, lift weights, swim, and fuck. We can send messages to their mobile screens."

"Why you mentioned their sexual prowess, I do not know," Millicent said dryly.

"They do five things really well, as far as I've seen. How callous would it have been for me to leave one of those things out? Then people would think they could only do *four* things." Seven men and women of perfect proportions and muscle tone stepped into the craft. Their skin was horrible, but their eyes were bright and filled with rage. None of them said hello, just walked to the rear of the craft and stood there quietly.

"That you've *seen*?" Millicent scoffed. "Where's Ryker?"

"He's on the way," Dagger called.

"True, I haven't actually seen them swim, but I am assured they are all excellent at it. The older ones have the skin lesions from the acidic water to prove it. Not talkers, though. They don't say much. Seem mad a lot of the time. I figured that was a good thing."

"I have all the crafts targeted . . . ," Millicent said.

"Kill them all!" Dagger yelled.

"They are most likely robots," Millicent replied. Danissa saw "Execute" flash. "So no one will actually die . . ." She paused. "Never mind."

An echo of thunder permeated their space.

"Control room, what is the status of the enemy crafts?" Millicent asked.

Over the comm unit, a voice said, "Direct hit on all. Fire is consuming most, and those are already losing altitude. Two are wavering."

Code flashed down the side of Danissa's screen, the mirror of what Millicent was working on. "Execute" flashed. Another echo of thunder drifted in.

"Control room, give me eyes," Millicent said.

"Why not just pull it up?" Danissa asked.

"I want them to maintain control with confidence. They'll be in charge as soon as we're out of here."

"Direct hit," the control room said. "They're falling like stones. We're preparing for impact. One will hit the landing strip hard."

"That's what it's designed for," Dagger said.

"What about the other crafts?" Millicent asked. "What will they hit?"

"Empty buildings. If those buildings topple, we'll be fine. The empty ones were strategic."

"Not so shit with defense after all, then." Roe sniffed. "Not when it really counted, anyway."

"Yeah, with us here," Danissa murmured.

"Everybody's a critic." Roe adjusted his belt and crossed his ankle over his knee.

Gunner ran into the craft. "We're good to go. I'll be flying this bird. Princess, update me on what I'm working with."

"Remember my old craft from when I was with the conglomerate?"

"We got five more getting into position," the overhead comms said. "There are a dozen more hovering above those. They are trying to force their way in with sheer numbers."

"We got bullets all day long," Millicent said before muting her microphone.

"Yes, I do," Gunner said, answering Millicent's question.

"I'll target." Danissa didn't wait for permission before bending over her console. Dagger closed the doors and walked to the lockers in the back.

"Well, this has ten times the firepower and smarter, more advanced tech. It's a pretty little vessel." Pride rang in Millicent's voice.

"You get to call things pretty, do you?" Dagger droned as he handed out utility belts to the clones.

"I'm thinking with my heart, not my nether regions."

"A woman's heart is either the most beautiful, giving, glorious thing in the world," Dagger said as though talking to himself. "Or, if you break it, the most horrible and violent thing. She'll save you with a kiss and a smile, or she'll smear your worthless ass all over the ground floor."

"You should probably stop taking lovers," Roe said. "Clearly you are doing something wrong . . ."

"This one"—Gunner hooked a thumb back at Millicent—"will stick a knife in your ribs when you're not looking. And if you *are* looking, she'll blow you up."

"I rather enjoyed when there was only one monster ego and horrible sense of humor to combat. Two of you security guys, plus a security dropout, might be too much." Millicent pursed her lips. Danissa couldn't help but laugh.

"Marie is on her way?" Millicent asked, her tone turning serious.

"Yes." Gunner's tone suddenly matched. "She's on the way to the safe house with Sinner and his team. If things go wrong, they'll get her off-planet. We have two other crafts loaded in other bays."

"Targets for all enemy crafts are locked," Danissa said. "Fire when ready."

"Transfer that program over to the second smartest of the rebels," Millicent said, executing her weapons program.

"Second smartest?"

"Yes. Managing the weapons will go to the smartest. We have fifteen or so minutes before we'll have a whole different set of problems. Ones that we've probably never seen before. It's time for battle."

Chapter 16

"Where are we?" Trent asked as he slithered through a charred hole and then reached back for Mira. "And how long does it take to make one of these rat holes?"

Billy crawled through next. As soon as he stood up, he punched Trent in the face.

Trent didn't see it coming. He flinched too late and threw his hands up to ward off another attack. "Why, Billy?"

"It's all dark, but they still see," Billy squeaked. "They'll get in and the other people will be confused." Billy danced about and then grabbed his crotch.

"You get used to it dangling there," Trent said helpfully. There was no point in asking Billy who "they" and "the other people" were. Billy wouldn't know, and he wouldn't be able to describe anyone. He seemed to spit out whatever flashed through his mind without any real idea what it meant. As his talent matured, Trent had every belief he'd be extremely powerful in precognition.

They just had to keep him alive so he *could* mature.

Zanda came through the hole as Mira started to wander off.

"Zanda, grab the baby!" Trent stuck his hands through the hole to help guide Suzi. They were slapped away, probably as Marie would've done. "Yes, I know, you can do it yourself. Go ahead."

"It takes a while to make these holes," Terik said when he finally passed through. "And a lot of effort to keep the fire from getting out of control."

Trent glanced at his wrist before taking two of the packs and slinging them over his shoulders. No communication from Ryker or Millicent.

"Your turn." Terik grabbed Mira and handed her to Trent. They'd had to leave the cart behind ten floors ago.

"How much farther?" Trent asked as he balanced everything.

"Two more floors." Terik took Billy's hand and then flinched away when Billy kicked.

They all paused for what would come. Nothing did.

"Sometimes it's a premonition, and sometimes he's just a jerk," Suzi said, pushing Billy away.

"These floors are connected." Trent looked into a burned hole. The layout resembled that of an apartment, with space for a cleaning stall, a bed area, and a leisure alcove. The walls were charred and furniture reduced to mounds on the littered floors. The inhabitants were long gone.

For all that, a faint glow of security lighting still ran through the debris-littered corridor.

"And you said there is a place for our people to land?" Trent asked, his voice hushed in the empty and destroyed space.

"Oh yeah." Terik pushed away Billy, who had tried another kick. "Lots of space. They have to get into it, though. It's basically a hollowed-out floor. I don't think it's very structurally sound, but it'll work."

Trent tried to keep his eyes open as they walked. Tried to keep his legs moving one in front of the other, staying strong for the children.

But he'd only had a very short nap on the craft en route to the children's hiding place, followed by another short nap at one of the eating stops. He'd probably been awake for nearly twenty-four hours and it was starting to slow him down.

There wasn't much he could do now, though. They needed to get to the meeting spot. Ryker and Millicent were counting on him.

A few grueling hours later, Terik finally stopped walking. He dropped his backpack to the ground. "Suzi, distribute food and get the blankets."

Trent blinked in confusion and focused his sandy eyes. They stood in the doorway of a huge, cavernous space. As he'd come to expect, various parts of the building and whatever used to be in it littered the floor in piles. At the other end, a gaping hole with jagged edges spoke of missiles, or a crash landing by a huge craft. Away to the right was another, much smaller, hole in a mangled, collapsed structure.

"Quaint," Trent said sarcastically, putting Mira down.

Billy rose up on his tiptoes, thrust Toad Man into the sky, and then spiked the stuffed toy with all his might. "Boom! Three will die, but two. Okay."

"Describe what you saw," Terik said, catching the little boy as he hopped by. "Say what you saw again. Use more words."

Billy's face screwed up before he punched Terik in the crotch.

"Oh!" Terik bent at the waist but held on to Billy's shoulder. "I said not to punch me there!"

"Three come in here, and boom! All go boom! Flip. Two land. Big people get out. Nice ladies. Flip! Boom! All go boom, and fire and light and heat. Flip. We get hugs and slap fives and better-tasting food. Flip—"

"Okay, okay. I got it." Terik let him go, braced his hands on his knees, and hung his head. "I should never have taught him how to punch."

"What does that mean, flip?" Trent asked, his wrist already raised to send a message.

"Two possible futures." Terik winced as he straightened up. "If your friends try to land three crafts in here, they'll all die. They'll explode somehow. Or crash, I don't know. I doubt Billy does, either. If they come with two crafts, they'll land safely."

Trent blew out a breath and shook his head. "You children are . . . exceptional. I don't agree with the experimentation they did, since it doesn't sound like it went smoothly for others, but with you children, their outcome was . . . just exceptional. Really awesome. I hope I can eventually look at your files, because you are something."

"Do you always talk this much?" Suzi asked.

Trent paused midmessage and couldn't help but scowl at the little girl. What people had against talking, he would never understand. Everyone was always telling him to stop babbling.

He finished his message, took a food packet, gagged because it was so disgusting, and then followed the others back through the doorway, where they'd be somewhat protected from the environment. The children more or less settled in a pile of bodies, probably accustomed to huddling together for warmth and comfort.

Trent sat in the space beside them. "We should probably take turns keeping watch," he said to Terik. "Just in case."

"Okay. Who goes first?"

"I can," Trent said, crossing his arms over his chest. He was the adult, after all.

Trent groggily came awake to someone shaking him. He blinked into the face of Mira. Suzi leaned against one side of him, and Billy was curled up on his lap. He'd clearly fallen asleep when he should've been looking out.

"Hi, Mira. What is it, honey?" Trent wiped the sleep out of his eyes. It didn't do much good.

That's when he heard the sound of engines beyond the doorway, working hard.

His heart started to hammer. He removed Billy and gently shook Suzi awake. Terik straightened up a moment later, wiping his face.

"Someone's here," Trent whispered, standing. "Get ready to run."

He edged to the door and took a deep breath. *Please don't be Toton. Please don't be robots.*

Something nudged him. A mirror was placed into his hand. He nearly groaned, remembering the last time he had attempted to look around a corner with a mirror. "I hope they don't shoot at me . . ."

In the shaking reflection, one craft was just touching down in the large space, and the other had landed safely. If they'd had a third craft, they'd taken Trent's words to heart and sent it away.

"It has to be them," Trent whispered as his wrist flashed with a message from Ryker: *I can see your mirror.*

The hard exhale was louder than his words had been. "It is them. Thank Holy."

Tiredness gave way to intense relief as he turned toward the others. All wore the same masks of apprehension, except for Terik, whose expression had closed down into a hard mask.

"I know them," Trent said. "It's okay. Help is here!"

"But what if they think we're freaks?" Suzi said, reaching for Terik's hand. Zanda's arms were wrapped around his leg.

Trent pushed away his desperate urge to rush through the doorway and glue himself to Ryker's side. Instead, he summoned up his patience and sank to the ground until he was on the same level as the children. "Their oldest daughter is here on Earth with them, and she's just like you. She's about the same age as Suzi. They are nice people, I promise."

"It's fine. I'll look after you," Terik said, his knuckles turning white where he held the girls' hands. He did a great job of hiding his own anxiety. Trent would bet his house that the conglomerate had been aiming for the superior-level security mold with Terik. And it looked like they had gotten it, plus some perks. Too bad they didn't value what they had.

"Come on, you'll see." Trent reached for Billy's hand. The little boy lowered his head, peering at him from under a furrowed brow. Without warning, he sprinted at Trent and head butted him in the chest. "Good grief, child!" Trent hopped up and dodged a kick, backing through the doorway. "No kicking! Remember? No kicking, no punching, no biting, no—stop that!" A small fist hit his hip. "Dang it."

He looked up in time to see Millicent coming out from around the craft. She surveyed the area. Ryker was staring at the hole to the right. Stern-faced troopers were stepping out of the other craft, and they immediately organized into rank and file. Ryker appeared to have brought the best.

"Trent!" Millicent walked over hurriedly before offering him a smile. "You made it. I'm glad. How could you possibly have known my cloaking device would only cover two crafts?"

Ryker was there next, sticking out a hand to shake. "Good to see you made it."

"This is Billy, who had a premonition regarding the number of crafts that could safely land." Trent stuck his hand out to grab Billy. It was slapped away with Toad Man. "He's violent."

Millicent kneeled. The children, huddled together, stared at her with solemn eyes. "Hello. My name is Millicent. I have three children who would fit right in with this group. What are your names?"

None of the kids answered.

"Well, I need to quickly fill you in on why we're here, and what we're doing. First—" She looked behind her. "Danissa, grab a portable screen and contact Marie. Have her get in front of a camera. I want her to meet the children she'll be working with."

Trent caught sight of Danissa, Millicent's sister, before she headed back to the craft. It was exciting to see them together. He looked forward to identifying similarities.

"I'm afraid you are caught up in a very dangerous situation," Millicent said to the children. "We need you to help us get through the collapsed building—through this tunnel. After that, we'll get you to safety. The problem is, I don't know where that might be."

"We'll leave two people behind who can fly the crafts out of here," Ryker said, his gaze roaming the space. "The children can return to this building through the tunnel and then be flown to the safe house to wait with Marie. You're sure that device will keep working?"

"No," Millicent said, still kneeling. "This environment tends to corrode that type of metal. It should work for a while, and it should only need to be cleaned once it fails. But just in case, we're going to switch to plan B, because if it fails for even a moment, they'll catch us. Our cover will be blown."

"What's plan B?" Ryker asked.

"Putting their cameras on a loop," Danissa said. "Here." She handed Millicent the screen. Marie's face filled up the whole thing. "I have the program ready to go. It'll trick the computers, most likely, but if a human digs into the feed or setup, they'll probably notice."

"What about a human computer?" Ryker asked.

"A what?"

"It'll need human *eyes* to look at the feed and find the little inconsistencies," Millicent interjected. "And it would need to be a detail-oriented human—or sentient being, anyway—at that. The setup, though . . . let's just hope they don't have a reason to look." Millicent took the portable screen. "Marie, introduce yourself to these children and tell them about how you can work computers with your mind."

"Trent, walk with me." Ryker laid a heavy hand on Trent's shoulder. Leaving Millicent to hopefully ease the children's anxiety, which would then make them more willing to help, Trent let the large man lead him toward the hole where another huge man waited. "Give me a rundown on exactly what we are dealing with when it comes to those children."

Trent went through their various abilities as Ryker studied the building layout on his wrist screen. When Trent finished, Ryker glanced at the other large man.

"I'd hate to endanger children," the other large man said, "but my, oh my, would they be helpful."

"Problem is, unlike Marie, who can help from a safe location, they have to be present." Ryker shook his head. "We need Terik, but . . . we should probably leave the rest behind. This is no place for children. Regardless of how helpful they'd be . . . I just can't rationalize endangering them."

Millicent straightened up and glanced at Danissa. "Get that program going. Time is running out."

"Time was running out when you left ten or so years ago."

"That doesn't make my statement any less true." Millicent gestured to the children, still gathered in front of her, and they followed, a few of them clutching stuffed animals or blankets.

"Round 'em up," Ryker said to the other large man. "Let's get moving."

Millicent was looking at her wrist screen when she neared them. "Four waves of Toton crafts have been taken down. Their systems are scrambled, thanks to Marie. I told her to back out, though. A good enough systems analyst could follow a hacker back to his or her source and disable it. Being that Marie's source is her *brain*, not a computer . . ."

"Is that possible?" Danissa asked.

Millicent shook her head. "I still don't know how her mind does what it does. I haven't been able to break her code—largely because she doesn't seem to *use* a code. It's an aggravating riddle to say the least. Enough to drive you mad."

"Bet I figure it out before you do."

Millicent's eyes lit with fire. "Doubtful."

"Ladies, stay focused, please." Ryker was looking down at Terik. His brow furrowed slightly, as though trying to figure out a riddle.

"Here we go, sir." The other large man stalked up with the same kind of killer's grace Ryker possessed. Clearly they had both been successfully bred for similar roles. "Ready when you are."

"The program is running," Danissa said.

"Hey, kid, my name is Dagger." The large man stuck out his hand. "Slap me five."

Terik didn't move.

"Good call. I might have germs. So you can see in the dark, huh?"

"Yes," Terik said with confidence.

"And you know the way through to the other side?" Dagger jerked his head toward the hole.

"Yes, but in a few parts it's going to be tight for a couple of you. I can burn the way, but that takes a while."

"Right, yeah, with your fire. That's cool. I'd love to burn shit." Dagger glanced at Ryker, and then back at the boy. "We have a couple cool things that should help us cut through, so don't you worry about that. We also have neat glasses that will help the rest of us see in the dark. You sure you don't need a pair of glasses? We got extra."

Terik just stared at him, not at all the brazen kid he'd been with his caretakers. He probably recognized that these new people were smarter and could easily kill him if they wanted to, regardless of his powers. Terik wasn't a fool.

"I'm going to be up front with you, okay?" Dagger continued. "We're going to lead together. How does that sound?"

"Fine," Terik said.

"And we're going to leave the others behind so—"

"No." Terik took a step toward the other children. "We stay together."

"It is going to be incredibly dangerous once we step through that hole." Ryker used a commanding voice that brooked no argument. "We don't wish to endanger any of you. The only reason we're taking you is because we have no choice."

Terik looked Ryker directly in the eyes, squaring his shoulders as he faced off against a man twice his size and width. "They go with me, or I stay with them. That is the only way you are getting my help."

Man and boy stared at each other, their breeding so similar Trent was now *certain* the conglomerate had been trying for another director. And they probably would've gotten it, too.

"Fair enough," Ryker said after a silent, tense moment. "But their welfare is on your head. You need to know that if one of them should die, it will be on your conscience for the rest of your life."

"Their welfare has always been on my head. I've already lost people since all this started. I'll be damned if I lose four more."

"That's the shits, bro-yo." Dagger patted the boy, dislodging his stare from Ryker. "But you're not alone anymore. Now you got help. More strong arms, and more brains than you know what to do with. We'll keep those little ladies and gents safe. Don't you worry."

"Let's get rocking." Ryker motioned everyone onward.

"That's our cue." Dagger patted the boy again before taking out his glasses.

"We are going in hot," Ryker said to the group, "but we are trying to keep a low profile. Use your silencer to kill if you have to. Try to go unnoticed. Remember your directives."

"What about the children?" Millicent asked. "Are they walking, or . . . ?"

"I'll take Mira," Trent said, picking up the toddler. "Watch Billy."

"I'll take his hand." Suzi tried to capture his hand. Billy swung his shoulders and pulled his arm into his body before swinging his hips and turning. "Billy, *come on!*"

"This is not how I envisioned this part of the journey," Millicent said, looking at the little boy. In a voice that made all her children stop acting up immediately, she said, "Take your sister's hand."

Billy's eyes widened. He stopped moving. Within Millicent's unwavering stare, he put his hand out for Suzi to capture.

"Good job." Millicent put on her glasses.

"Careful kids, she's tough." Ryker laughed.

"How will they see?" Trent asked. "How will *I* see?"

"Here." A trooper handed Trent a pair of glasses, and passed others out to the kids. "We don't have anything smaller. We have one extra pair besides this. Don't break them."

Dagger put out his hand for Terik to lead the way. One by one, they all filtered into the hole surrounded by twisted metal and sharp points. They were crossing enemy lines.

Chapter 17

Butterflies filled Millicent's stomach as she followed Dagger, anxious about the danger they were sure to find on the other side of this war-made tunnel. Her wrist screen was lit, distorting her vision somewhat, but she had to keep track of the assault on the headquarters. So far, Toton hadn't gotten past her preliminary defenses, whether swooping down from above or attempting to come up from below. She doubted Toton was used to the kind of smart firepower she'd been working on while on Paradise. Ironic, how a peaceful place could inspire such extremely violent ideas.

They turned at a twisted beam and then stepped through a hole that looked like it had been burned around the edges some time ago. She bet it was from the time Terik had explored early in his occupation of the building, creating a path through the twisted rubble. The ceiling pressed down on them, making her stoop to keep moving. Claustrophobia reared its ugly head, squeezing her chest.

"Don't touch anything you don't have to," Dagger whispered to her. "Pass that back."

"Why?" she asked. Her wrist screen started to dim. She was losing signal. Soon it would be off altogether.

"Terik said this place is not structurally sound. I'm not paraphrasing. The kid is damn smart for his age."

Millicent ignored the commentary and passed the message back to Ryker. He pulled his hand away from the wall before conveying it to the others.

Her screen flickered, and then went out. Something snatched at her suit. She slowed and put her hand out to Ryker so he wouldn't run into the obstacle. Before she moved on, she saw him doing the same thing to whomever was behind him.

The structure groaned. A loud pop had Millicent jumping.

"The kid says that always happens," Dagger whispered back. "Pass it on."

"How many times has he been down here?" she asked.

A moment later, he said, "Twice."

"*Always*, huh?" Millicent shook her head and attempted to ignore her rapid heartbeat and the sweat coating her forehead. The walls pressed in next, the tightening space lacing her thoughts with panic. She focused on breathing, on not losing her cool. Ryker grunted behind her. Dagger had to twist to fit—his shoulders were too broad for him to move straight ahead. The big men would have a hard go of it.

A bang sounded from behind them. A child's voice rang out in the space, and then Ryker's hand fell on Millicent's shoulder. She snatched Dagger's suit and pulled. He stopped when she did.

"What's up?" Dagger asked as Ryker said, "We need to go faster. The little boy is talking about exploding crafts."

"Go, go, go!" Millicent pushed at Dagger before repeating the message.

"What's the point of the darkness?" Dagger asked.

"Trent said that's how we should go through," Millicent answered, panic now bleeding through her thoughts.

"Terik says we got a ways to go. There are no openings. Sound might carry, but the light won't until we get closer. I say we ditch the glasses and light this baby up. These things aren't showing me the fine details."

"Yeah, fine." She passed the message back, but before it could even make it to the end of the group, blue fire crawled up the walls around them, casting a strong glow. Millicent's mouth dropped and she jerked away from a reaching flame. Surprisingly, there was very little heat.

"He says the fire won't hurt you unless you touch it for a long time," Dagger whispered. "Pass it on."

Another bang. A stuffed toad went flying past Millicent's head and hit Dagger in the shoulder. Billy's voice drifted up again, the words not discernible.

"Faster, faster!" Ryker pushed Millicent's back.

She snatched the stuffed animal off the ground and handed it back before repeating the message to Dagger. Their pace quickened. The building groaned above them. Fire-laden metal jutted out from the sides. Twisted debris snagged at her feet.

"RUN TOAD MAN!"

She heard Billy clearly that time.

She shoved at Dagger.

"Hurry!" Terik said in front of them, no one worried about sound now. "Zanda, can you harden the ceiling?"

"What?" a girl's voice called up.

Millicent passed back the question even though she had no idea what it meant. She barely missed a sharp bit of metal at hip level. Ryker grunted behind her.

The sound of an explosion rumbled down the tunnel way. The building groaned. Metal screamed, and pops sounded above them.

"Go!" Ryker yelled, pushing her. "The boy is crying and saying we're going to die. *Go!*"

Blind panic rushed through Millicent. She couldn't die. Not while Toton and the conglomerates still held the power. Her children would be left defenseless, one of them still on this Holy-forsaken world.

She shoved Dagger. "Tell Terik to get his kids to make a miracle happen. And hurry, you donkey!"

"Bring up Suzi and Zanda, he says." Dagger's shoulder knocked into a twisted beam. The building rumbled again. A slab shifted and dropped, thunking Millicent on the head.

She flinched away, her hand coming up in reflex to rub the offending spot. Wetness coated her fingertips. She glanced at the glistening red while passing the message back. More pops went off, sparking her anxiety. What sounded like a smattering of gunfire preceded another explosion that shook their tiny tunnel. A deeper groan from the building made Millicent grind her teeth.

Two girls hurried past Millicent, squeezing through the space like they'd been doing it all their lives. Dust shifted down from above, accompanied by a worrying vibration. The fire-coated walls started to shake.

"This whole place is going to fall down around us," she muttered as bile rose in her throat.

A solid metal support cried as it bent next to her. She hurried onward, moving at a breakneck pace. Metal sliced at her legs and arms. Pieces of building shimmied as she passed. The groan of the building got louder.

More metal squealed, but this time in front of her. Things clanked. As Millicent pushed against Dagger, she saw materials shifting. Being bent out of the way by an invisible hand. Cracks lined the walls, or warped them. Fire burned hot on anything wood.

The children were doing what they could to clear the way.

Dagger bent, his butt pushing out and nudging Millicent back. Suzi wrapped her thin arms around his neck, leaned her head against his shoulder, and closed her eyes.

"What's happening?" Millicent asked.

"I have to focus," Suzi said in a wispy voice.

A pop sounded above their heads. The building's groan turned into a roar. The whole place was about to collapse on them!

"Almost there!" Dagger said. His voice was small in comparison to the roaring all around them. His body bounced around, knocking into the walls like Millicent's was.

Someone screamed, a blood-curdling sound. Dust whooshed past Millicent from the falling building. The ceiling crushed down toward them, narrowing the space by half. Suzi's fingers turned into claws on Dagger's back. Her face screwed up in pain or concentration, and beads of sweat dribbled down her temple. "I'm . . . not . . . strong enough . . . to . . . hold it."

They turned a corner and Dagger fell to his hands, crawling. Suzi still held on, eyes closed, her feet sliding against the floor between Dagger's legs. Millicent dropped down, too, barely able to breathe through her panic. The ceiling crunched down another several inches. They'd be squished!

She hurried around a corner, her knees scraping something sharp. Pain sliced through her as the tunnel suddenly fell away. With a gasp of combined surprise and relief, she rolled out of the tunnel—and found herself in a fire-blackened building with straight walls and skeletal casings of work pods. Ryker rolled out next to her, holding Billy. Danissa and Trent came next, white-faced and panting. Roe, panting so hard he looked like he was trying to heave out a lung, collapsed on his side. The clones and a few troopers made it out before the rumbling and shaking intensified. The tunnel roof heaved and dropped. Someone screamed. Blood washed out of the tunnel. Still, the building groaned and shifted.

The tunnel had been closed forever.

"This is who's left," Ryker said into the continued low rumble, looking over the dozen or so faces that had made it out. Their starting numbers from headquarters had been cut down by about a third.

Suzi's eyes snapped open. She looked around wildly and then held out her hand for Terik. Deathly pale, like Mira and Zanda, Terik inched over and took her hand. "You did good."

"I couldn't hold it anymore," she said in a tiny voice.

"You held it long enough. It was all you could do."

"It was more than we could do." Millicent took a moment to breathe before looking at her wrist screen. It lit up. She had internet, and the headquarters was still holding its own. She wished she could say the same.

"Looks like they cleared this place out." Ryker, the first to recover, which wasn't much of a surprise, ran his fingers along the walls. "This scorching is old. Years and years old, I'd bet. It looks like it was offices. Their own, probably."

"Before they started the war, you think?" Dagger asked, standing.

"No way to tell."

Millicent pulled up a map before looking back at the collapsed tunnel. "Think they'll look into what two pirate vessels were doing in that hollowed-out building?"

"Doubt it," Roe said, sitting up and draping his arms over his knees. Sweat ran down his face. "If I were them, I'd assume a group of rebels had stopped there to wait out the battle at headquarters. We got vessels without firepower camping out all over the city. That should've been a perfect place to hide."

"Makes sense." Ryker bounced on the floor. "The floor is good. Walls are good. Just the inside was gutted. Why set fire to it?"

"Keep people from wandering back in and settling." Dagger stalked across the large expanse toward a distant window. "They're probably watching this place, right?"

"Feeds are coming from this building," Millicent said. "From this floor, even. I think this place is doing the watching. You should see cameras looking out."

"Okay," Ryker said. "Now let's get moving. Toton is bound to be suspicious at this point."

The group took off toward the middle of the floor, where, judging by the map, the stairs were located. Once there, Marie confirmed over their comms that she could find no mention of surveillance on that stairwell.

"Why would they watch the whole city, but not their own buildings?" one of the troopers asked, looking around.

"They are confident that their defense will keep people out," Millicent answered. "Hopefully that overconfidence lasts."

"Hopefully," Roe said. From his tone, it didn't sound like he was convinced.

Millicent wasn't, either. Despite their brush with death in the tunnel, this felt too easy.

They filed into the stairwell quickly. Concrete steps wound upward. Each floor was marked with a mundane sign, giving the number and its braille equivalent.

"We're going down, right?" Ryker whispered. Even with the lowered voice, his words bounced off the walls and echoed through the shaft.

Millicent held up four fingers, then pointed downward and nodded. They weren't positive of their destination, but earlier, while they were still at headquarters, Marie had done some extensive poking around while Millicent and Danissa created interference. She had found a sort of black hole beneath the fourth flour, indicating a hard port. A private loop that could only be accessed physically, with wires leading to an intricate yet hackable wireless system that was boosted by a great many towers throughout the city.

Or else it was a wasteland. That tunnel had showed up as a black hole as well.

Soft footfalls reached Millicent's ears. The swish of fabric and hard breathing were an unwelcome reminder that anyone within earshot would know they were there.

A hard hand landed on her shoulder. Dagger held his finger to his lips; Ryker threw a fist in the air. Everyone stopped on cue.

She heard it. The faint scraping sound of many legs scurrying across the ground. It was probably a robot, a spider or something similar, and it was coming up the stairs.

Eyes wide and heart racing, she looked at her map, wondering why she hadn't seen the sentry sooner.

It wasn't there. This must've been the next-generation robot, because her software was not reading its proximity.

She swore to herself, fingers moving furiously as she searched for schematics on the floor they were standing near. Level fifteen, with video uplink and not much else. Could they dare to hope it was a blackened, hollowed-out floor like the other?

"Do we kill it?" Ryker whispered near her ear.

She shook her head. "It's a sentry. They'll be monitoring it; I have no doubt."

Ryker gave a nod and looked at the nearest door before flicking his gaze upward. He was waiting for her decision, preparing for either possibility.

Gritting her teeth, she pushed through the closest door, feeling an iron grip on her shoulder before she could finish the action. Ryker ripped her back and took her place, entering the floor first.

The scraping quickened. The children pushed in around her legs, half knocking her aside. A foot scuffed the ground. Danissa's body barreled into Millicent's back, and they rolled onto the floor together. Rough blackened char smeared across Millicent's hands as the others filed in behind them. Then the door clicked shut, cutting off the glow of the stairwell.

"I sent the last couple of troopers back up the stairs," Dagger whispered from the doorway. In the soft illumination from a portable light, he stood broad and tall against the wall, his hand on the door handle. It looked like he expected an army to barge through. "That thing moved fast. We wouldn't have all made it in here, and they were closer to the upper level."

"I'm just glad I made it with this group," Trent muttered, shifting Mira on his hip.

Millicent was glad the children had made it, too. Their age aside, they were a valuable asset. One that had so far kept them alive.

Another light flared to life in Ryker's hand, this one stronger. It showered the floor and walls around them, revealing exactly what Millicent had hoped for—a dead floor that had been burned through. Embarrassingly, her sigh was audible.

"Terik, light," Ryker said, standing in front of them, facing the vast empty space.

Fire pulsed along the floor and along the wall, bright yet artificial. Ryker shut off his light and stowed it away in his utility belt.

"Now what?" someone asked.

Millicent touched the communication command on her wrist. "Marie, can you see any robots patrolling the stairs? Do they show up on your thermal map?"

"No, Mommy," she said. "Looks clear."

"They are there, honey. If you can, try to figure out how we can track them."

"Okay."

"She can do all that with her mind?" Terik asked in a flat voice. His eyes were wary.

"You're the last person I'd expect to be weirded out." Trent frowned at him.

"I'm not weirded out. Just asking." The flames pulsed higher for a moment, reacting to whatever emotion Terik was trying to hide.

"We can search for an open stairwell," Ryker said. "Moxidone had their fair share when departments were multiple levels, but this far down . . ."

"Gregon did, too," Danissa said.

"There is a void on the map." Millicent angled it so Ryker could see. "We could try it. Otherwise, we're going to have to make a run for it in the stairwell."

"Dagger, inform the others to stay put," Ryker said.

"Yes, sir. Should I hang out near the door?"

"No. We can use a siren for that. Put it high, though."

"What's a siren?" Danissa asked, getting to her feet.

"It's a device that'll give us a warning when it's disturbed." Millicent tried to familiarize herself with the level beneath them, but all the information was the same. Toton didn't keep thorough records of these floors—at least, not in the files Millicent and the crew had hacked. If they weren't in the right place, they would be trapped in the belly of Toton's empire.

"I hate this," she said in distaste. "I had a nice life set up back home. Boring, but paradise compared to this. Now I'm stuck in this trash heap, in danger, trying to save a planet that sucks."

"Well, if you think about it—"

"Don't." Ryker shook his head at Dagger, cutting him off. "She gets aggressive if you try to reason with her venting."

Dagger's mouth snapped shut, but his eyes twinkled.

"Let's go," Millicent said, setting a fast pace.

The floor creaked under their footfalls, weakened from the blast of the heavy flames Toton must have laid down.

"They must've used a lot of explosives to get the floor looking like this," Trent said softly.

"I'd say a flame thrower, or else there would be craters in the floor." Dagger looked down as if to check.

"Twenty feet or so," Millicent whispered, looking down at her map. Ryker's hand stopped her. She glanced up at a gaping hole, closer than her map had said it should be. If there had been a banister once upon a time, there wasn't one anymore. Nor were there stairs—just a hole in the ceiling, and one in the floor.

"I got a strap," a trooper whispered, stepping forward while digging in his utility belt.

A strap was thicker and more durable than a rope. It responded to mental commands—attaching and detaching at the user's will. They were fantastic devices that had saved Millicent and Ryker on multiple occasions in their initial escape from Earth.

"We all do," Roe said, edging up to the opening.

Click.

"Roe, run!" Millicent backed away from what was surely one of those bombs.

"No! Don't move!" Danissa held up her hand before pointing at a floor-level panel at the edge of the hole.

"Well, which is it?" Roe demanded.

Millicent squinted into the gloom. The small panel flashed red, reminding her of those smart doors from so long ago. No other lights blinked to life.

"What is that, do you reckon?" Millicent asked.

"Is it dangerous?" Roe followed their gazes. "Because I'm sitting here like an idiot with my balls out if it is."

Ryker crossed around behind it. He bent and grabbed the edges. "It's partially embedded in the wood."

Click.

"Do you feel anything?" Millicent asked, breaking out in a sweat.

"My head is buzzing." Ryker and Roe both touched their implants.

"That's their mental warfare device." Danissa checked her wrist screen. "We need to move on. It will eventually overcome the implants."

"Why did they use this to protect an interior stairwell and not the one we were just descending?" Dagger asked.

Danissa shook her head. "I don't know, unless this is acting as a sort of sentry. Maybe spiders don't patrol in here . . ."

"Just step away," Millicent told Roe. "They work based on proximity." To Dagger, she said, "Tell the people on the upper floor to swing down to us. Then we can all swing down to the next floor."

"It's the proximity to the edge of the hole that's the problem, not this control-panel thing." Ryker checked the far side of the hole, and nodded at something that must've validated his theory. He stepped back and his hand came away from behind his ear.

"What about the former clones?" Roe asked, moving back. "They'll have to cross that threshold when they swing down, but they don't have implants."

"Why did you bring untrained clones instead of rebel troops?" Trent asked incredulously.

"I wanted to encourage the rest of the former clones to join the ranks." Roe braced his hands on his hips. "Had I known we would only get a few choice picks on this venture, rather than the three craft loads we'd started with, I would've done things a little differently . . ."

"What about the children?" someone asked as someone else said, "How long does it work? My implant was disabled."

"Does anyone hear that?" Dagger tilted his head, looking behind him.

Everyone fell silent. Only then did Millicent hear the deep hum vibrating through the floors and up the walls around them. Something sputtered high up, off to the side. The same sputter then came from the other side, on the wall.

"Get moving," Ryker said, suddenly all action.

The troopers rushed toward him, yanking out their black straps. Dagger stooped down to tie a strap around Terik's waist. Then he looped it around Zanda, tying them together.

Billy stomped on the ground. "Tek. Just like Tek!" He stomped again. "Ouch!" He hit his head.

"What's just like Tek?" Ryker asked.

"We don't always know what he means." Terik clutched his strap.

Dagger stopped in front of Trent. "Can you lift your body weight?"

"How should I know?" he answered with a blanched face.

"Normal people know that information." Dagger wrapped a line around Trent's middle. "I'll assume you can't."

Billy skipped toward Ryker.

"Someone grab the little boy," Danissa called.

A roar drew their attention to the far wall.

"Was that metal pole always there?" Trent pointed a shaking finger at a sort of nozzle made of shiny metal protruding from the blackened wall.

"They're all along the walls, look!" The trooper pointed to add emphasis to his words.

Something dripped out of the farthest nozzle, barely seen because of the distance. Then flames erupted. The nozzle started to turn, sweeping the air and ground, as another roar sounded from the other side of the room. The vibration of the floor increased. The hum got louder. Closer.

"They're going to burn us out!" Millicent dug into her utility belt. "Hurry!"

Chapter 18

Flames shot out of another pole. And then another. Heat blasted them. Ryker anchored a line and threw someone off the side. Trent screamed as he plummeted through the air. Ryker didn't stop there. He anchored another line and threw in a trooper holding Billy. And then another.

"Step right up for your chance to ride the strap of death!" Dagger grabbed a trooper, anchored him, and pushed. The trooper screamed, but he managed to clutch on to the rope as it swung downward. "Oops. He didn't have an implant, I guess."

Sweat dribbled down Millicent's temples as the closer poles flared to life, pushing more heat at them. Working fast, she dug through Toton's systems, trying to find the logs that pertained to blasting fire.

"Hold on, bro-yo," Dagger said, grabbing Terik. "Hold that little lady tightly."

Terik didn't reply. He was frowning as he stared at the fire. A second later, he was flying through the air. Zanda cried out in fear and pain. Terik didn't make a sound.

"What's going on down there?" someone yelled from above. "We're still getting ready."

"Get away from the edge!" Ryker yelled. He slapped down a black strap and handed the line to a clone. "Tie yourself in and jump. It'll probably hurt like hell."

Surprisingly, the clone didn't hesitate. She tied herself in with quick but calm movements and jumped. If she made any sound, it was washed away by the roaring of the flames behind them.

"Time is running out," Ryker said, handing off lines. "Best get jumping or you'll be toasty. Tie in, cupcake. I'd hate for you to let go and drop like a stone."

"Oh, lovely image, thank you."

Ryker grinned at her, tightened the strap, kissed her, then flung. She barely kept from squealing as she flew out over empty space. A face looked down at her from the floor above, a trooper who clearly hadn't heeded the warning of his buzzing implant. Or maybe he was safe on that floor.

The strap tightened around her gut and squeezed. Holding her breath as pain flared in her middle, she swung. Her feet scraped the char and a trooper pulled her in. Flames were already roaring from another nozzle at the far end of the floor.

"Oh shit," she said, breathing hard. The other end of her strap snaked through the air as people gathered around the opening above, waiting.

Danissa grunted as her strap tightened, and then she swung in. Another nozzle coughed out more flames.

"We can't wait much longer," one of the troopers yelled at Millicent before looking behind him.

"Thanks for waiting at all." Millicent was jostled to the side as Danissa was hauled in. Dagger sailed through the air next, followed by Ryker, each holding a child. Billy punched Ryker in the face instead of screaming with fright or pain.

"Why are we waiting?" one of the troopers asked. "Shouldn't we keep moving down?"

"Because the fires are triggered by our presence. We can't send someone out too far ahead, because then the people who come last will land on a fiery floor." Millicent pushed at the troopers near her. "Okay, go. Go, go, go."

The clones slapped down their black straps and jumped down first, not needing prompting. The troopers, clearly harried by the fire coming up behind them, went next. The one without an implant screamed again.

A trooper fell down through the empty space above them, his arms windmilling. One of the men who'd gone up a floor in the stairwell. He hadn't reacted quickly enough to the shock of the fire blasts to get his black strap properly secured in time.

Ryker set Billy down for a second time and flicked his wrist. His strap released from above. He shook his head. "The people on the floors above us aren't moving fast enough. They're going to get caught."

Dagger set down Suzi. "Unless they use a—"

Another body fell down the gap, screaming. His hair was on fire. The second soldier from the other floor. A third came down on the end of a strap, but he was engulfed in flame. He swung down toward them, screaming. Ryker and Dagger both stepped up to grab him, but the trooper didn't make it that far. He slammed into an invisible barrier. Blood spurted from his nose and mouth. His screams cut off and his body went limp, knocked out or dead, it was hard to say.

"Probably for the best," Dagger said evenly.

"Release that invisible barrier, Suzi, and I'll cut him down." Ryker waited a moment before stepping forward and grabbing the strap. The body fell a moment later.

The roar of flames behind them increased in intensity.

"We gotta go!" Ryker slapped a strap down and flung the person attached to it.

"Why don't you ever warn me!" Trent screamed, once again swinging out over the abyss.

Ryker chuckled as he reached for Terik.

Millicent secured her own strap and then swung out over the void. Ryker followed a moment later.

"I have no idea why this kid keeps punching me," he said as he skidded to a stop and put Billy down.

"You deserve it, that's why." Millicent glanced back at the first sputter of flames on their floor.

"What awaits us at the bottom of this?" Ryker asked ominously.

"No escape," Millicent said through a tight throat. "I need to figure out how to stop the chain reaction."

Roe peered out over the edge as the next wave of people swung down. He shook his head. "Better think fast. The fun ends two floors down."

"This whole trip has been nothing but bad news," Millicent muttered, hunting through Toton's logs. Danissa bent over her screen as well.

"Here we go, ladies." Dagger scooped up Danissa and flung her down. Millicent was next. But Millicent was just as stumped when they reached the next floor.

"What about that sensor?" Danissa asked, clutching a trooper by the suit and keeping him on the floor. "Can we physically get into it?"

"Try," Ryker said.

Millicent nodded and flung herself down to the next floor, Danissa right behind her. Without someone to catch them, they skidded across the burned ground. Millicent rolled to her stomach and crawled to the sensor, thankfully in the opposite direction of the bodies littering the floor. Her implant buzzed from the mental warfare.

"The invisibility device," Danissa said, looking around her as though it might have followed them like a pet.

"Crushed in the tunnel." Millicent ran the pad of her finger over the smooth cover of the panel. She hooked her fingernail under the edge, and then took out a utility knife and popped the cover. Wires and more sensors greeted her, not controlled from this location but vulnerable to damage.

"You need to hurry, princess," Ryker yelled.

"I'll say," Roe's voice drifted down.

"I need your strength, Ryker," she hollered back.

A moment later, he swung down, Billy once again in his arms. As soon as they stopped moving, the little boy gave Ryker a good kick.

"This is the first time I am intensely curious about breeding," Ryker said as he stooped near Millicent. The roar above them now competed with the one behind. "What do you need, love?"

"Rip these out." She circled her finger over the wires.

Ryker's arm bulged as he grabbed hold of them and yanked. His jaw clenched. "It's shocking me."

"Can you bear it?"

"Cupcake, I can bear anything." He yanked again, ripping the wiring. His grunt almost sounded like a groan as he flexed his fingers. His hand shook.

"Hurt a little, huh?" Millicent dug into the mess of wires with her pliers. She cut two connections that had stayed intact. The buzzing in her head stopped. A long low beep sounded in the distance. It repeated—and kept on repeating. "That's not good," she said, looking for the source. But it was hidden in the blackness of the floor.

"We gotta come down," Roe yelled.

"You first, old man," they heard.

"There is nothing wrong with my trigger finger. Remember that." Roe swung down.

The fire roared behind him as more people jumped out over the void and swung down. Ryker pushed Millicent to the side before helping to bring the others in safely.

"It didn't turn off the fire," Trent said, gasping for breath.

"No crap, Trent." Millicent went back on her wrist screen. She looked up, panic starting to overcome her determination to stay calm.

"We can run. There is an elevator at the very end. Even if it's not working, we can crouch in the shaft until the fire stops."

"What else do we have?" Ryker said, glancing behind. Another nozzle roared to life, spurting fire into the air.

"Me. You have me." Terik stared at the flames, curling his fists into balls, his skin covered in a sheen of sweat. "I can feel what is creating the fire. There are chemicals involved. But I can . . ."

Half of the nozzles stopped blasting fire, followed by another three. Liquid dripped from them.

"Mommy," Millicent heard.

She unmuted her implant comms. "Yes, honey."

"There are a whole bunch of notices posted to their system. Warnings and lots of activity. And a malfunction with some sort of weaponry."

One of the nozzles near them sputtered. Terik's fists clenched. "I can squelch the fire for a time, but the device needs to be turned off." His voice was laced with strain. "I don't know how long I can hold it."

"Can I help?" Suzi asked, sitting down next to Terik. She peered at him anxiously.

"What is the malfunction," Millicent asked Marie. "Quick, honey."

"Something with the plumbing . . ."

"Shut it off. Or break it," Millicent said as the closest nozzle sputtered. "Shut it down, honey."

"Does she have it?" Danissa asked in an urgent voice. The group had moved away from the flames, except for the children, the programmers, Ryker, and Dagger.

"She has *something*. She called it plumbing."

"Could be," Danissa said, scowling down at her wrist. "I can't find anything. I can't find *anything*! Where are they keeping this info?"

"Behind thicker walls, I'd imagine." Dagger reached down for Danissa. "We need to move, pretty lady."

"You, too, Millie," Ryker warned.

There was a hiss as the rest of the nozzles died down, then cut off. Liquid dripped, pooling.

Terik heaved a big sigh.

"Did that work, Mommy?" Marie asked.

"Yes, baby." Millicent matched Terik's relief. "Yes, it did."

"*She* did that?" Terik's brow furrowed. "From a remote location?"

Millicent didn't have time to answer as someone shouted, "We got company!"

"Run!" Trent yelled. Billy started screaming about heading toward the stairs and slapping at Toad Man.

"What is it?" Millicent hopped up.

Ryker grabbed Zanda and shoved her at Danissa. "Help her."

"Spiders! A ton of robot spiders!" Trent sprinted by with Mira hanging around his neck.

Millicent ripped out her EMP gun as troopers rushed past her. Ryker grabbed her shoulder and yanked. "Let's see if we can get out first. Save the charge!"

Millicent let him turn her. She ran, following the others. Their feet pounded against the creaking and wobbly floor. It would probably only take another few blasts of fire to eat away the ground entirely. Breathing heavily, fear tingling up her spine, she caught up with Roe.

"Keep going," Roe said as Millicent matched his speed, slower than everyone else. "Keep going."

"We got weapons. We'll make it."

"Save the others," Roe panted, limping.

Ryker bent and grabbed him around the middle. He flung Roe over his wide shoulder before resuming his run. "Holy strike me, you need to go on a diet, fat man," Ryker said.

"Put me down, you idiot!"

They made it to the stairwell doorway, where the rest of the crew waited with fear or expectation covering their faces. Zanda screamed and pointed.

Millicent looked over her shoulder. A line of large, gleaming robots ran at them, faster than the other spiders—and sleeker. They moved gracefully, as though oiled and cared for instead of rusted. They were larger, too, with shining claws at the end of each of their legs.

"Go!" Millicent screamed, shoving one of the clones. "Go through the door. Kill any robot you see. The word is out."

"These probably aren't as easy to kill—oh shit . . ." Ryker's words died away.

As everyone jammed into the doorway, Millicent turned and ripped out her gun again. That's when she saw what Ryker saw. A sort of animal, like a panther on Paradise, but more robust. Long and glittering claws clicked at the end of mechanical paws. Its head, more of a block than an animal head, had spikes for teeth in a mouth that was perpetually open. On its back was a sleek metal sphere.

"We should've blown the shit out of that warehouse when we passed through it the last time we were on Earth," Ryker said in a dangerous tone.

"That thing is just for killing." Millicent backed into someone.

"It's for catching people. It'll be fast. I bet it jumps high, too. Like a watchdog on Paradise."

"That is not at all like a watchdog on Paradise." Millicent brought up her gun and gritted her teeth. "It doesn't have hands. We just need to get through this door. Everyone needs to move faster!"

"Here we go, sir," Dagger said.

Millicent backed through the door as the panther robot took a running leap. The spiders skittered forward.

"Hurry!" Millicent yelled, diving to the side.

Dagger kicked a spider. His foot made a solid thunk as it sent the robot thumping back. It didn't curl up. The panther sailed through the air at Ryker, who knocked Dagger through the door and ran after him, yanking the door shut behind them. The door bowed in as the robot slammed into it. Scratches, visible through the wood, slid down to the bottom. Something slammed into the door again. The dents increased.

"We need to go," Ryker said, shoving everyone downward. "Fast!"

"I'll take front." Dagger squeezed along the sides so he could get in front of everyone. "Those spiders are going to take more than a kick to kill."

"Spiders two-point-o," Roe said, looking back at the door they'd come through. "Let's hope they respond to Millicent's weapons."

"Yes," Millicent said. "Let's hope."

"Mommy!"

Breathing heavily, Millicent unmuted her comm. "Yes, baby."

"I think I know how they're tracking their robots. It's like tracking staffers. Like how you can find people by their implant? These have a little chip, I think, that emits a sort of communication frequency—like a walkie-talkie on Paradise. If I search for that, they're all over the place. The building is alive with them. Except on the upper-middle floors, which have these other chips. Like . . . blue versus red, kinda. The top of the building has nothing but the red ones, though."

Millicent shook her head, thrown by the influx of information. Dagger shouted. Ryker ripped out his gun as something metallic made a *donk* sound. And then a lot more *donk* sounds, like a heavy piece of machinery falling down the stairs.

"Kick their brains off," Dagger yelled.

Made sense.

"Okay, send that information to me," Millicent told Marie. She remembered what Trent had told them regarding the number of robots in this building, but hoped he was mistaken.

A moment later, she sucked in a breath. Marie was most likely right, and a horde of those robots, which Marie had colored with red dots, were pouring from the top of the building, down the side and middle. Heading right for them.

"We need to get going and barricade ourselves in somewhere," Millicent said through a numb face. "Preferably where the hard port is."

"Should we release the viruses now, Mommy?" Marie asked.

"No, sweetie. Not yet. We're not ready yet." Millicent stumbled down the stairs, trying to run and look at her wrist screen at the same time. "Stay off the line for now, Marie. Help headquarters."

"Okay, Mommy."

"Got another one," Dagger yelled up.

Millicent checked her screen, returning her focus to their surroundings. Red dots were running upward toward them, and those they'd left behind were headed back the way they'd come. Four floors down, however, there was nothing. An absence of red or blue dots. That was the sugar pot, it had to be.

"Almost there," she said, ignoring the burn in her legs.

"I can do it," a child yelled. It sounded like Suzi.

A crash sounded. A dull metallic *dong*, followed by the sound of something metallic raining down on cement. A moment later, Millicent saw why. Suzi must've picked it up with her power and slammed it against the wall harder than even Ryker could've done. The brain had come off and the machinery had burst apart.

"If only I had been born a generation later," Ryker said as they jogged past the ruined remains of the bot.

"No kidding," Millicent said. Two more robots were running up to them from the next floor down. Millicent could just see them both lift into the air, their legs spasming wildly, and then slam into each other. Their bodies mushed against each other before being thrown to the ground by invisible hands. The metal clunked down the steps before them.

By the time they reached the intended floor, another eight bots had met the same fate.

"Does she get tired?" Trent was asking when Millicent pushed her way through the bodies to get to the door.

"She *is* tired," Terik said. "We're all tired. But we want to live, so . . ."

"Got it." Trent turned Terik and dug through the pack on his back. "Then eat a pouch. Keep your strength up."

Millicent hovered in front of the stairwell door. There was no handle. Her skin prickled. Her wrist screen glowed with incoming red dots. The blue dots were the ones that jarred her, though. She didn't know what kind of sentient beings they were, or even if they were human, but her crew would be meeting them soon. Millicent had a team of the very best the planet had to offer, and she intended to extend a very warm welcome, equipped with as much firepower as she could muster.

"I have no idea what is behind this door." Millicent slid her hand along the smooth surface.

"I will go." One of the clones stepped forward. "I am not afraid to die."

"Oh. He speaks." Roe hooked his thumbs in his utility belt with raised eyebrows. "And now we know."

Ryker nodded as he pulled an instrument from his utility belt. It elongated in his hand, probably the result of a mental command. The end turned into a flat surface, and he stuck the tip into the door crack and pulled. Muscles flared along his powerful frame, but the door didn't budge.

"Here. Stop! Here." Danissa put her hand on his arm in a shoving position. Millicent recognized the irritation that crossed her expression. Ryker didn't move unless he wanted to.

"Let her try, Ryker," Millicent said. He took a step away. "Hurry, Danissa. We don't have much time."

Danissa put the instrument into the crack again and then motioned for him to hold it. She touched the end with a small device from her utility belt. "I designed this a while back, and it has saved my life more than a few times." Her expression turned troubled, probably remembering the lives she hadn't saved.

The door clicked. Danissa adjusted the device. The door clicked again. Something sputtered, and the size of the crack increased.

"Okay, shove," Danissa said to Ryker, stepping back.

"Need a hand, sir?" Dagger said.

Ryker yanked on the instrument. The door squealed as it was forced open. Apparently that was a no.

Ryker motioned everyone away and stepped to the side. His gaze fell on the male clone with the hard face. "You sure?"

"My sole purpose in life is to save someone. Here I will be honored as the saver of a world." The clone stepped toward the crack in the door.

"That's a lovely way to look at it," Trent said.

"Might as well stay positive if that's all you got," Roe growled.

"So if you have a lot to live for, like yourself, you should be negative all the time?" Trent asked Roe.

"Keeps me honest." Roe shifted to nod at the clone. "Good man."

The clone pushed the door open and rushed through, clearly prepared to meet danger head-on. Everyone held their breath.

Nothing happened.

"It can't be that easy," Millicent whispered, watching her wrist screen.

Ryker peered through the door. After a moment, he pushed it open a little more.

The clone stood in the middle of an empty room. The walls looked like patches of light-cream fabric. White tiles covered the floor, so clean they reflected the clone's image. A door at the other end had a panel with a blinking green light. Only one.

"It's a smart room," Millicent said into the hush, looking around the walls. "My wrist screen is flickering from being this close. It'll probably cut out if I step in. I'd bet anything it's a sterile zone. No wireless."

"Nothing is happening to him. Did we throw it off by breaking in?" Ryker asked in a low voice.

"We got company!" Dagger shouted.

"Too many," Suzi yelled. "That's too many. I can't handle this many."

"Need to make a decision, princess," Ryker said.

"Marie?" Millicent said, touching her implant unconsciously.

"Hi, Mommy."

"Hi, baby. We're about to be cut off from the internet, but—"

"Hurry up, bossy lady. These things are out for blood!"

"—we'll still need help. I'm sending you our coordinates. Try to find a system that is running down here as soon as we cut off, okay? And if it is running, try to stop it."

"Do I use the EMP?" Dagger asked. He grunted. "Trekking things are heavy as a metal craft turd."

"What does that even mean?" Danissa asked, tinkering with her device.

"They're hard as shit to kill, that's what it means!" Something metallic rammed against the wall.

"Okay, Mommy," Marie said. "Sinner says to tell you that the first line of defense has been breached at the headquarters. They are showing up in larger numbers. We're going to roll out the bigger guns. Oh sorry—big guns."

"Tell Sinner to stick to the plan. Okay? If he tries to take you away, you go. You go, baby, okay? And I'll see you back on Paradise."

"Will I get to meet the kids?" she asked.

Millicent bounced in place, hearing the scrape of claws on the ground. This was a smaller group of red than the one that was coming down through the building, but it was still plenty big. "Yes, baby. You'll get to meet the other kids. Okay, baby, I have to go. Bye-bye."

"Okay, Mommy. Bye."

Millicent stifled a biological need to sob uncontrollably as she clicked off, knowing that it might be the last time she ever heard her daughter's voice.

Knowing what was likely about to happen, she stepped forward anyway. Into the heart of the smart room.

Chapter 19

Danissa hurried after the others, crowding into the strange white room. Dagger pushed the door shut behind them, leaning against it heavily. "We need to find a way to lock this thing—"

The door clicked as a lock engaged. Across the room, another lock engaged.

"Danissa, did you do that?" Dagger asked softly. Everyone turned to look at her.

"No. Millicent?" she asked in a quavering voice.

"No. This room is intelligent. It traps its victims. Now the fun begins." Millicent looked up at the ceiling before turning in a circle to survey the blank white walls.

"We'll make it through this," Dagger said softly as he put a reassuring hand on Danissa's arm. "Ryker and I can handle it."

Danissa laughed, a hysterical sound that she needed to tamp down. Her screen flickered and went out. No wireless of any kind was accessible in this room. The room had shut off their eyes and ears. So what came next?

As if in answer to her question, a strange *whirr* sounded deep within the walls.

"Getting that other door open is probably step one," Gunner said, eying the walls.

Millicent reacted first, grabbing Gunner's prying instrument and running toward the far door. Once there, she looked back for Danissa, probably wanting the device Danissa had engineered on the run a year or so ago.

"We don't know what's beyond this room," Danissa said as she ran over. "Maybe this is the lesser of two evils."

"I doubt that," Millicent murmured as she took Danissa's device. "Is this self-explanatory?"

"For you it will be." Danissa thought back to all her narrow escapes. No immediate memories surfaced that would help. She went deeper, trying to recall any important details from all the run-ins she'd had with Toton. With her photographic memory, which extended to any and all visual images, she had a wealth of information to pull from.

Screaming erupted in the room. Those without implants grabbed their heads, unable to use the protective programing to beat Toton's mental weaponry. Every one of them sank slowly to their knees, their screams rising in pitch until they hit the ground, writhing. At once, the sound cut off and the figures went limp.

"I am sure glad I let you talk me into another implant," Roe said in a gruff voice, bending down to check Mira's pulse. "Still alive, though her heart is beating fast. Whatever's going to happen, is going to happen now-ish."

"Yes, extremely helpful," Millicent muttered.

Trent bent to the children as well, checking the others and straightening them out. "Thank Holy we didn't bring Marie."

"It's a shame we brought any of them," Gunner said.

"They've saved our asses a couple times." Roe ran a finger along the fabric-covered wall. "I'm happy they've been along. We just need to make sure they make it."

"Is that your thing?" Dagger asked, his eyes scanning like Gunner's. "You announce the obvious like some oracle?"

"Yeah. I think it's working for me, too." A mechanical sound filled the room, like a low groan deep within the walls. "Here we go."

"I could sure use your help, Danissa," Millicent said.

Danissa didn't move. She squeezed her eyes shut and *thought*. That sound was familiar.

Past experiences flashed through her mind's eye. She compared each one to that sound in a flash, trying to find one that fit.

"Are those fire poles?" Trent asked from across the room.

Danissa shook her head. Fire poles had a different hum. Guns made a different groan. What was that—

Like lightning, it hit her.

A stained and brown-smeared room crystalized right behind her eyes. Flickering, pale light from worn-out bulbs had made shadows jump along the walls. One door had latched, and one had made that familiar clicking sound without engaging.

Her craft had made an emergency landing. She'd run through that room to escape the spiders. Trying to get out of the strange building with the odd mechanical equipment and empty warehouse shelves.

"Mechanical arms," she said, rushing toward the opposite side of the door. Dingy material peeling away from the wall flickered over reality, her memory overriding what she was actually seeing for a moment. "Arms with surgical equipment will extend from the walls. They don't have much movement. I remember wondering what the point of them was. They're easy to dodge. Slow moving."

"Not if you're lying on the ground, passed out," Roe said.

"There you go again." Dagger stalked toward a metal object extending from the wall.

"Not everyone is as smart as you. They might need a commentator." A pole protruded from Roe's sleeve. "A sledgehammer might've worked better than a freaking pole, Millicent. Some weapons designer . . ."

"How about this?" Dagger grabbed something out of the fallen trooper's utility belt. "Cut it."

"Why don't I have one of those?" Roe looked closely at what resembled a small saw.

"You didn't grab one off the shelves when you filled your utility belt."

"Now who's stating the obvious?" Millicent muttered. She shook her head. "I can't find the right code."

"Sometimes it takes a while. Keep trying." Danissa hacked at the material of the wall with her small knife. "I need a bigger knife over here!"

Dagger jogged over, his eyes constantly moving. He reached behind him and extracted a large serrated knife from his belt. "Will that work?"

"Thanks." She jabbed it into the fabric and raked it downward. A small line of tiny holes opened up. "Actually, you do it. This will take me forever."

The mechanical *whirr* turned into a whine. Poles elongated from the walls until the arms' joints came through. The bottom sections swung to the side as more poles emerged.

"Dodge them for now," Gunner said, letting the pole drift over his head. "I want to see what they do before I interrupt their programming. This looks surgical, but who knows what sort of defensive maneuvers this room has."

"Instead of smashing this, I bet I could just hang on it and break it," Roe said, looking at the pole above him. "They're fragile-looking."

"Again . . . surgical." Gunner leaned toward the end of a pole where something extended. A gleaming blade with what looked like a razor-sharp edge cut into Danissa's memory of a dull knife with rust stains. This room appeared to be kept up, unlike the one she'd traveled through.

The sound of fabric ripping drew Danissa's eyes. "Well, I'll be starved, look at this." Dagger's arms flexed and he jerked the fabric away in small yanks. "We got a control panel."

Millicent's head jerked their way. Her eyes widened. "How did you know?"

K.F. Breene

"I'll explain later. Keep working that door. I've seen one of these before, but never worked on one. I might not be able to figure it out."

"I doubt there is much you can't figure out, pretty lady." Dagger squeezed her shoulder. "Good luck. Holler if you need anything. Except brain power. I can't compete."

"This is a six-fingered hand," Gunner said. "An extra thumb, one thumb opposite the other. Think that has any bearing on the designers?"

"I'd bet so," Trent said in a tight voice. "Hopefully the size doesn't, though."

"Yeah. They'd be big fuckers," Roe growled. "These things are precise—they keep aiming for my neck. How do they know?"

Danissa tried to block out the voices and focus on the small screen in front of her. Three red lights blinked. Two groups of strange characters, arranged top to bottom, were layered beneath that in glowing white. Under that, a circuit board.

"This is definitely a panel. And I'll bet those are words. But what do they say?" Danissa bit her lip.

"I find it absolutely amazing that you two share the same thinking tick," Trent's voice drifted into her thoughts. "I'd always thought that was a learned behavior, but here you both are, biting your lips and thinking. Extraordinary."

"Shut up, Trent," Millicent barked. "You're distracting."

"I'm glad you said something." Danissa wiped her forehead.

"Soon I'll get a complex about speaking at all," Trent mumbled.

"If you haven't already, I doubt you'll start now," Roe said.

A loud crack ripped Danissa's mind away from the circuit board. Gunner ducked out of the way of a swinging knife and jumped up. His large hands wrapped around one of the higher poles. He jerked his legs to shift his weight. Another crack had the pole angling downward. The sound of multiple saws came from the other side as Roe and the two remaining troopers cut off the mechanical arms.

"This part isn't so bad," Dagger said.

A long low beep issued from the control panel. Danissa whipped her head around as the *whirr* started again, pulling the poles back in.

"Time for defense," Gunner said ominously. "Get that door open, cupcake!"

"The damn thing isn't responding," Millicent yelled, jamming Gunner's instrument a little farther in the crack.

Danissa grabbed a pair of computer leads from her utility belt, basically two small prongs at the end of wires. She connected the clamps to a portable screen. The screen stayed black. She adjusted the clamps at the other end of the panel, hooking them to anything she could, trying to bring up some sort of code. Nothing would show up.

"Damn it," she said under her breath, bending forward to take a closer look.

Another sound permeated the space, one Danissa hadn't heard before. She glanced up as an echoing click sounded under the floor. The walls jolted. The floor started to rise as the ceiling lowered.

"What the—" someone muttered.

"Hurry, ladies," Gunner yelled. Something else pushed out from the walls—a whole lot of somethings. There were two rows of them, one on top of the other. They stopped extending after about five inches of each was exposed. They were in the very middle of the walls, between the floor and ceiling. The room was forcing the occupants toward the devices' line of fire.

"They're guns!" Dagger yelled, only getting one fist around the barrel. He covered one hand with the other and yanked. "And they are heavy-duty. It's not budging."

The end of one barrel was pointed at Danissa's head.

Her heart sped up. With shaking hands, she used the butt of her knife and smashed the control panel with the glowing characters. The screen pixelated. She did it again, opening up cracks. Wasting no time, she jammed one of the clamps attached to her device into the crack. The screen flared to life.

"I have no idea how that worked," she muttered, jamming the other end in there. Her portable screen flickered, but the image was good enough. Right away, she saw the code in its depths.

"This device has locked on to the door code, but the lock won't click over," Millicent said in a harried voice. Out of her peripheral vision, Danissa could see Millicent throw a frantic look over her shoulder. Then her vision shifted to the barrels of the two guns that were waiting patiently for the room to put them on the right plane.

"Help me," Danissa said breathily. She couldn't seem to get enough air. Her hands wouldn't stop shaking. "Hurry."

"What have you got?" Millicent was beside her a moment later, looking at the screen. She pointed at a piece of code. "I've seen that before. Here." She took the screen and started flicking buttons and making commands.

Danissa ducked under Millicent's arms and searched through the other woman's utility belt. All her devices were organized as Danissa would expect, the portable screen next to something she didn't recognize.

"Do you have any computer leads?" Danissa asked in a slurry of words.

"Not like you do. Mine won't work on this. They'll connect to Toton's robots or anything that has a specific type of port. I wasn't able to work with this type of console on Paradise."

Danissa looked over Millicent's shoulder, bending with the other woman as the room buckled in on itself. Millicent executed her program. Another string of code flashed across the screen.

"What's this?" Millicent asked.

"Give it to me!" Danissa snatched back the portable screen without thinking. Yelling erupted behind her, but she didn't hear the words. The ceiling pushed her to bend lower. The floor rose, forcing her to her knees. She stooped, all her focus on that screen. On that string of code she'd seen before.

Her fingers flew over the screen. The room forced her to her stomach. The barrels pointed along her body and at her head. If those guns went off, none of them would survive.

"We are in a bit of a pickle," she heard Dagger say.

She slapped "Enter." The console beeped, a long, lonely sound in the suddenly quiet room. She heard the sound of a heavy lock disengaging. The floor dropped out from under her.

"Whoa!" Millicent said, followed by a grunt when she hit the ground.

Danissa rolled over and up onto her feet. She snatched Gunner's instrument and her own device before taking to the door again. The correct opening code was already loaded, thanks to Millicent, and the door popped open easily this time.

"It will reload," Danissa said. "At least, their defensive programs have in the past. We need to get out of here. I don't want to race their computers again. If they can learn, we'll be screwed."

"Don't need to tell me twice. But what about them?" Roe pointed down at the prone bodies.

"Grab them." Gunner bent and picked up two clones. Dagger did the same. "Ladies, carry the smaller children. If you can't, drag them. Hopefully they'll shake it off once they're outside of this room."

Without delay, they moved the unconscious to the door, and then Danissa set Mira down and ran for the other side of a corridor, which featured the same cream-colored fabric lining the walls.

"Dagger!" She reached the other side as the door she'd just come from clicked shut. Heavy locks engaged.

"Think these go through the cycle faster?" Dagger asked. He raked his knife down the fabric, ripped it back, and exposed the exact same console.

Danissa sighed in relief.

A hiss made Danissa look up. Smoke spewed out of the upper walls and then drifted down. She smashed the screen, plugged in, and called Millicent over. "Tag-team effort, Foster. Time is *not* on our side."

"Has it ever been?" Millicent's fingers worked faster than before. She slapped "Enter" and handed over the portable screen.

Danissa's eyes started to water.

"Lower down, ladies," Dagger said, bending with them. But the leads were only so long. Danissa couldn't go far.

"Do we have any gas masks?" Gunner called.

Danissa's eyes stung. Tears dripped down her cheeks. Fire raked her throat. Her eyes drooped.

"Here." Dagger held a mask to her face. "Finish that."

She meant to say, "I'm fine, you take it," or something to that effect, because he was once again sacrificing himself for her, but the words didn't reach her lips. Her mind was whirling, and she pushed her fingers as fast as they would go without making errors.

The mask dropped away. The hissing stopped and the doors clicked.

Confused, the smoke accosting her, Danissa glanced down at Dagger's lifeless body.

"Oh Holy Heavens, no!" She snatched the mask off the ground as someone grabbed her arm. Clean air swirled in through the newly opened door. Someone dragged her. "No! *Dagger!*"

Chapter 20

Millicent tore off her mask in the next room and squinted. Her wrist screen flickered to life. "Mommy? Mommy!"

"I'm here," Millicent whispered, looking around at the space they'd stepped into. "I'm okay. Give me a moment, baby."

"Help him!" Danissa yelled as Ryker dragged her out of the smart corridor.

"Quiet!" Millicent hissed, analyzing the walls and then the floors. Everything was white tile glossed to a high shine. Bright lights reflected off the surface, producing an almost unbearable glare. In the middle of the floor were two chrome pipes ending in black flaps. As she watched, one of the flaps popped open for a moment before shutting again.

"An exhaust system," she said to Ryker before realizing he wasn't beside her.

"Thank Holy, he's alive," Danissa said, relief dripping off her words. She was crouched over Dagger, peering down into his face.

"That smoke put him to sleep, but he'll be fine." Ryker went back into the room to get more people.

Terik roused, followed by Zanda. Trent was next.

"Ow." Trent palmed his head. "I feel like I have a hangover."

"Everyone stay quiet," Millicent said aggressively. Toton would know something had gone on in the smart room and corridor. Even if they didn't know for sure that their "visitors" had escaped, they'd check it out. Or at least send eight hundred robots. Time was short.

But then, time was always short. She should be used to it by now.

"I'm okay, pretty lady. All part of the job." Dagger coughed.

Millicent gritted her teeth at Dagger's echoing voice, but spared herself from glaring back. She ran her hands over the smooth tile at her feet, then along the wall. The ceiling was a completely continuous surface, not marred by vents or lights of any kind. The cool air seemed to come from little cracks in the corners where the floor connected with the walls. Light originated from round spotlight-type fixtures along two of the walls.

She looked down at the exhaust valves. One of the flaps moved, letting hot air out. The other didn't have a flap at all—Millicent had been mistaken. Instead, it was a sort of vent, almost like a filter. The metal rim was cold to the touch.

"The room below this must house some heavy computer systems," Danissa whispered as she walked up. Her feet made tiny squeaking noises on the clean tile. "Any systems that need this much ventilation are probably large. This is a good sign. Your theory about this being the hub might be correct."

"Hopefully. But why the light in this room?" Millicent asked, wondering when the next atrocity would present itself. "Why all the white? Most importantly, how do we get out of here?" She looked back toward the smart corridor. That was the only doorway, and she really didn't want to go back through it.

"They have secret doors," Danissa whispered, walking toward one of the walls of lights. She screwed up her face and shielded her eyes behind her arm, moving forward as if walking through gale-force winds.

"Puda—" Her voice hitched. She blew out a breath, something that clearly cost her a lot of effort. "Puda found one by accident once. We all thought we were trapped. I was with security. So they were covering us, and Puda—"

She shook her head and stopped talking. "I don't know if they are all the same, but the one we found was directly opposite the door. The lights in that place were out, though."

Millicent jogged to the adjacent wall and then turned back to motion for Ryker to go to the other lit wall. Shielded from the intense glare by her raised arm, she watched the path of Danissa's fingers. When the other woman shook her head and moved down the way, Millicent followed that same movement, searching for the secret door.

"Got it," Ryker murmured. Even still, his deep base vibrated through the room.

A ratchet sound preceded an enormous door swinging inward.

"This is the second indication that we are dealing with a very large species of humanoid," Roe growled.

"If it *is* humanoid," Trent muttered.

"Is everyone ready to move?" Millicent asked, seeing the host of red moving down through the building. They were close, with only a handful of floors to go. They'd likely have access to all floors.

Strangely, the blue hadn't moved location from the upper-middle floors.

Mira sniffled and hugged on to Terik's legs. He picked her up in jerky movements. One of the clones stepped up beside him, much more graceful, and reached for the baby. "You look in pain. Let me help."

"I'm fine," Terik muttered, but he relinquished the toddler, who went solemnly.

"You're not in pain, huh?" Roe asked, prodding the female clone closest to him.

215

"I have a headache and my body feels like bugs are running along my bones, but I've been through worse," she said. "I can handle it."

"What was worse?" Roe motioned her forward.

"The pool, the cleansing detergent to rejuvenate our skin, the bone treatment—"

"*Shhh!*" Millicent said as she peeked through the door. Another large room decked in white tile greeted her. Dim lighting, so dark she couldn't see to the other side of the room, masked the interior. "Terik, step forward," she whispered.

He stepped up beside her as she swung the door nearly closed. Only a small amount of light trickled through the crack now.

"What do you—"

Loud noise cut her off. It blared through unseen speakers.

"What do you see?" she yelled over the din.

"Door. Straight ahead. Has a handle." He plugged his ears, wincing.

"Check for hidden doors in the darker room," Millicent told Danissa. To Ryker, she yelled, "Check out the door across the way. It might be a trap."

Millicent didn't find anything on her side. Danissa shook her head as she met Millicent back in the middle, where light spilled out of the previous room.

"Let's go," Millicent whispered to the rest of them, starting off toward Ryker.

The door of the darker room swung inward again, just as large.

"Stairs," Terik murmured. "The walls are normal. Not tile like in this place. It's a normal stairwell."

"Nothing in this building is as it seems." Millicent braced her hand on Ryker's arm.

With Terik and Dagger leading the way, they grabbed the smaller children and walked down the stairs in the pitch black. Millicent didn't trust using a light. If something at the bottom didn't show on her scanner, she didn't want to alert it of their approach. Granted, the slide of hands on the walls, paired with the scuff of shoes, wasn't exactly in keeping with a low profile . . .

Ryker paused in front of the door at the bottom of the stairs. "Any idea what we're getting into?" he whispered.

"Stop talking! Your voice still carries even when you whisper." She checked her screen. Her stomach flipped and her skin started to crawl. "In there, nothing. Back the way we came, every robot they got in this building."

"Did you say—"

"*Shhh!*" someone said.

"Every robot in the building?" Trent whispered.

"We can cut them out." Danissa sounded determined, though her voice slightly quavered. Millicent felt her sister's hand on her back, lightly urging. "If we can get into their root computer, we can cut off the signal to the robots. To everything. We can bring it all down."

"I really, really hope we're in the right place." Millicent took a deep breath and urged Ryker on with a hand to his arm.

He yanked the door open and surged forward, EMP gun drawn. The other troopers followed. Two light orbs rolled out ahead of them. They flared to life, illuminating the space.

Millicent stayed close behind and passed through the huge door. "Holy . . ." She lost her breath for a second. Danissa's loud exhale said she had, too.

The largest computer Millicent had ever seen sprawled across the floor. Lights flickered and blinked in various machines, and the whole setup was so loud the hum vibrated up Millicent's spine. "This is absolutely the right computer."

"It's all here," Danissa said, walking as though in a daze to the nearest screen. They coated high tabletops, all lying flat. "Their whole system has to be rooted right here."

"Yes . . . ?" Millicent looked at her sister in confusion.

Danissa's eyes cleared. "I rooted several points in our system. I was trying to connect them all when the last of my security was taken out. That port was taken out, too, but the others should've been live. If I could've . . ."

"Sounds genius. We don't have time to discuss it." Ryker leaned into Millicent with serious eyes. "You need to do whatever you need to do, and we need to keep those spiders—or whatever—out of here. So hurry. I don't feel like meeting any more of their mechanical creations."

"They must celebrate life," Trent said as Millicent hurried along the various screens, looking to see if there were any differences in function. "They are making robots out of life, to resemble life. Maybe not ours, per se, but they are trying to duplicate the natural world. That has to say something."

"You don't celebrate life by hacking it up and putting it into robots," Roe said, cocking his gun.

"We create humans, and then hack them up and use their parts in other humans," Trent countered. "We end one person's life to prolong another's."

"Yes, but we don't celebrate life. We're a cold, ruthless, barbaric species that don't look far beyond material good and our own selfishness. So if they do celebrate life, we'll win over them because we don't celebrate nothin' but power."

"Great Divinity, you are a real downer, bro-yo," Dagger said.

"That's one word for it," Trent muttered.

Millicent could barely see Roe's grin as she dug into the computer, easily batting aside their sign-on parameters. She opened it up to the pirate network and basically waved her daughter in. "Okay, Marie, you have front-row access. On my say-so, we'll destroy all their systems beyond repair. We'll seal in some viruses afterward in case we didn't do a thorough job crashing things."

"Okay, Mommy. Wow, this is complex."

"Just do what you can, baby."

"I'm excited. This is a real challenge," Marie chirped happily. "Not like when you have me do those exercises, because those aren't really—"

"Quietly, baby," Millicent said with a shock of irritation. "Do it quietly."

She ignored Ryker's dark chuckle.

"She's right, though," Danissa said, her fingers flying over one of their screens. "This is complex. And if not for binary code, we'd be lost. Their warnings are all in those strange characters."

"What'd you think, that they would speak Standard?" Roe asked with humor in his voice.

"What's that?" Suzi asked as a strange clicking sound permeated the space at the far end of the room next to a second door.

Dagger rolled another light orb her way and immediately followed, checking the handle. Thankfully, it was locked.

Millicent glanced at her wrist. Her stomach rolled again, and a burst of perspiration coated her forehead. "Those are robots. They'll be coming down the stairwell we just emptied, too. Make sure it's closed and locked. A barricade wouldn't go amiss, either. Their goal is probably to chop us up and use us for parts."

"The door we came through is already closed and locked," someone hollered. "Here, help me grab—"

A loud thump cut off the trooper. Dagger moved Suzi back from the second door as another thump shook it. A loud bang hit the first door.

"We're trapped," Terik said.

"No, we are in a prime defensive position." Ryker stood at the front of the room, equidistant from the two doors. "Arm yourselves. If you get wounded, fall back and watch the children. If someone has already fallen back with the children, you get the glorious privilege of fighting wounded. You'll be in good company. Millicent, we are counting on you."

Millicent bit her lip as she scrutinized the strange security measures. She hadn't seen anything like them before—complex didn't even describe it. It didn't take a genius to know that once she was past this, she would have their beating heart resting in her hands.

The question was, could she, Danissa, and Marie crack it open before the robots got into the room?

She glanced at her wrist screen—specifically, at the blue dots now roaming around the floors. "I'll be seeing you shortly," she said with fierce determination. "I will *not* die down here. I will *not* become one of your robots."

Chapter 21

Trent clutched his gun with white knuckles. "Am I fighting, or watching the children?"

"Are you wounded?" Ryker asked, surveying a big block holding other smaller blocks. Trent had no idea what any of it was, other than that it was computer related.

"That's rhetorical, isn't it?" he asked drolly.

With a show of incredible strength, Ryker grunted and slid the huge piece of possible furniture toward the door. Dagger joined a moment later, and even though the odds were not in their favor, these two incredibly strong men made Trent grateful he was on this side of the equation.

He actually hoped Roe was right. They'd need barbarianism to get them out of this mess, Trent had no doubt.

"Let's get the other side," Ryker said to Dagger, and jerked his head toward the other door.

"Children." Trent put out his arms to herd them. "Let's get you back."

"No!" Billy ran at him. Knowing what that meant, Trent braced himself and caught Billy's shoulders as the little boy neared, effectively dodging his kick. "Stay here! Right here. Because they can chew through the ceiling."

As one, everyone but the two systems workers looked up.

"That's not good," Roe said.

A scratching sound was the only other warning they got. A square of ceiling, topped with a strange sort of animal, dropped from the sky and landed on a computer. A spark flew up. Something sizzled.

It flew up a moment later, its four legs, each ending in claws, writhing in the air as if it were running. The body smashed against the wall. It broke into pieces and rained down onto the floor. Out of the hole in the ceiling, spiders and other insects crawled like a disturbed hive. Black-and-silver shiny bodies scrabbled upside down across the ceiling. One dropped, its legs flailing. It landed, upside down, near Millicent.

Before Ryker could even move, Millicent jumped up. A gun propelled out of her suit and into her hand. She aimed and shot, landing three bullets in its exposed abdomen. The thing spasmed and curled up. Dead.

"Can you burn with that fire?" Ryker shouted at Terik over the din. A thud hit the door. The large, extremely heavy blockade bumped forward. "Or is it just for light?"

"I can kill faster than a real fire could," he yelled back, seemingly unafraid. If not for the boy's shaking hands, Trent would have assumed the kid had no fear.

"Then kill the bugs on the ceiling!" Ryker shouted, his gun pointed upward. "How many are coming, Millie?"

"Hordes. Scores of them. Buy us time, Ryker. Use everything you've got and buy us time."

Fire raged across the ceiling, so hot half the people in the room threw up their hands. The flames didn't lick at the walls or reach down to the floor. It corroded the metal of the spiders and blistered their strange mechanical faces. High-pitched whines and spasming bodies dropped onto the supercomputer. They bounced off and fell, consumed by flames.

Still more robots poured out of the hole. They started dropping quickly out of the burning heat and hitting the ground and bouncing. Barely scorched, they righted themselves, ready to do battle.

"Here we go!" Ryker surged forward, launched over a component of the supercomputer, and landed on top of a spider.

The door bumped again. The blockade shifted forward another few inches. A thunk hit the other door as well, with the same effect.

"What the hell is behind those doors?" Trent asked, his gun out. He shot at a spider going for Millicent. The bullet hit its mark, knocking the robot off course. Trent followed it up with another shot, curling the thing up. "Kicking might not work on the new ones, but guns still do."

"Should I use the EMP gun?" Ryker shouted.

"No!" Millicent yelled. "It'll affect the computer. Use guns if you have aim. We're halfway there."

Gunshots popped through the room. Another two thumps pushed the blockades forward. Trent heaved himself against one of them, but he wasn't strong enough to move it back. Whatever was on the other side of that door had to be massive. Either that or there were a lot of them.

Something slashed his leg. He called out in surprise and turned. A spider sliced at him. Before the blade landed, the thing was flying across the room. It hit the wall and crunched.

"Save your strength, Suzi," Ryker hollered, much to Trent's dismay. Ryker kicked one spider and shot another. With hands as fast as lightning, he bent forward and ripped another bot's leg before grabbing it and hurling it against the wall.

The blockade bumped forward. The door behind it crashed. A thick robotic arm ending in six razor-sharp claws curled around, groping for Holy knew what. Mind buzzing and body primed with adrenaline,

Trent opened fire. The bullets struck the claw and arm. Smoke curled away as something mighty roared on the other side of the door.

Millicent and Danissa both glanced up with wide eyes. Millicent looked back at the computer first, her brow furrowing.

Spiders dropped to the ground like rain.

"Hurry!" Roe yelled, shooting at the robots running at him.

Trent shot, too, his aim loose, not that it mattered—they were packed in so closely, he'd hit one if not another. Another swipe from a clawed appendage had him gritting his teeth. The robots were backing him against the wall now.

Ryker kicked and shot at the same time, over and over. They were backing him up, too. Pushing him toward Millicent. Dagger was at Danissa's back, his face hard and drenched with sweat.

Billy yelled something. The thumping behind the door increased. The blockage pushed forward, and this time it fell. The items in it crashed to the floor. The door cracked and then wobbled, broken from its hinges. Trent's insides pinched.

A massive robot filled the door frame. Humanoid in form, it had tree-trunk arms and even bigger legs. Made of something like chrome, it should've been jerky, like the spiders. Instead, it moved with the grace of a living being, lethal and dangerous, clearly intensely strong.

"Now you can help, Suzi," Ryker said, barely heard over the roar of the flames and skittering of spiders.

The humanoid robot roared like an animal, louder and deeper than the bears on Paradise. The noise shook the room. Tendrils of fear curled around Trent's bones.

"We're out of time, princess," Ryker yelled, bracing himself, his eyes rooted to the huge robot.

"Almost," Trent heard. He hoped he had heard, anyway, because in another few minutes, they'd all be dead or captured.

A slash above the knee made him stumble. He shot downward until he heard click, click, click.

"Shit." Trent kicked at a spider as he dug into his utility belt for more ammo. Pain vibrated through his foot. The spider barely bumped back.

The huge robot lunged for Ryker. Another massive robot crashed through the blockade on the other side of the room.

Ryker leapt up and grabbed hold of a massive arm. Somehow he twisted his body around, dragging the arm with him. It went behind the robot's back. Ryker, half the thing's size, wrapped his legs around its waist and shoved the thing's elbow upward. A satisfying crack preceded a deep-chested roar. The robot swung its other arm, trying unsuccessfully to reach Ryker on its back. It then swung its whole upper body.

Ryker wrenched the arm again and then yanked it clear off. He dropped to the ground and raced back toward Millicent, where an invisible wall created by Suzi protected her from the spiders.

Dagger ran at the second massive robot.

A sharp pain in Trent's leg drove him to the ground, submerging him in a sea of spider robots. One of the arms came out near Trent, what had seemed like mostly useless appendages by the strange robot face, and snatched his chin. More robot hands grabbed his wrists. They pushed in. A claw aimed for his neck as, somewhere in the background, a thrushing sound overrode people's screams, making cold dribble down his spine.

Suddenly he knew exactly how they collected brains for their robots, and he was about to experience it firsthand.

"Trent is under fire," Ryker yelled, his voice dim in the roar surrounding Millicent.

She bit her lip, not allowing herself to look up. Not allowing herself to focus on anything but the complex code at her fingertips. She could see Danissa's efforts and the mysterious unraveling that was Marie's work, but they still had so much more to break. They had to move faster.

"We need a miracle," she muttered before wiping sweat off her brow.

A roar made Millicent clench her teeth. Dagger screamed.

Still Millicent watched the screen.

"Is Daddy okay?" Marie's voice sounded in her ear.

"Daddy is fine, baby. We have to hurry. Hurry, Marie."

"Can I cheat this time, Mommy?"

Millicent wiped her brow again, sweat trickling down her temple. Trent's ear-piercing scream froze her for a moment. She couldn't help glancing back. A robot was slicing into his neck.

"Cheat, baby!" Millicent said, having no idea what her daughter meant by "cheat" and not caring. A gun filled her hand. She turned back and shot into that cluster of bodies. Her bullets slammed home. Robots shook and curled. Blood ran down Trent's neck. His eyes, still open, looked around in panic.

He was still alive. For the moment.

A roar cut off abruptly. A loud crack preceded a heavy metal head rolling across the floor. The robot body followed a moment later, hitting the ground and shaking Millicent's screen. Blood drenching one side of his body, Ryker jumped onto the computer desk, ran across it—cracking one of the screens—and then launched himself at the other massive robot heading toward Millicent.

"Holy," Millicent said, fear stealing her breath. The lights in the room flickered. Her screen fuzzed with snow. Suzi screamed at the exact moment a spider slashed Millicent's thigh.

"I'm locked out," Danissa screamed, terror screwing up her face. "I'm locked out! They've locked me out!"

"No." Millicent shot at the spider. Another took its place. Loud thrushing filled the room.

"They've come to collect us." Danissa's face bled of color. "They're here to take us."

The fire on the ceiling sputtered. Billy was screaming. Toad Man flew across the room. Millicent slammed her hand down on the screen again, trying to break it. Trying to force her way into their system like they'd done in the smart room. It was too strong.

Remembering the screen Ryker had cracked, she tried to move toward it, but spiders blocked her way.

"Help!" Trent yelled. Another spider was preparing to swipe his neck.

The second massive robot reached over its shoulder and caught Ryker by the suit. It brought its hand back. Struggling, unable to get free, Ryker dangled in front of it. The robot reached for his neck.

"Blow us up," Danissa said, her voice somehow calm over the pandemonium. "Blow us all up." Her gaze was imploring. "Kill us. Don't let them turn us into robots."

"We'll try the EMP," Millicent said through a burning throat.

"We'd never get out of this building. Kill us."

Breathing heavily, her heart thudding, Millicent dug an explosive out of her pouch. She looked at Ryker, who was staring back. He nodded once as the robot's fingers encircled his neck.

"I love you," she said, the explosive hot in her hands.

She saw him mouth it back. Saw the feeling in his eyes. Heard, "There," in her daughter's voice.

Then everything went black.

Chapter 22

Her hand shaking, she held the explosive a little too hard when metallic thuds crashed to the ground. Her leg throbbed. Her heart hammered.

She was still alive.

"What's happening?" she asked the strangely quiet room. She heard panting and movement, but there was no skitter of spiders from the hole above, no heavy tread of those massive robots.

"I cheated, like you said I could," came her daughter's chipper voice through the implant comms. "I had to cut out the pirate network for a moment, but it's back up. You have to physically destroy the root now, but I cut off their wireless and disconnected almost everything. They had it all running off that computer. Everything. They'll be down all over the world now, like you said, Mommy. Not very smart. Aunt Danissa's system is much better. I can't even get into her roots, and there are bunch of them it looks like."

A screen glowed to life, illuminating Danissa's tear-streaked face. Millicent tapped her screen, firing it up. Behind her, metal clanked.

"They've stopped moving," Trent said in what sounded like disbelief. "What happened to the light?"

"I don't know," Ryker said, the velvety drum of his deep voice music to Millicent's ears. "The light spheres shut off. They don't work anymore."

"I got one." Dagger's voice was thick with pain. "Got any meds?"

Sudden light illuminated the room, pulling Millicent's attention away from the screen. The spiders stood upright, as though awaiting instruction. The hole in the ceiling was clogged with inactivity. One of the massive robots lay on its stomach, the other on its back, apparently unable to stand on two feet if they weren't receiving computer instruction.

"The brains must just be for problem-solving and program enhancement," Millicent muttered, looking over all the spiders.

"They probably rely on the mother computer to organize the robots' movement," Danissa said.

"Suzi and Terik are passed out, but they're alive," Ryker called. "The rest are okay. We lost three clones and the rest of our troopers."

"Take that, you bastard," Danissa said, a fierce gleam in her eyes. Red characters flashed in the upper right of her screen. "That'll disable the root."

Millicent's screen went dark again. Her sister had entirely crashed the system.

"I need help," Trent said in a scratchy voice. He held his neck with a bloodstained hand. His face was pasty. "I feel cold and weak. That's bad."

"Got it." Dagger moved to the other man's side. "We'll get you patched up."

"Do you have any blood synthesizers?" Trent asked, sitting up amidst a cluster of robots. It was an indication of the shape he was in that he didn't move away.

"Probably." Dagger kicked the spiders away, stomping on one before he saw to Trent. His aggression was evident.

"What about Roe?" Millicent asked, backing away from the screens. She belatedly realized the screens were all at a strange height. Too high to sit at, but she had to stoop while standing. All were the same, and it wasn't until she noticed a massive rolling chair at the back of the room that it struck. These beings were giants.

She looked at her screen. A horde of red dots gathered around her position. The blue dots were racing around their floor, but still contained. They were probably preparing to leave.

"What about Roe?" she asked again, kicking a spider out of her way. It felt better than moving around it.

Ryker looked up with a stern face and tight eyes. His lips made a thin line. He shook his head.

"What . . ." A weight pressed hard against Millicent's chest. "What do you mean?"

Ryker moved away from his location, his feet out of Millicent's sight. "They were in the act of harvesting," he said in a rough voice. "Part of him was still alive, but . . . it wasn't attached." Ryker shook his head. "He didn't make it."

Millicent's eyes prickled with heat. Her vision blurred, the loss crashing down on her. She leaned heavily against the desk. A moment later, she felt Danissa's hand on her shoulder.

"The fallen have saved the world," an angelic voice said. A singer's voice. It took Millicent a moment to realize the speaker was a clone. "They will live on in our history records."

"It's times like this that I wish I believed in one of the gods," Trent said, bowing his head even as Dagger worked on his neck. "I'm going to miss him."

"We have to keep going." Danissa's voice was loud, clear, and hard. "We cannot stop now. We aren't done yet."

Blinking away tears, Millicent checked her wrist again. Danissa was right. And it was something Roe himself would've said. "We'll see that Roe's dream becomes a reality. We'll dismember the conglomerate."

"It's already dismembered," Danissa said, taking Millicent's explosive and attaching it to her utility belt. "Toton was effective. We just need to bury it now."

"Looks like you found the hardness in your blood," Trent said as Dagger helped him stand. "You two are very alike. More alike than any of Millicent's children. Mother Nature is so interesting."

Confusion spread across Danissa's face.

"Even half-dead, he won't stop babbling about genetics." Ryker picked a gun up off the floor and jammed a fresh magazine into it. "What's next?"

"Those are big fuckers," Dagger said as he looked down on the fallen robots.

"They are probably scaled to life." Millicent reloaded her own gun.

"Do you think they're all robots?" Ryker asked.

She shook her head. "I have some blue dots that say otherwise. They're moving around, which indicates they aren't affected by the computer shutdown. Do they have computers integrated into their thinking, like we do?" She tapped her implant. "I wonder."

"We have to keep fighting?" Trent bowed in defeat.

One of the children started crying. Trent staggered forward but was stopped by Dagger. "I'm not done doctoring you."

"Well, can *someone* help them?" Trent swung his arm toward the children.

Millicent and Ryker started that way at the same time. Ryker probably missed their children as much as she did. It was Suzi who was shedding tears, her face a blotchy red and her fists pressed against her eyes.

"She's overwhelmed and tired," Terik said by way of explanation. "We need to eat and rest before we can use our . . . powers again."

"I'm afraid we don't have time to rest." Ryker picked Suzi up.

The sound of a foot hitting a spider preceded Billy yelling, "We need to catch them before they fly away!"

"I should've stayed on Paradise," Trent muttered.

Millicent grabbed Mira and motioned for Danissa to get Billy.

"Dagger, can you carry Zanda up a shitload of stairs?" Ryker asked.

"We'll see."

After checking weapons and choking down tears at the blood spreading from Roe's lifeless body, Millicent followed Ryker out of the room and through the sea of strangely still robots. A red light was blinking on the face of every one of them, no matter the shape or size of its body.

"Is there any way to use these to do the work for us?" Trent asked, lugging himself along behind Millicent. It wouldn't be long before he was good to go.

"In the time frame we have left? No." Millicent shifted Mira to the other hip as she reached the stairwell and started climbing the steps. Her breath came in heavy pants with each step. "And that is excluding the morality issue."

"I want to go home. I don't give a shit about morality issues right now. I'll let guilt eat at me later." Trent clutched the railing and pulled himself to the next step.

"This route will take too long," Ryker said as they passed the floor with the smart rooms. A few floors later he shook his head and stopped. "Are those fire throwers inactive?"

Millicent grimaced. "Should be . . ."

"Yes," Danissa said with assurance.

He pushed the door open and stepped into the charred room. "How about their crafts?" he asked, walking across the floor to the windows. At this level, all they saw was blackness.

"I'm sure their crafts still run," Danissa said. "At least on manual. The question is: Who is flying them? There would have to be someone to take over the manual setting."

"It looks like they have someone capable in this building," Millicent said, checking the blue dots. "I'd imagine there are more of them around the city. But in what numbers? The ones here don't seem inclined to move."

Ryker blew out a breath. "We'll have to chance it. I'm calling in the rebels." He kicked a sleek video unit out of the way, his mood bleeding through his actions. "We're going to blow them to hell."

"Get the Moxidone rocket site active, sir," Dagger said. "Let's clear them out and take over their merchandise. I'd rather take that to Paradise than the old thing you've been using."

"There will still be work to do here." Ryker operated his wrist screen. "You don't have to retire just yet if you don't want to."

"Don't think I'll stick with being a lifer." Dagger hooked his thumbs on his utility belt, staring at the window. "It might be nice to adopt a kid or two, and have a family."

"Oh?" Trent sidled closer. "I wasn't aware they were sterilizing men of your intelligence and breeding under the age of fifty . . ."

Dagger's brow furrowed, then his nose crinkled. "That's kind of a strange thing to talk about . . ."

"You get used to it," Ryker said, looking up from his wrist screen. "I have a pickup on the way."

Dagger snorted. "I'm not shooting blanks, no. But that doesn't really matter, because it's been a long time since I've met a woman who could breed. Does Paradise have a breeding lab?"

"No," Millicent said in distaste. "No breeding labs."

"Well, then." Dagger shrugged. "Looks like we have kids who need a home right here." His gaze swept over the exhausted children. "And maybe a woman will take a liking to me. Eventually."

"Doubtful." Ryker laughed. "We got fifteen minutes. Two crafts were docked relatively close. Either they were outside of Toton's parameters, or they were well hidden."

"What did you mean about Millicent and me?" Danissa asked Trent, her voice uncomfortable. "You compared us to her children. And people keep throwing around the word *aunt* . . ."

"And they said you were intelligent . . ." Ryker grinned as his eyes swept the sky.

Before Trent could launch into one of his long-winded explanations, Millicent said simply, "We were bred from the same parents. We are biological sisters."

Danissa stared at Millicent as if she'd spoken a different language.

"Now, tell me." Trent shifted so he could see Danissa's face. "Did they breed you at all?"

"Another funny thing to say. He has an odd way of talking to a person." Dagger moved away a little.

"Again, you get used to it." Ryker squinted out the window. "The craft should be close, but I can't see through this environment."

"I birthed one staffer. I mean, child," Danissa said. "A boy."

"Just one, huh? Hmm." Trent held his chin as he gazed at Danissa with a furrowed brow.

"Do you know what happened to him?" Millicent asked.

"The clones are organizing around the rocket," Ryker said, back to looking at his wrist screen. "They don't know how to fight, but their speed and stamina is apparently way above the Curve."

"Oh great." Dagger pointed at two lights coming closer, hazy in the sky. "They can run around in circles and make our enemies dizzy."

"I don't know," Danissa answered Millicent evenly. If she had any emotion on the subject, she was not showing it. "I took their medications and walked away. I wasn't like you. I didn't fight back."

"Why didn't they breed you again?" Trent asked.

Dagger shifted as though uncomfortable. "He's starting to get on my nerves, now . . ." Ryker huffed out a laugh.

"They tried," Danissa answered. "It didn't take. I can't have any more."

"Because they then sterilized you?"

"Because I couldn't get pregnant. My body won't breed anymore. I thought you were supposed to be a lab rat or something?"

"Yes, which is why I'm asking." Trent shook his head. "You were not only misinformed, they possibly missed a huge opportunity with you. That is, if you are anything like Millicent. And it seems you are."

"Stand back, everyone." Ryker yanked out his gun and shot a hole in the window. He kicked out the glass. A blast of putrid-smelling, frigid air assaulted them.

"They've moved up a level," Millicent said, watching those blue dots. "Slowly, though. They don't seem to want to move far from their location."

"Good." Ryker's hair blew around his head. The craft drifted in close. "Hopefully they stay and fight. I've got more forces on the way."

"With some women," Trent went on as if they weren't about to board a craft and prepare for another battle, "they undergo a secondary infertility. This means that after they have the first child, they cannot conceive again. There are many reasons for this—"

"Do we have to hear any of them?" Ryker asked dryly.

"But the bottom line is, just because you were able to have one child, does not guarantee you can continue to conceive. Secondary infertility sounds like the diagnosis they gave you. Simpletons."

Millicent waited for the platform to extend from the craft. A trooper threw a line at her. She didn't bother tying it around her waist. Instead, holding tight, she quickly boarded the craft and handed the line off. It was thrown back to Danissa, who tied it securely around her waist and walked across.

"I didn't realize he was quite so chatty," Danissa murmured as she settled opposite Millicent in the craft. Her brow rumpled as she glanced up at Millicent's face. She was probably trying to work out what it really meant to be of the same blood. It wasn't a common idea on Earth.

"He babbles, yes," Millicent said as Trent came through, holding Mira. The other children were passed through and helped to settle.

"But that might not be the case." Trent sat right next to Danissa, easily picking up the hanging thread of his one-sided conversation. She shifted away. He followed. "Sometimes it just takes longer to conceive, but it is possible. They only gave you three rounds of attempted fertilization, right?"

"Two," Danissa murmured.

Trent rolled his eyes and gave a derisive laugh. "Ridiculous for someone of your caliber. They should've kept you in the program. I read about a woman who took one full year, trying every month, to get pregnant. And she did, in the end. Without anything special, her body did finally accept the fertilization. She carried to term."

"He's still talking about this?" Dagger asked incredulously, boarding the craft. Dried blood caked around his side where a large slash had opened his suit and coated his pronounced obliques. Stitchers and his quick healing ability had served him well, since his skin was already fusing together.

"He won't stop until someone shoots at him," Millicent said. "Roe usually took on that role." A surge of pain rose up. She clenched her teeth and looked away right before she felt Dagger's hand on her knee.

"I'm sorry for your loss," he said in a low voice. "Ryker called in a squad to retrieve all the bodies. We'll give him a proper farewell."

Millicent nodded, not trusting her voice.

"Get your gear ready," Ryker said as he entered the craft and took a seat near the cockpit.

"I was with a man for years after my attempted . . . fertilization," Danissa muttered. "Still didn't happen."

"Oh really? Huh." Trent rested his chin on his fist. "Was he natural born, too?"

"No. Lab born."

"Oh. Well, he was probably sterilized, then. That doesn't count, obviously. No, I bet you could still procreate. I wouldn't stake my life on it without running some tests, obviously, but if you found it difficult, I have three different concoctions I've created that would help your body naturally prepare for fertilization. They are enhancers, really. Only about one percent of women were still not be able to conceive. They aren't miracle concoctions, after all."

"Fascinating," Danissa said sarcastically. "But didn't you leave behind your lab?"

"I was able to make the concoctions there." Trent patted her knee and smiled. "If you want, we can organize continuous samples from Mr. Dagger. Actually, he'd be the best fit, going by the Foster-Gunner model. You'd have to do your own stimulation, but as a woman who was sexually active, I'm sure you know all about how to manipulate—"

"Trent," Millicent said, shaking her head. "The children."

"I'm not a dispensary," Dagger said aggressively, making Millicent's small hairs rise.

Trent's mouth snapped shut and his eyes widened. He cleared his throat and winced when he crossed his ankle over his knee. "He's usually so nice, I forgot the extreme violence his kind are capable of." He looked out the window as Ryker huffed out a laugh.

The craft drifted away from the building as it rose, giving them distance.

"Okay," Ryker said, standing. He went through his utility belt before heading to the back of the craft. "We'll restock for an invasion. Anyone without an implant will be left behind. They probably have mental warfare geared up. Those without implant defenses won't be helpful."

"Sure would be nice to take the kids," Dagger muttered, scratching his chin.

"Sure would be nice if they were grown, had implants, knew how to fight, and how to shoot," Ryker said, changing places with Dagger and heading back to the front.

"Yes. All of those things, yes." Dagger checked his guns.

"See? Fun and jovial most of the time. You forget what he's capable of," Trent muttered.

"Do you forget with me?" Ryker asked Trent as he passed.

"I just try to avoid you when you're hurt, feeling protective of Millicent or your children, or in a bad mood."

"So that's why I don't see much of you."

"Yes."

"It's worrying when they are in an upbeat mood right before a battle," Millicent said to Danissa. "It means there is extreme danger ahead."

"It has been a long time since there was anything but extreme danger to look forward to." Danissa studied her hands.

"A little longer." Ryker leaned into the cockpit before checking his wrist. "Just a little longer. We have to knock out these trespassers, and then we can wrap it up and go home."

"As easy as that, huh?" Danissa shook her head, glanced at her wrist screen, and then peered into her utility belt. She stood and headed to the weapons bays in the back. "Do you have a deflation valve on your ego? As is, it's clouding your judgment."

"Where's the trust?" Ryker's grin didn't match his eyes as he looked out the window. In the upper levels, where the air was clearer, they could see the top of Toton's building. Black dotted the sides, the spiders stuck to the outside like they were glued on.

Dagger's arm and back muscles flared as he leaned against the side of the craft. He peered out at the building. "It bears repeating—those fuckers are bound to be huge."

"Let's hope they move as slow as those robots." Ryker worked at his wrist screen.

"And are half as strong." Dagger shook his head. "I hope you got a lotta guns headed in with us."

"Millie, work with Marie to execute your prison program on the leaders of the other conglomerates," Ryker said as more crafts joined them. "Right after we're done here, we save the world."

Butterflies swarmed Millicent's stomach.

First, they needed to face the beings who'd put the world in danger. And somehow make it out alive.

Chapter 23

Millicent stood at the console in the craft, ready to execute her many programs. This particular vessel wasn't equipped with all the weapons she'd designed, but it had a few, and those were high-powered. It would work.

"Ready, cupcake?" Ryker asked as he stopped next to her.

Trent, the children, and the remaining clones had been transferred to another craft. The clones had asked to join the fight for the rocket. The children had asked to stay in the craft with Millicent and company. The clones would get their wish, but the children were being whisked away to safety. They'd get to meet Marie, who had promised to be nice.

As soon as Terik, who seemed strangely familiar, though Millicent couldn't figure out why, tried to throw his weight around, Marie would dig in her heels and go back on her word. Hopefully that was the worst of their problems.

A weak and pale Trent would be chaperoning. It would probably be harder than joining the battle.

"Yes, I'm ready," Millicent lied, glancing back at the fresh faces who'd had to take a backseat last time. Ryker said they were the best they had. Millicent sincerely hoped so; she wasn't sure what weapons they'd be going against.

"What's their twenty?"

"What does that even mean?" Millicent checked her wrist screen. "Where are they?"

"Then just say that. They've moved up three floors while we've been sitting here. Unnaturally slow for someone under fire. It's making me very nervous."

"Clearly they don't think they have much to be concerned about." Ryker shifted, blocking most of the door. "And clearly, they are wrong."

"They have to know what we're capable of. We're going in blind, though."

"You know their tech. You know their code. I know their approximate size and possibly build—if they created those robots in their image. I don't call that *blind*."

"You've always been overly optimistic."

"Confident, princess. The word you are looking for is *confident*." Ryker glanced toward the cockpit. "Counting down."

"We're ready, sir," Dagger said from off to the side, standing with his hands on his utility belt. Danissa stood near him, her face pale, a gun in her hand. Her determined expression warred with anxiety.

The craft jerked and then accelerated.

"Troops B, C, and D, follow closely," Ryker said through the comms. "We're leading the way."

"Ready for it, Millie?" he said in a low tone, not on the comms. A muscle in his jaw flexed. "We need to go in hot. I want to make it out of this alive."

Millicent's fingers hovered over the "Execute" button. They were near the top, where the air was as clean as it would get, making visibility nearly clear. The building enlarged in the windows, with its black spots on the side like warts.

"Ready to fire in three," Ryker counted. "Two . . . fire!"

Millicent slapped the screen. The craft rumbled. Streams of smoke followed two points of fire that smashed into the building. The twin explosions blasted fire into the sky.

"Fire!" Ryker said again.

Millicent hit them with a shrapnel rocket, designed to lodge in the holes she'd just created and spray them with metal.

"One more and we attack, in three . . . two . . . fire!"

She loosed more power and then sprayed the building with rounds as they neared. The blue dots on her wrist screen were moving within the confines of what was certainly a room, and a rather big one at that. Three didn't move at all.

"I think we got a few," Millicent said, out of breath even though she'd barely moved.

"Then let's get the rest. How many are we dealing with?" Ryker readied his weapons as the craft drew up next to the building.

"Two dozen, give or take. And that's if these dots are really them. And if there aren't more of them. I can't be certain."

The craft hovered beside the gaping hole in the building. Flames crowded in patches on the floor and coated the walls.

"It's going to be hot," Ryker said as the door slid open. To punctuate his words, a blast of hot air hit their faces.

"Of all the places we could enter, we choose the most volatile?" Danissa asked over the roar. More crafts hovered in close.

"This is the least volatile as far as the enemy is concerned." Ryker ran across the extending platform.

"We hope," Millicent said, waiting for two more troopers to follow Ryker before she ran across. She jumped over two feet of hollow space before landing on the wet floor of the building. Rain pounded the blackened carpet.

"Wait over there, ladies," Ryker said, pointing to the side.

"Will we be participating?" Danissa asked as the rest of the troopers and Dagger filed out of the craft. The vessel pulled away and was immediately replaced by another, emptying more rebels to join their cause.

"Always," Millicent said.

After a few moments, Danissa said, "Is Trent very knowledgeable about breeding? I mean, in practicality and not just theoretically."

"Very. It was because of him that Marie is what she is. It's because of his research that those kids are what they are. He knows his stuff. Annoyingly so."

They both fell silent as the next craft was emptied. And then the final craft.

"Their position?" Ryker asked from his place near the windows. The light showered his squared shoulders and powerful frame. All eyes focused on him, and then followed his gaze to Millicent. Ryker was making it clear she was also in command.

Millicent rolled her eyes. These men and their fanfare. "They've slowed their movements. I'd bet they know we're on their floor. I have no way of knowing what that means."

"Everyone pull up your maps." Ryker looked down at his wrist. "You already know what sections you've been assigned to cover. Now you'll see your route. This might change as they shift position. For now, we'll try to surround the room they're holing up in. Then we'll go in as one."

"There is no way this will work according to plan," Danissa murmured. "It never does."

"I know." Millicent checked her route. Naturally, it coincided with Ryker's team. "But you can't tell them that. It'll make them afraid. People do stupid things when they're afraid."

"Shouldn't Dagger be in charge of a different team?" Danissa's brow rumpled. "He's the second best at security, right? Behind Ryker?"

"Ryker knows what's bound to happen. He'll choose to protect us over taking the building. Don't bother trying to make him see sense. He has none where my safety is concerned."

"I wasn't going to try and make him see sense. I'm no hero—I'm all for this plan."

Millicent couldn't help a grin.

"Move out!" Ryker waved his arm through the air, and everyone turned and jogged off in their approved direction. The remainder was a group of hard faces and chiseled bodies, with scarred eyes and set jaws. These men and woman had seen plenty of action, by the look of it, and they were grizzled.

"Nope. I definitely won't be making him see sense," Danissa said in a low tone.

Millicent went over all the commands for her suit. If she was about to be thrust into close combat, she wanted to have all her weapons ready.

The group of troopers fanned out, leaving a hole at the center for Ryker to fill. Dagger stalked toward Millicent and Danissa, completely devoid of his usual good humor. He didn't let fear rule him, either, by the look of it, and he had no illusions regarding what might be waiting for them.

Shivers raced across Millicent's skin. "Here we go."

"Ready, ladies?" Dagger asked.

"Protect Danissa if shit goes sideways," Millicent said, walking forward. She shared the ability to check whatever those blue dots were with Ryker, letting him pass it on to whomever needed it. "I'll be fine."

"Gunner already gave me that directive. He said you're good in a pinch. Violently so."

"Yes. Today is not my day to die." Millicent stopped beside Ryker. She nodded.

He matched it, then turned.

They walked slowly, avoiding the dwindling flames and pausing every so often to check on the status of the blue dots. The creatures had spread out around the perimeter of the room, probably preparing to defend themselves. One blue dot was still moving, though. Upward, toward the roof.

"Send crafts to check out the top of the building," Millicent ordered. "They've been heading upward since their systems went down. I bet they have an escape system in place."

"Already on it. So far, nothing." Ryker paused at a doorway. He peered into the room, which, according to their maps, was supposedly empty. Then glanced back the way they'd come. "It's all dark. Not burned, but dark. The only light is from the windows."

"Because of the bombs, you think?" Dagger asked.

"No." Ryker fell silent, using hand signs to direct his men through the doorway. They fanned out around the perimeter of the room as Millicent entered.

Huge couches and chairs filled the vast space, their cushions compressed as though they'd been sat in often. In the corner there was a table-screen with an enormous chair that had been pushed back. A few hefty tablets lined a shelf along the wall, and three standlike robots on wheels had some sort of blue stuff piled on them.

"Is that food, do you think?" Dagger asked as he peered at the blue material. It was almost claylike. He bent forward to smell it.

"Those robots look like serving trays of some kind." Ryker's eyes scanned the room.

"They are definitely big." Dagger looked under the furniture. "Twenty-five percent larger than us, I'd wager. Smaller than their robots, thank Holy."

"So I'll just shoot from a distance, then, will I?" Millicent asked, running her fingers along the rug. "This is silk, I'd bet my life on it. I had floor coverings like this in my old apartment."

"You had silk in your apartment?" Dagger asked, lowering his gun somewhat. She could barely see his expression of incredulity through the gloom. "Weren't you only a director?"

"I did, too," Danissa said. "I picked it out myself."

Chuckling echoed across the room. "We have *two* members of royalty with us," Ryker said.

"I'll say. I guess I was slumming it without even realizing it." Dagger shook his head and continued his approach, slowing as he neared the far wall. "Another robot over here. Looks like some sort of cleaning device. Still has one of those . . . brain units."

"I'm getting a soft vibration from my implant," Danissa said, putting her fingers to the spot behind her right ear. "They are using their mental warfare. It just started, so whatever it is, they can remotely activate it, and it doesn't need to be connected to their system."

"Any energy source will do." Millicent surveyed the lights along the ceiling, all blackened. Not merely turned off—lightly painted over. "They don't like the light."

"What's that?" Ryker asked.

They moved through the room on silent feet. That one blue dot made it up another level.

"They don't like the light. That one vacant room with the hidden door was blasting light. You had to shield your eyes to get to the door. That was a defensive mechanism for them. Like guns. They probably can't tolerate intense lighting."

"Or sound," Danissa said. "That makes sense. The guns would indicate that their bodies are susceptible to punctures, like ours are."

"They also think we are largely stupid." Dagger looked down at video equipment set up along the base of the windows.

"Well . . . maybe some of us are . . ." Millicent paused at the next doorway, one customized to be much taller and wider, almost hitting the vaulted ceiling. "Looks like they got tired of stooping."

"There are huge apartments on the other side." Ryker studied his wrist. "And something for food storage. These must be living quarters. Robots are their servants."

"Humans are their servants," one of the troopers growled.

"That was their second mistake," Dagger said.

"And their first?" Millicent watched the ground where she walked. Something was niggling at her. This was all too easy. These beings had

had time to run, or hide, or create traps. Yet they'd gathered in one room and waited for Millicent's party to come to them. They weren't a dumb species, nor could they be a young one—at least in terms of humans—to have accomplished so much. So why were they letting the enemy waltz in?

"Coming to Earth in the first place," Dagger answered. "At least, if these aren't humans in disguise. Which, judging by their furniture, they are not."

Millicent's mind drifted back to that blue dot that had been moving faster from the others—and away from them. It was up one more level. It hadn't broken away from the rest until the systems had gone down.

"This is a distraction," Millicent blurted out.

An explosion rocked the floor. A body flew out of the doorway and skittered across the ground. Millicent ducked behind a massive chair.

"Keep your eyes open," Ryker yelled.

Another explosion flung a second trooper. He hit the wall with a sickening crack and slid down to a crumpled heap at the base.

"Make a new doorway," Ryker yelled, clearing to the side.

Three men heaved a massive couch out of the way while a muscular trooper dropped to one knee, swinging a long metal weapon onto his shoulder.

"Clear away," Millicent yelled, waving her arm to the side. Troopers got out from behind him just in time. A small flare of heat and fire erupted out the back of the weapon as the rocket sped away from the front. It hit the wall and blasted through. Debris rained down and the ceiling cracked.

"Not the best weapon you could've used," Millicent muttered, jogging forward with her gun in hand.

Another explosion sounded to the right of her. Pieces of wall and plaster rained through an open doorway. On the side Millicent could see, little discs waited in the walkway.

"Look where you're stepping," Ryker said, clearly noticing the same thing. "They've got land mines in clear view."

"Dagger is right—they think we're idiots." Millicent stepped around the land mine.

Dusty Eagle, Millicent thought. A heavy handgun with maximum power and great balance filled her hand. These beings might be big, but if a gun would hurt them, *this* gun would blast them into tomorrow.

There was another explosion in the distance. The rebels were closing in, surrounding the enemy. Whatever these giants had planned would happen soon.

Millicent checked their whereabouts. The blue dots had slowly gathered together in the middle of the room, clustered. They knew they were surrounded and were waiting for the showdown.

She shook her head again. That lone blue dot was up yet another level, nearly to the top of the building. Was it going to the roof?

"Nothing is on the roof," Ryker said after she voiced her suspicions. "While we were being picked up, I had our crafts survey the building."

"Then where is it going?"

"I don't know. I can send them up again to try and get a closer look." Ryker eyed the door in front of them. Troops moved through the darkness on the right, gingerly picking their way from one place to another, stepping around the explosives. Through the windows, which had been covered with a sort of film, Millicent could barely see a silver craft drifting past in the distance—one of theirs. Soon, the open space amidst the furniture was covered by more rebels.

"They've gathered in a position that can be totally surrounded," Millicent said, taking a step back and having no idea why. She itched to run. This was wrong. "The room is massive. It's taking all of our forces to surround it, spreading us thin. Getting here was easy." She took another step back. "It was too easy. Nothing in war has been too easy."

"Think they are the type to sacrifice themselves?" Ryker asked, passing out charges to waiting hands.

She thought again of that one blue dot working its way up. She cataloged her team's movements and that of the enemy. Their defenses. Their offense. And now this . . .

Danissa's fingers curled around her upper arm. Her sister squeezed, a silent comment on her own matching hunch.

"Let's blow them to hell and get out of here," Millicent said in a rush. "I don't like this."

"I agree," Ryker said, suddenly all action.

"You were right, sir. She's got good instincts." Dagger ran forward with Ryker. "Let's go, let's go! Place those charges, men and women!"

"Danissa," Millicent said, flashing through the various scenarios of what the enemy might be doing. "We need a heat map on this building. Can you break into Moxidone and work with their satellites?"

"I don't have to break into anything. I have access to both conglomerates. But we already know where they are . . ."

"We know where their tagged organic matter is within this building. That is what Marie was tracking. The brains in those robots and the beings locked in that room. I want nonorganic heat. Crafts, specifically. Then get information on the organic heat in the other Toton buildings. Send that to the headquarters. I imagine the rebels and conglomerates will need it when we get out of here."

"What are you going to do?"

"Fight, what else?"

"Go!" Ryker dropped his hand. A pulse passed through the charges the rebels had planted—the system checking the spacing—before small explosions blazed across the floor. Walls disintegrated, crumpling to form jagged holes. With the spacing, the wall's integrity would remain intact, keeping the ceiling from falling down on top of them. It would also prevent them from having to use the doorways.

"Light and sound!" Ryker yelled, rolling light spheres into the now-open space one by one. "Max power."

"Blare it!" Dagger yelled. He fiddled with something. Loud, jarring music with a deep bass blasted out from his hands. With a big grin, he tossed in the portable speakers. "Oldie but goodie."

"They carry music into battle?" Danissa asked, not looking up from her wrist until a loud female moan drifted up from a pair of glasses that were being thrown in. "And porn? They carry *porn* into battle?"

"I've long since stopped asking questions." Millicent jogged forward. More light spheres went in, and then the troopers followed. Ryker glanced over his shoulder at her before ducking through the wall. She followed a moment later. For all her big talk, she wanted to stay in sight of Ryker. She didn't always make the best decisions . . .

Through the wall, with music and light assaulting her senses, she got the first look at their enemy. Giants all, easily topping Ryker's height by three feet or more, their chests broad and heavily padded, though not defined with muscle like Ryker's. Humanoid, with two arms and two legs, they wore heavy masks covering their faces and much of their bodies, except for their arms and feet, which each had six digits and scaly skin.

They crouched within a self-made blockade of furniture. As the troopers swarmed into the room, one of the creatures held up a strange sort of metal implement Millicent had never seen before. It held its arm in front of its face, clearly trying to block out the light.

A mad vibration started in Millicent's head and worked down her bones, making her jittery. As she jogged forward, it got worse, turning her movements jerky.

Before she could raise her gun, Ryker was already there, leaping on the overturned chair in front of the being and ripping the instrument out of its hand. Dagger was in the midst a moment later, slamming down an object onto one of their heads.

Another weapon went into the air. One being stood. It ripped its arms up, and a chair went rolling across the room, bowling over troopers.

"They're strong fuckers," Ryker yelled, kicking one in the face. The being swung at him, the movement almost lethargic. "But slow as shit!" Ryker wrapped his big arms, though small in comparison, around the being's head before whipping his body around.

"Just shoot the damn thing!" Millicent yelled. "Stop messing around." To punctuate her words, she took aim and fired. Her bullet hit the mask and blew a hole through it. Green splattered out the back.

"Ew. Their blood isn't red." Millicent surged forward, looking down. Her toe nearly hit a mine. "Watch your—"

An explosion tossed bodies into the air. She gritted her teeth and shot the being reaching for Ryker. Ryker stabbed down with a knife and then flicked off the creature's mask. A toothless mouth gaped, black inside. Four eyes clustered in its face, almost like a spider. It didn't have a nose. At least, not in the center of its face.

"Do they not smell?" Dagger asked, standing on a couch and shooting downward at them.

A shiny point emerged from the huddle of enemies. Dagger jerked away just in time. The spearlike weapon hit a trooper right behind him.

"Even their weapons are slow," Ryker said.

A metal tubelike gun extended from Dagger's suit as another being exploded upward. It swung its arms in a big sweep, sending a trooper sailing. He crashed to the ground ten feet away, the strength and power of the being's movements awesome. The speed laughable, which perhaps explained why they relied so heavily on their robots.

"Fee Fi Foe Fum, motherfucker!" Dagger roared. His guns spat out automatic bullets, peppering the beings' bodies. One, sheltered by another's body, aimed something around its comrade and fired. Dagger rolled away right before a flash of light sliced through the air. It cut a trooper in half, sliced off someone's arm, and then scored the wall way behind them.

"I take that back," Ryker said, his own automatic guns extending from his suit and fitting perfectly into his hands.

"Holy shit!" Dagger yelled as he rolled and then jumped up. "They have better weapons than we do."

"Don't give them a chance to use them!" Ryker launched himself into the fray.

"Millicent!" Danissa yelled. Millicent glanced back to see horror plastered across her sister's face. "We have—get—" A deep rumble shook the walls and the floor. Millicent barely heard the windows blast in the distance. Every few words her sister said was lost to the noise. "Huge—ship—*now*!"

The beings stopped fighting. They sat down as one, folding their hands over their chests, and succumbed to death.

That was a very bad sign.

Chapter 24

The rest of the troopers kept shooting, but Ryker retracted his guns and ran toward Millicent before she could even take a step. His expression was filled with grim determination.

She had good instincts. His were great. He was bred to survive.

"RUN!" Millicent screamed, turning.

Ryker grabbed her hand as he passed and yanked her along faster. Danissa was already running ahead of them.

"What's happening?" Millicent asked as she caught up to her sister.

"Huge ship. Huge, huge ship, from the looks of things."

"We need a pickup, *now!*" Ryker was yelling with a hand to his screen, obviously on comms.

Once they left the room, Millicent's eyes widened when she saw huge chunks of debris falling outside the window.

"Is that . . . *building?*" she asked, her heart hammering. A surge of heat pumped through her core, fear and adrenaline mixed together.

"Huge ship," Danissa repeated, panting but pushing faster. "Huge heat index."

The floor shook harder, making everything on it dance. Millicent swayed, trying to keep upright, running harder. A giant piece of building hit off the small ledge outside. The wall cracked and then crumbled, shedding more structure.

"Holy shit, this is bad," Millicent muttered as they sprinted through the next room and toward the area in which they'd initially landed. The floor shook harder, like an earthquake. The ceiling cracked.

"How did they hide a huge vessel in the building?" Millicent yelled, trying to make sense of things and failing. They stopped at the pickup location. Chunks of building fell outside like rain.

"What's happening?" Dagger asked, running toward them. Troopers trailed behind him. A crack enlarged above them. It split open. A metal beam crashed down and flattened one of the troopers. "Holy—"

"They created mayhem when they first took over the systems. They could've done anything. We were scrambling—how would we have known?" Danissa staggered, her arms windmilling, as the structure shook violently.

"How are we going to get out of here, sir?" Dagger asked, his cool tone evidence of his impeccable training.

More of the ceiling cracked like an egg. Metal swung down. Millicent dropped to her knees, narrowly avoiding a blow to the side of her head.

Ryker grabbed her around the middle and dragged her forward. "Keep your feet, Millie." He didn't answer Dagger. That was probably the scariest thing of all.

Ceiling tiles fluttered down before heavier stuff crashed to the floor. The whole building swayed, as if its structure was slowly deteriorating.

"How is this possible?" Millicent screamed. "What the hell have they rigged up?"

Rebel crafts waited outside the windows, far enough out not to get caught by the huge chunks of building pouring down. A violent lurch dumped the whole party to their knees. The crack above them turned angry, a huge black chasm spewing out wires, materials, and metal.

Something deep and fundamental went off, like a blast. Another, deep in the floor. The building lurched again and shimmied. More blasts, working closer.

"They're blowing up the building!" Dagger yelled.

"Time to hope for miracles." Ryker yanked Millicent closer and gave her a toe-curling, bruising kiss. A "this can't be the last time I see your face" type of kiss. He took one moment to stare down into her eyes as the world collapsed around them before roughly spinning her around. "Ready?"

"For what?" she asked, and then he started running. Tugged along, she went with it. At the window, she screamed as she launched herself out as far as she could, no planning.

Gravity dragged her downward. A giant chunk of building sailed down just behind her and slightly above. If she'd jumped a moment later, it would have hit her in the head.

She looked down, because that's the direction she was going. A mass of gray waited for her, blocking her view of the ground ninety floors away. Eighty-eight floors away, actually. Eighty-one.

"What now?" she yelled, not reassured by the strong fingers clamped around her wrist.

Ryker fell like he had a parachute strapped to his back.

Of course, he didn't, so he had no reason to be so calm.

His mouth moved. The words didn't reach her.

"What?" she yelled.

A horrible rumble sounded behind her. She glanced over her shoulder. Plumes of dust coughed into the air as the walls buckled. Or, continued to buckle, really, since they were already on their way. Above them, fire gushed into the sky like a rocket taking off.

Millicent had a sickening feeling that that was exactly what was happening. Toton had planned for this eventuality. They were always way ahead of the idiots on Earth.

Seventy-one.

"We need a plan!" Millicent shouted. "Or to finally choose a god."

Ryker affixed a strap to her wrist.

"Oh perfect, yes. A magical strap with nothing to attach it to." Millicent eyed the building, imploding on itself. Those charges had been set up perfectly to collapse the building onto all the tech and secrets Toton had stored within it.

She bet other buildings around the city were doing the exact same thing. Then wondered about the rest of the world. Were they all evacuating?

"Damn them!" she swore as time slowed down.

Sixty-five.

"At least they made their home at the very top of the building." She nodded as the stinging rain smacked her in the face. "It gives me more time to talk to myself before I hit the ground."

Ryker affixed a strap to her other wrist and then tied a rope around her middle, all while they were falling to their death.

Fifty-some-odd. Probably.

It was amazing, really, how cool he was under pressure. There he was, tying the other end of the rope around his middle. He'd already had the straps on.

The sky turned murky gray, darkening the longer they hovered in the air. Because that's what it felt like. They'd reached terminal velocity. The air pushed up against them, making her feel like she was stationary in the air.

Of course, she *was* falling, no matter what it felt like. And eventually, the ground would catch her.

A yank on her arm brought her out of her dismal reflection. Ryker pointed at a shape moving through the murk like a giant Paradise shark.

"Ready?" she barely heard.

No, she was not. But they didn't have much longer to fall. The hum of an engine beat at her senses, but she couldn't see a craft. He brought her in close, and she wrapped her arms around his waist. If he stopped suddenly, her arms would lose their grip, and she'd eventually get jolted by the rope. She'd been here before. This was going to hurt; she had no doubt.

As long as it doesn't snap my spine . . .

The craft's motor whined as it accelerated, charging at them. Ryker whipped the rope around in circles before letting go. It sailed at the vessel, but fell just short.

"Shit," she heard. "C'mon you bastard."

Thirties. Hopefully. But probably more like upper twenties.

He swung again and tossed. A rock pinged off the craft. The strap held.

"Hold—"

His suit fabric ripped out of her hands and her arms scraped down his body, exactly like she'd expected. Also like she'd expected, she hit the end of the rope and it squeezed, stealing her breath. Without time to groan in pain, she was yanked upward, tethered to Ryker, who was climbing the rope despite her weight dragging him down. A hard thing scraped her face and smacked her toe as it passed by. The craft rose, lifting them up and away to safety.

Screaming caught her attention. Millicent barely caught sight of a falling woman, her arms windmilling through the air, before the craft, still on the rise, sought shelter behind an intact building.

Danissa!

Heart in her throat, Millicent was flown through the sky in a cloud of putrid dust, barely able to breathe. She dug through her utility belt, hoping against hope. With a straggled sigh, she affixed her air breather and took a lungful. Her eyes watered from the building's destruction, making her close them. She tried to see what had become of her sister, but the craft was rising through the air. They passed one building, and then another, while they climbed.

"You okay, princess?" Millicent heard through her comms.

Comms, unmute.

"Danissa," she croaked through a scratchy throat.

"Hang on," Ryker said, ignoring her panic.

They continued to rise until the air was clearer and they were no longer choking on dust from the collapsing building. Shivering from the cold and wet, Millicent wrapped her arms around herself. The craft slowed to a stop. Ryker was attached to it with a black strap. Someone helped him into the vessel, and then he pulled her up. Blood marred his bicep, but he didn't let it hinder him. Once she was safely on board, he yanked her to his body, hugging her so tightly it hurt.

"That was close, princess." He kissed her head and squeezed her. "Too close."

"What about the others?" she asked through a constricted chest. She barely knew her sister, but she was blood, and she'd dreamed all these years of finally meeting her family. Of living together on Paradise.

"We're good," Dagger said over the comm. "We're okay."

"Who is *we*?" Millicent begged.

"I got her," he answered. Another craft rose out of the murky gray sky. A large man crawled into the vessel in the distance. A dangling woman was then hauled up.

"He saved her," Millicent said, letting tears overcome her. "Oh thank Holy, he saved her."

"I couldn't let something so pretty go to waste," they heard Dagger say. He didn't mute his comms. "Here we go, pretty lady. Are you okay?" A moment later. "She's good. She probably hurts like hell, but she's good."

Ryker hugged Millicent close for another few moments as more crafts rose out of the murk, some carrying a great many dangling troopers. Ryker had been the example, and the rest had followed his lead, only with more warning.

Millicent let Ryker stand them both up. "All better, princess? Ready to get back to it?"

"Not really." She let him cut off the line.

"Ground level is swamped in dust, sir," one of the troopers in the craft said. "Two crafts were downed by debris, and we didn't save as many as we would've liked."

Ryker's jaw clenched and he minutely shook his head. "You did what you could. There was nothing else any of us could do." He stood at the console. "Let's go to headquarters."

As they flew over the city, Millicent saw four other destroyed buildings. Her theory had been correct. Expertly placed explosives had taken them down on top of themselves.

"Not as many as I would've thought," she said. "I wonder how long they planned their takeover. With so few people, they really took this place by storm. They crippled the conglomerates."

"They could've been there for decades, rotting the hierarchy of Toton. The other conglomerates just assumed Toton was faltering. Thinking they could swoop in and take the scraps. Greed is blinding. I wonder—did those beings take anything with them?"

"I'm sure they've been shipping back their spoils all along. They've had a decade or more to harvest."

"Think they'll be back?"

Millicent huffed out a laugh, staring out the window at the many desecrated buildings they passed. "What would they come back to?"

"This is one city of many."

"Yes, but now we know about them. They'd have to fight their way back. Why not find another world where they can slither in and start the harvest again."

"We'll never know."

Millicent looked back at him with a silent question.

"We did our part," he said as the vessel lowered into the rebel headquarters. "Let the Earth residents handle it."

"Children, this is no way to behave. You have the intellect of teenagers, for Holy sake. Act like it!"

Five hours after her brush with death, Millicent smiled in relief as she walked into the safe bunker in a dilapidated part of the city mostly devoid of smart tech and any sort of movement. She didn't know what had caused Moxidone to bomb the hell out of the area, but it had created a great place to squat and not be noticed. Millicent and Ryker had purposely stayed away until they were certain Toton was not still around the city, following them. It was paranoid, but where their daughter was concerned, they didn't mind acting a little crazy. They hadn't spent the time idly—they'd been directing efforts in other parts of the world, making sure the robots were all frozen, and hunting for any enemies that might be left. The reports from other cities mirrored the situation in LA—it seemed whatever creatures could escape the planet had done so, and the rest had sacrificed themselves.

Trent stood in the middle of a tiny room with his hands on his hips. He stared down at Marie, who sat with her arms folded and a stubborn expression on her face. Terik was off to the side, fuming. The rest of the kids, aside from Billy, were looking back and forth between the two young people.

"Going well, is it?" Millicent asked, stepping into the room.

"Mommy!" Marie jumped up and wrapped her arms around Millicent's neck. "Is it over? Did we do it?"

"We did it, baby. Now we just have to clean up. Where's Billy?"

"Found him," Ryker said from a room off to the side. "He's in here with Sinner and the other troopers, causing havoc."

"I heard what happened," Trent said, patting Millicent on the shoulder. That was the equivalent of him hugging her—even after all these years, she still wasn't great at touching nonfamily members. "Close call. And they just folded up and died?"

"Very close call," Ryker said as he walked in. He held a dangling Billy by the ankle. "It's beyond me how nobody noticed Toton getting such a large craft, or a small rocket, into that building. How did they even do it?"

"The people here say things have been mayhem," Trent said. "Have you checked into the other parts of the world?"

"Load up, everyone, we're headed out of here." Millicent motioned everyone out of the room. Marie eyed Terik, who gave her the stink eye. "Does he seem familiar to you?" Millicent asked Trent.

"Yes. I wanted to ask Danissa to give me access to their lab's files. I'm curious about all these children. Rumor is, there are still more, spread around the city. We need to find them. But how about the rest of the world?"

They walked toward the door, where the small collection of troopers that had been sent to guard the children waited. Billy wriggled like a fish as he dangled in the air, trying to get a punch off at Ryker. The kid was more violent than the security guys.

"Most of the other cities were better off than LA," she said. "There were a lot of people hiding. The cities weren't as barren."

The environment assaulted them as they exited the bunker and walked along the pockmarked walkway thirty floors above a pile of rubble. A craft hovered next to the only undamaged part of the floor's bay. The docking didn't work, so they helped the children over the small gap before throwing in Trent, who kept hemming and hawing about a safety rope.

Once inside, Millicent stood near the console, afraid to sit down lest she instantly fall asleep. She had barely slept in three days—her body was trying to mutiny.

"I sent more troops to pick up children," Trent said. "There are . . . quite a few of them. Over two hundred from both conglomerates in this city alone! Most of them are normal kids, but some have exceptional abilities. Or so the files Danissa sent to me say. From what we can gather, none have been sterilized. We have a real starter seed for Paradise. Another generation to live on and naturally create a future."

"I was looking forward to populating Paradise with Millie," Ryker said with a smirk.

Millicent rolled her eyes. "No. No more. The creation lab in *this* body is closed, indefinitely."

"Yes, childbirth is certainly hard on the—"

"Move!" Marie shouted at Terik, cutting Trent off. Trent's expression immediately turned to annoyance.

Terik stared at Marie, blank-faced, blocking her way. He didn't so much as flinch.

"Is that so?" Marie asked in a dangerous voice. Her father's voice.

"They have been at each other since they met." Trent sighed in exhaustion. "I have no idea what the problem is."

"He's a pompous asshole—"

"Marie! Language!" Millicent said with a warning.

"—who thinks he's the only one who ever had any hardship. Well, *I've* got rare abilities, too. And *I've* been rescued from a lab, too. And yes, I was in a battle. He's not any better than me!"

"I didn't say I was better," Terik said in a deceptively calm voice. "I said that I'm different, and nothing will ever change that."

"You're not different!" Marie balled her fists. Ryker rubbed his eyes, minutely shook his head, and looked away, something he always did when Marie got her dander up for reasons he couldn't understand.

"You're natural born. I'm lab born. I'm different."

"I was lab born," Marie shouted. "My brother and sister were the natural-born ones, not me!"

"Get in the craft," Ryker said in a deep, commanding tone.

Still glaring at each other, the two children did as they were told, followed by the others.

"I'd like to look and see if these children were flagged to be sterilized," Trent said, rubbing his chin and staring at Terik.

"Does he talk about you like that?" Terik shoved a finger in Trent's direction, staring down at a seated Marie.

"Yes! He talks about literally *everyone* like that!" Marie stood from her seat. "I'm not afraid of you, you know. That flat stare? My dad does it better than you. I've half a mind to put my foot up your—"

"Marie," Ryker said. Silence immediately filled the craft. The two troopers in the rear straightened up, the children's mouths formed thin lines, and Trent's eyes popped. "Enough."

"Yes, Daddy," Marie said, sitting back down. Terik clasped his hands on his lap.

"Have you heard any word on the Moxidone rocket?" Millicent asked into the blessed silence. Securing it had been a cinch. It turned out, Toton—or whatever those beings called themselves—had been hell-bent on destroying themselves, along with all evidence of whom they were, what they'd done, and why they'd done it, once their chosen few were safely off-planet. That had left the rocket ripe for the taking.

"Perfect working order," Ryker said. "It was tested in small flights after it was built, and was deemed ready for the journey to Paradise. We should cut our travel time in half."

Millicent sagged against the console. She wanted to be home so bad she shook.

"Is *he* coming with us?" Marie asked quietly, glaring at Terik again.

"You know," Trent mused, folding his hands in his lap with a small smile. "On the other side of hate, there's often love. Strong emotions mean a strong connection . . ."

Marie switched her glare to Trent.

"Yes, Marie," Millicent said. It was her turn to run her hand over her eyes. "They are coming with us. Soon we'll all get separate rooms, we'll take a long nap, we'll clean up this planet some, and we'll leave. Okay? Until then, not another word. Out of any of you."

"Fat chance," Ryker murmured.

Chapter 25

Danissa wiped a tear off her cheek as she stood next to the incinerator. Puda, dressed in a clean suit with his hands folded over his chest, lay peacefully on the tray, waiting for his return to the elements. She would take his ashes to the top of the tallest building and release him into the environment to drift down over his home. She'd briefly thought about taking him to Paradise, but it didn't seem fitting. This was the life she'd known with him—in this place. He needed to rest where their connection was strongest.

She stared down on to his face, remembering their time together. Remembering the long, pleasurable nights, and the many stands she'd made within Gregon to grant him special privileges. It had always been worth it. She regretted none of the time she'd been with him, until the end. By allowing him to take risks with her, for her, she'd ultimately led him to his death.

Guilt tearing at her, she took a step back.

"Wait," Dagger said in that supportively strong voice Danissa craved. "What happened?"

"What do you mean?" she asked, wiping another tear as sobs threatened to take over.

His gentle but firm hands landed on her shoulders. He made her take a step forward, back to where she'd started. "Are you feeling guilt?" he asked.

She sighed. "I don't like how you can read me."

"I'm great at reading body language, and yours is as telling as anyone's. Why are you feeling guilty? Because he was with you when he died?"

She couldn't utter the affirmation, not while the sobs were bubbling up, making her body shake. Millicent, Ryker, and the children stood behind her, lending their support. She didn't want them to see her break down. It wasn't something that someone in her position was supposed to do.

"He chose to be with you, right?" Dagger asked, his words coated in velvet. She nodded silently. "He didn't want to leave your side. He died to protect you. He died a hero. Give him that. Remember him for his valor. For his act of bravery. You didn't kill him, Danissa. He saved you. Send him to the afterlife with a vow never to forget him. *That* is what every hero wants."

Sobs finally broke free. She heaved with them, knowing Dagger was right. Knowing that Puda would've wanted exactly what Dagger said. She nodded and forced herself to remember the good times as the door to the transformation coffin opened. She fell into the memory of his dazzling smile. As his body moved into the lit interior, she let the tears subside and said good-bye to her best friend and lover.

When it was over, and the ashes were cooling, she followed the others out of the room, belatedly realizing that Dagger still had his hand on her shoulder. "Thanks," she said.

"I've been through this more times than I would like. I've seen people go through it more than that, especially these last few years. It gives a man perspective—helps show him what's important."

"Thanks for saving me, too. I don't think I ever said that. I wasn't going to jump." And she hadn't. Dagger had thrown her out of the building, and she'd screamed the whole way down. She'd been no help at all. It was more than a little embarrassing.

"You did say that. Right before you punched me, remember? I had just pulled you into the craft." He gave a cute, lopsided smile, showing his natural-born origins. "It was a good punch, too. Well executed."

"Oh yeah." Her memory was hazy—fear and adrenaline had been waging war in her at the time. "Sorry about that. But thanks again. For saving me."

"I'd be lying if I said I didn't also want to be remembered a hero." He shrugged.

"What about Roe?" she asked a moment later, slightly uncomfortable and not really sure why.

"Gunner and Foster are taking him back to Paradise. That's where he was the happiest. They bury their dead in the ground there. So they'll do that with him."

"In the ground?" Danissa crinkled her nose in disgust.

"I hear that place is really different. They live on the ground. Their homes only go two floors up, at the most. Their crafts don't even fly. I can't wait to see. It'll be a trip."

"So you're really going? You were serious about that?"

He shrugged again. "I think so. You?"

"Yes! I want out of this place. I want a better life."

"You know . . ." He scratched the stubble on his chin. "I didn't like what Trent said to you, but if you do want to try for a child, I can help." He held up his hands. "No touching or anything. I'm not saying that. Just . . . if you want to try and reproduce, I can give you all the . . . samples you need. The labs peppered me for them often, so I know how it works. Just throwing that out there. No strings attached or anything. But if you need it . . ."

It was her turn to shrug, something warm and soft infusing her middle. She smiled to herself, remembering what it had been like to hold her newborn all that time ago. Wondering how it would feel to get to keep her child this time. To watch him or her grow.

She bit her lip. "Thanks. Again. I might. It probably won't work, but it's worth a try."

A day and a long sleep later, Millicent stepped onto the walkway in front of a department much like the one she'd left in San Francisco all those years ago. Black scarred the side of the building, and half the bay had been torn away. The computer generation above her was absent, revealing the torrid sky. Even as she glanced up, lightning flashed down in the distance.

She turned and looked out over the changed silhouette of the horizon. The battle that had lasted years had made its mark. Buildings were scarred or missing entirely. An entire block had been leveled, leaving behind nothing but piles of brick, stone, metal, and glass. Countless lives had been lost, mostly innocent, some not. The city had been ravaged. Rebuilding would take decades.

Ryker stopped by her side and waited for her to turn toward the entrance of the building. Danissa, Dagger, Trent, and the children were behind her, along with a half dozen troopers. There were a few remaining tasks before they turned matters over to the officials, who had only recently been elected by the rebels to start rebuilding the city while also helping other areas strengthen their acting government.

One of those things was to further tear down the old regime.

"We probably should've left the kids at headquarters," Trent said as they walked. "It's not too late."

"I'm going," Terik said in a hard voice. He hadn't wanted his family unit to be separated from Marie. It wasn't out of fondness, either, if their constant fights were any indication. Millicent had a feeling it was a matter of survival. Terik knew that Millicent and Ryker would always make sure Marie was cared for, and he wanted his little family in on that. He hadn't lasted this long by making stupid decisions. Millicent had to respect him for that.

"This is just a quick stop since it was on our way." Millicent checked the time. They had plenty. "We're here to organize the pickup, mostly. We shouldn't find any resistance."

"We're probably safer with them here." Dagger chuckled.

He wasn't far wrong.

"You know," Trent said. Millicent glanced back. He had pushed up between Danissa and Dagger. "I couldn't help but overhear your private conversation yesterday. I am so excited, let me tell you. I think you have the groundwork to make intelligent, beautiful children. Don't worry about the excessive violence from Dagger's side. With Millicent and Ryker—"

"Step away," Dagger said in a rough voice.

"Oh. Of course," Trent said. A moment later, he continued, "With their children, all three, the balanced analytical brain of the mother has counteracted the more violent intensity of the father. It's still there, of course, as you can see when Marie loses her temper. I have never seen her pick up a stick and try to brain someone, like she did yesterday with Terik, but when pushed, she does react strongly. Still, she is mostly a mellow child of extreme intelligence. And I can certainly help with the procreation, as I said, and even with natural enhancements of the child. It is perfectly safe, I assure you."

"You aren't going near my possible child, or its mother," Dagger growled.

"Oh interesting. Danissa, you are a lucky woman. It looks like you're in his protection bubble already. I'm lucky enough to be in Ryker's. Although, if you decide you don't like him, it could really present problems down the line. Thankfully, Millicent chose Ryker, but if she hadn't, we would've seen some real problems in the community. Still do if anyone flirts with her. Everyone is terrified of him."

"Trent," Millicent said, not bothering to hide her smile. "Now probably isn't the time."

"Oh sure. Right, yes. Of course."

They were quiet for a moment as they neared the large entryway. Millicent took a deep breath, half feeling like she was going back in time—and dreading it.

"But talk to them about me, will you, Millicent?" Trent spoke up again. "They'll trust you. I would love another chance at a couple like you and Ryker. I think I am on to something new . . ."

"Does he ever stop?" Dagger asked incredulously.

"No, he doesn't." Ryker grinned as his arm came up in front of Millicent to stop her. "Do you have that heat map active, princess? It's not showing up on my screen."

"Sorry, Daddy," Marie said. "I just gave it to Mommy. Here."

"Sloppy," Terik murmured, so low Millicent barely heard. She did hear the grunt of pain that followed, though.

"Marie! See, Danissa, this is what I meant," Trent whispered. "She isn't usually this amped up. But it is quite clear that she has learned the proper way to punch. I bet she'll be an even better fighter than Millicent. We'll see if Terik can match her."

"Trent," Ryker barked. "Shut up or go back."

"Sorry," Trent muttered.

There were no spiders or organic robots showing on the map. No blue of Toton. Only green dots indicating humans. The distinction programmed by Marie was hopefully correct.

"Good afternoon, Ms. Foster," the AI security said as Millicent crossed the threshold.

"Good afternoon, Mr. Gunner."

"Good afternoon, Ms. Lance from Gregon Corp."

The welcomes continued for everyone who still had an implant, all of which had been mostly restored to their factory settings. Millicent wanted to see what systems were still in place within the building, and what kind of warnings or errors, if any, they triggered.

"Did you put your name back into the system, or had they left it?" Danissa asked in a hush.

"Removed the notices and triggers from our files," Millicent answered, holding up her gun. "That was all."

"There is a security breach. Unidentified personnel warning," Ryker said, his eyes on his wrist screen. "For the children. There is an alert for Gregon staffers visiting without the proper paperwork—that's Danissa. This would've been normal protocol from before the war."

"That was to be expected," Millicent said. "Is anyone coming to answer it?"

"Not so far." Ryker glanced around the floor. Most of the work pods were intact. Chairs were scattered, some screens broken, and a few stations demolished, but the floor was mostly in workable order.

"Why didn't this floor get attacked?" Millicent asked, looking over the empty space in disbelief. The hollowness and lack of human activity were surreal.

"Toton had no reason to come here," Danissa said. "I was never here, none of my hard ports were here, and most of the staffers had already been moved or had vanished. The question you should be asking is why Moxidone didn't blow it to hell like all of the Gregon and Toton buildings they demolished."

"I don't need to ask that question," Millicent said with butterflies in her stomach. She wondered how the upper-level staffers would react to seeing her face. "I surmised relatively quickly that Moxidone was using this upheaval as a means to economic domination. They took out Gregon in the name of taking out Toton. If they ever defeated Toton, which their arrogance must've assured them they would, they would have been the last man standing. Gregon would need loans to rebuild. Toton would need to be taken apart and consumed. Moxidone would've been in a great position."

"That must've been before half their staffers vanished," Ryker said, his gaze constantly scanning.

"Idiots," Dagger said.

"Always have been idiots." Millicent shook her head. "It seems only idiots are ever in charge, doesn't it?"

"Says the woman in charge," Trent muttered.

"Keep to the middle of this path." Danissa motioned with her hand.

Random objects littered the sides of the makeshift walkway, from chairs to empty food pouches to cast-aside suits. Off to the right, a skeleton lay in pieces, like it had been blown up years ago and allowed to decompose. Which was surely what had happened.

They turned a corner and confronted a barricade made of office equipment. It was only as tall as a person—not a great defense. Millicent said as much.

"Quick, get to the side!" Trent yanked at Danissa, trying to pull her back to the corner. "They are excellent shots!"

"There is no one there, Trent," Millicent said, checking her screen again.

"They should've done this and also sprinkled mines along the walkway." Ryker surveyed the makeshift wall.

"All their top security abandoned ship," Dagger said. "When the shit hit the fan, and our superiors were sending us to basically die, we gave them a one-finger salute and joined the rebel ranks. I wasn't interested in protecting them any longer. Not when I had a choice to get out. Without anyone intelligent in security, you get these shoddy defenses."

"I say thank Holy," Danissa said. "Otherwise I wouldn't still be alive."

"This is . . . interesting." Ryker started forward, watching the ground. They all climbed up and over. Another barricade waited down the hall.

"Where is everyone?" Dagger asked.

"In the center of the floor. Conference rooms." Millicent and Ryker led the way, climbing over barricades and pushing through the makeshift defenses until they came to a heavy door. Once there, Ryker put his ear to the wood while looking at his wrist screen. He knocked.

"How many of them are immobilized by your program?" Danissa asked.

"Half, at least. All upper-level staffers who aren't security."

"Who is it?" someone yelled through the door.

"Gunner. I was once a director of security for Moxidone. I also have Ms. Foster, Ms. Lance, and Mr. Dagger with me. I assume you recognize many of those names."

There was silence from the other side. Green dots moved toward the door, clustering together.

"How do we know it's you?" the voice called.

Ryker shot Dagger a flat stare that conveyed his irritation. "Check your security logs."

"What's the difference?" Millicent said through the door. "We're human, not robots, we found you, and we knocked politely instead of blowing the door down. Toton is gone. We are the survivors. Open up, you fools!"

"Good*night*." Dagger grinned. "That is exactly the Ms. Foster I've heard so much about. What about you, pretty lady?" He turned his smile to Danissa. "Do you get sassy and commanding?"

"Of course she does. She was excellent at her job—no sense to let that go because her job is gone." Millicent readied her charges. She would force her way in if need be. After this she could go home. *Impatient* was a small word for her need to get going.

Before she committed herself, the lock disengaged and the door swung open. Tired and gaunt faces full of worry stared out at her before turning toward Ryker. One of them said, "It *is* you!"

"Out of the way," Ryker said, stepping forward. As one, they nearly fell over themselves to skitter backward and to the side. "Where are the superiors?"

"In the back, sir. But . . . something is wrong with them. They are lying there, like they's dead, but they ain't dead . . ."

"We know. We're here to collect them. Lead the way."

Two men jogged to the front of the party, and then wound them through an empty corridor and into a stuffy room. The man on the bed looked like he was in his sixties except for his gnarled hands. He was probably closer to a hundred and fifty, and had obviously made use of his clones. "This is the VP of the industrial supply department."

"And the rest?" Ryker asked. "Are Gregon officials here as well?"

"We got both Gregon and Moxidone, yeah. Top-level. Three are in their rooms, kind of collapsed like this one here, and eight others are in their various living spaces. They all kinda . . . stopped moving. I don't know what happened . . ."

"I put them under arrest," Millicent said, stepping out of the room and looking down the corridor. "Things are changing. Public officials will be elected to rebuild your society. Once the survivors come out of hiding, a general election will be organized and a new leadership chosen. Two of you can take him to the front of the building. Just put him down near the front doors before you come back for the others."

She walked away down the hall, wanting to check on the others. "They'll need to be fed intravenously," she said to the remaining trailing security man. "We'll be moving them to a prison until officials are elected."

"Like . . . the government?" the security man asked.

Millicent bent over a man lying on his face, stiff as a board. She checked his pulse. "You didn't think to move him to his back?"

"Ah . . . no, miss. It hadn't occurred to me—us." The security man wrung his hands.

She shook her head and glanced at Ryker. "He suffocated." She straightened and moved on. "Maybe I should've waited a bit longer before I applied the program."

"You couldn't have known they were guarded by Curve huggers," Ryker said. "If you'd waited, I'm sure we would've had to deal with people at the barricades."

"True. Changing how these people live, especially since only one city has been affected this badly, will be a huge undertaking. Are you sure it's even possible?"

"The other cities might be intact," Danissa said, "but their systems and hierarchies aren't. They abandoned their positions to hide. They wanted to save themselves. They were of no help to us—not even when we requested aid. Their finances are down the drainpipe. There is so much they'll have to rebuild, that they are vulnerable. This is the time. It can happen. With new blood will come change."

As Millicent checked the others, she knew Danissa was right. But despite her desire to stay longer and help see the transition through, she wanted to get back to her other children. To her home. They'd defeated two tyrants—Toton and the suffocating hierarchy of conglomerates who had way too much power. It was more than anyone else had done.

"Let's organize the others to be collected and let's go home," Millicent said, entwining her fingers in Ryker's as they headed back to the craft.

A few hours later, Millicent stood with Danissa in front of the pods in the Moxidone rocket. They had both checked over the computer systems and agreed it was rock solid. The children had already been nestled in, the youngest going with Dagger. Millicent had every belief it would result in him adopting her eventually, but Terik would never let that happen until the rest of the children were settled with other families.

The only thing left to do was actually get into the pods and go.

"So," Danissa said as she stared down at the pod. It was clear something was on her mind, and had been since all the danger had ceased. She'd attempted to start a conversation like this a great many times but never went through with it.

"Yes?" Millicent asked, checking her screen. They had fifteen minutes to be safely stored inside. They were cutting it close.

"We're really blood, huh?" Danissa's face turned red. She wouldn't look Millicent in the eye.

"Is that a surprise? We look similar; we act similar; we have similar abilities . . ."

"You are better in battle."

"You'll be better at something else, we just don't know what yet. Maybe gardening. I truly hate gardening."

Danissa's brow furrowed and she shook her head.

"Never mind," Millicent said, checking her screen again.

"So . . . we're sisters," Danissa said softly.

"Both our parents are the same, so yes, we are sisters. We're family, and on Paradise, you'll get a better sense of what that really means. You have nieces and a nephew. You have a sort of brother in Ryker. And if you are able to have your own kids, they will be cousins to my kids. It's really a remarkable feeling. Belonging. You have no idea."

"I want that," Danissa said softly. "I want all of that."

"Great. So get in the pod and let's get going."

Danissa exhaled audibly. "I'd hate to have gone this far only to die on the journey."

"I hear you, trust me. But otherwise you have to stay here in a ruined world."

"Okay, okay." Danissa gingerly stepped into the pod and slowly lay down. It was clear this was taking all her willpower.

"Afraid of small dark spaces?" Millicent asked with a grin.

"A little. More afraid of not having control to get out."

"Yeah. That's a bitch. Too bad. See ya."

"Wait!"

Millicent clicked on the pod, waited for it to seal, making sure Danissa went into the life-stalling sleep before she hurried to her own pod.

"Are you ready, Ms. Foster?" the controller said over the loudspeaker.

"Ready and eager, zip me up." Millicent settled in and closed her eyes. As the oxygen-rich fluid washed over her, she envisioned her family in her mind's eye, Danissa included, and held the image. She couldn't wait to get home.

Epilogue

The whole community stood before the open hole in the ground and looked down on the body of Roe, wrapped in a white sheet painted with flowers. Millicent allowed the tears to flow down her cheeks, unabashed, already missing this man who had given her a new life.

They'd been back on Paradise for a month, getting everyone settled who'd made the journey. The new rocket had flown fast and true. The old rocket had left at about the same time, taking those who wished to go. It still wasn't due to arrive for some time.

Millicent's children pushed in close, sandwiched between Ryker and her. She'd been away from them for a little over two years, and in that time, they had grown out of babyhood. They blessedly slept through the night. But still, she'd missed so many milestones with them. Going to Earth to defeat Toton had been necessary, but she loathed the time she'd lost with her children.

"Good-bye, brave Roe," the speaker said as she took a shovel. She threw a ceremonial pile of dirt down on him, something Millicent had always thought was crude, but at least it added a sense of occasion.

"Now what happens?" Dagger asked from beside them, more relaxed on Paradise than he'd ever been on Earth, even after the fighting stopped. His broad shoulders held no visible sign of tension, and his eyes gleamed.

Danissa, standing with them, ran her fingers through her loose brown hair, an action Dagger followed with his eyes before looking at the ground between his feet. Clearly he was infatuated, but she was still getting over her loss. If they ever did get together, Danissa would have to make the first move, Millicent was sure. If there was something Dagger wasn't, it was pushy. He was the opposite of Ryker in that way.

That hadn't prevented them from attempting to conceive, however, something Trent was eagerly helping them do. Dagger had offered his sperm, no strings attached, but Danissa had asked that he play his role as a father if it ever came to pass, something that had earned her a beaming smile.

"We go for a celebration of his life," Millicent said, motioning for everyone to follow the horde of people down the small hillside marked with gravestones.

"I can't get over the beauty of this place," Danissa said, looking out over the green hills. "The animals, the sky."

"Wait until you see your waves." Millicent smiled. "Good thing there isn't anything set up out that way, or you'd force us all to move with you to the beach."

"It has to be set up sometime." Danissa laughed.

"I solved the riddle," Trent said as he jogged over. "Hi, Danissa. Hi, Dagger." He looked directly at Ryker before glancing at Terik, who was walking a ways in front of them, arguing with Marie. "He was lab born, all right." Trent waved his wrist with the screen. He didn't have access to the files on Earth, but he did have five huge backup drives of information about all the lab activity since he'd left. He'd been poring over it since their return to Paradise, acting like a man on a mission.

"We knew that, Trent," Danissa said dryly. "All of them were. But good work finding the obvious."

Trent wiped his forehead, then wiped his glistening fingers on his pants. "Yes, yes. But even though he—they—were lab born, they weren't made like a lot of lab borns were in my time. Terik had one mother and two fathers. Gene splicing did occur, but only to weed out the more unfortunate characteristics of one of the fathers, replacing them with more agreeable ones. He seems to have been bred for upper-level security, much like Ryker or Dagger—may I call you Kace?"

"Still no," Dagger said.

"Yes, okay. Fine. I keep hoping. Anyway, he was bred to fall into their role. Billy, too, it looks like. He had different parents, one mother and one father. Still lab born. Very violent, that little boy. We really need to work on that. I am pretty sure he'll come around."

"Is there a point to this that we'll care about?" Ryker asked.

"Yes. You especially, Ryker, regarding one of those fathers." Trent swallowed. "It was Mr. Hunt."

Millicent staggered. She grabbed Ryker for no reason. "But . . . how? Hadn't he been sterilized? And we killed him! I thought these experiments didn't happen until we were gone?"

Trent wiped his hand through the air. "You're correct on both counts, yes. But as a natural born, he was given the benefit of the doubt for many years. He did not get sterilized until a few breeding failures and his own personal issues could no longer be ignored. At that point, any sperm in the vault was *supposed* to be discarded. Clearly that didn't happen."

"Is he a danger to my daughter?" Ryker asked in a rough voice.

"Mr. Hunt . . ." Dagger looked ahead at Terik. "Wasn't that the insane security director that you took down, Gunner?"

"Yes. He wasn't right in the head."

"But"—Trent held up a hand—"I've pored over Terik's records and, most especially, his evaluation reports. We've all seen firsthand how he acts with the other children. Always loving. Always protective of them. He is balanced, more so than Marie. When she throws things at his head, or tries to beat him with blunt objects, he acts in defense only. He has never struck out against her. He has never initiated an attack. He has *never* lost his temper. I think they created something excellent in him."

Millicent had watched her daughter argue with Terik. He had always seemed level. He verbally sparred, but Trent was right, he never engaged physically. "Why did you tell us, then?"

"Oh." Trent dropped his hands. "Should I not have? The thought didn't occur to me."

"At least I know he won't keep secrets when we try for a baby," Dagger said.

"No. He'll blabber about everything, no matter how trivial." Ryker was still looking at the son of his old nemesis.

"Like all the children, we'll watch him." Millicent wiped the hair out of her eyes. The cool breeze felt good on her face. "As a community, we'll give him, all of them, a loving home. If his behavior changes for the worst, we'll figure out a solution." Millicent shook her head. "I will not condemn him for his heritage. That's not fair."

"I don't think we should let Marie be around him so much," Ryker said. "If he snaps, she'll be the first in the line of fire."

"She'll be fine, Ryker." Millicent slipped her hand into his. "Stop being overprotective. She's smart and she knows how to defend herself. She'll cut him down, no problem."

He didn't respond, which meant he'd go with it, but grudgingly so.

"I keep forgetting to ask," Trent said as he went back to his screen. It was almost like he was determined to read all of the research overnight. "What does *hometown* mean?"

"The town you call home . . ." Millicent stared at him in confusion.

"No, I mean, as a nickname."

A smile curled Dagger's lips. "Why do you ask?"

"It's nothing. Just that someone kept calling me *hometown* when I went to get Terik and the children."

Laughter burst out of Dagger. He grabbed his stomach and shook with it. "They were calling you stupid. Extremely stupid, actually. Too stupid to function."

Trent's face reddened and his brow pinched together. "Oh, that's rich, coming from them!"

Dagger laughed harder, followed by Ryker. Millicent had no doubt that Trent had just acquired a new nickname.

They walked down to the community garden as the sun worked its way toward the distant horizon. Standing together, they watched the children play and the adults chatter, safe on Paradise.